HEARTH AND HOME

GOLD SKY SERIES

REBEL CARTER

VIOLET GAZE PRESS

Cover Design by Najla Qamber

Edited by Lena Tudor

Published by Violet Gaze Press

20-22 Wenlock Rd

London

www.violetgazepress.com

Created with Vellum

For THE Becci Deckers.
You're right. I'm Aladdin, not Jasmine.
You're always right.

CHAPTER 1

Julian stepped inside of the boarding house and cautioned a look around him. He knew the establishment was reputable. His sister's glowing recommendation of not only the facilities but the proprietress had made him hopeful for a comfortable stay, but a cursory glance around the well-appointed space had convinced him of it.

Miss Alice Hill's boarding house was entirely unexpected on the frontier but would have fit in among the businesses of the city's most affluent streets. The furniture was tasteful, luxurious drapery decorated the French style windows, the hardwood flooring gleaming and spotless... and then there was the woman who greeted him at the door.

Violet Shield.

Something coiled and tightened in his chest at just thinking her name. The woman was like a vision in the desert, the warm smile on her face touching a softer part of himself he'd turned away from. A part of him he hadn't realized he'd pushed away until the moment the door had opened and there she had been.

She'd been garbed simply enough in a starched apron and muslin dress of a shade of lilac that brought attention to her dark waist-length hair which had been pulled back at the crown of her head. She wore no jewelry or adornments save for a thin gold chain at her neck that caught the light when she turned toward him.

"How long will we have you in Gold Sky, Mr. Baptiste?"

Julian's eyes left the glint of the gold chain to meet the eyes of the smiling woman he'd been trying very hard not to stare at. It was impolite, ill-mannered, and—well, he wasn't a man who stared at women.

He was no stranger to beautiful women, women who donned only the finest fashions, possessed advantageous familial connections, and moved through the world with only the kind of grace a charmed life could offer.

It wasn't even that Violet was refreshingly unlike certain women who had scorned him, or even that she was like ones he found himself helpless to resist.

Violet captivated him. Violet simply *was*.

She spoke plainly enough but Julian warmed to her husky tone that reminded him of summer nights. Her Mexican accent, light as it was, brought to mind the sound of flint striking steel.

There was strength in her. He could see it. He could hear it.

Julian chanced a glance at her profile to see high cheekbones and full lips. Dark lashes rimmed large brown eyes flecked with gold—and he suddenly chastised himself. He should not have noticed that about her, that her eyes held an ochre color unlike he had ever seen, but here he was feeling unnerved by this woman and fighting the urge to gawk at her.

Julian Baptiste III had been brought up better than to stare at a lady.

Or at least until now.

He was gentleman enough to admit that he had been struck dumb the second Violet Shield had opened the door and greeted him with an easy smile, a genuine smile, so unlike what he was used to seeing from strangers.

Life in New York City, even as a man with means and an influential family, was still exhausting, because even if he was a gentleman, he was still a man of mixed heritage. Those who balked at shaking his hand or serving him were forced to bow before the Baptiste name, and so he'd learned to wrap that power around himself, clothe himself in it like the finest bespoke attire.

He clasped his hands behind his back, careful to keep his eyes trained just over her shoulder. The woman's dark eyes were too soft for him to trust himself with. Julian was no stranger to guarding himself around women who might seek to find themselves in a compromising position with an heir to a fortune, but this was different. Violet's looks weren't of the trapping sort, but were the kind that disarmed for all their promised safety; tempted one to relax, and that was dangerous.

If he wasn't careful, he'd forget himself and say something he would regret. He could feel it in his bones with the way she drew him to her.

He cleared his throat. "I'm unsure. Through the summer, possibly longer if the area suits me."

"You won't find our little town...lacking for entertainment?" Violet asked, scribbling in the ledger book the boarding house used to record guests.

He smiled, finally moving his gaze to meet hers, and felt his heart squeeze.

"No, I expect I'll have plenty of entertainment on account of my sister and her family."

Violet beamed at him and Julian felt himself go warm at her sunny expression. The coronary squeeze became nearly unbearable at the weight of such an expression. "Seylah is gorgeous. You must be very happy to have such a perfect little thing in your family."

Damn it all. He'd been right about the ochre in her eyes. He nodded, looking away from her. "Quite. Maman is overjoyed by the new addition. I expect to have spoiled her entirely rotten by the time I return to New York."

"Of course." Violet shut the book and picked up a key. "It's your right as her uncle."

Julian cracked a smile, steadfastly avoiding looking Violet in the eyes again, and instead focused on the key in her hand. "My responsibility, I suppose."

"One might say a sacred duty, even," she said, coming around the desk to stand beside him.

"Ah, yes, the age-old tradition of spoiling a sibling's progeny until they are ruined to the core. A time-honored tradition, and we Baptistes are nothing if not sticklers for tradition."

She was close enough now that he could smell the faint scent of rosewater. Sweet and light as the laugh that slipped from her mouth at his joke—sweet and light, just like her.

Or rather, what he supposed she was, Julian reminded himself.

He didn't know this woman even if it was like something had woken up inside him the moment their eyes had met. Like lightning, it was. Electrifying every part of him that had been put to sleep by the city and constraints of polite society. The shell around him had cracked, that perfect facade he kept in place that showed how unbothered he was by everyone and everything around him had splintered with a simple hello...and the mad thing was, Julian did not hate it.

Julian could think of only one time he'd ever heard anyone describe meeting anyone like that.

His father and mother.

He swallowed hard and took another half-step away from Violet, aiming to maintain his distance. It was only proper, no matter how much he wanted to walk closely to her as if they were familiar, not strangers newly met, but...intimate. His skin flushed hot at the thought and he bit back an angry groan at himself for letting his mind get away from him—again.

What was he? An untried boy in his first season?

"Are you all right?" Violet asked, stopping to look at him strangely, and Julian knew he had almost been found out.

"I'm quite alright—better than, in fact."

"But just then..." She pointed at him and tilted her head to the side, the movement causing her dark hair to slip over her shoulders. Julian's fingers itched to see if her hair was as soft as it looked. He clenched his fingers together for a second before he shoved a hand into his pocket.

"Just then?" he prompted with as guileless a look as he could manage.

Violet blinked at him. "You growled," she informed him.

"Ah, that," he said, and chuckled, turning away to examine a painting on the wall as if the watercolor landscape were the most captivating art he'd seen since the Louvre. "That was a cough."

"A cough?" Violet's brow furrowed. "Are you unwell?"

"It's a, well... it's a small condition I have," Julian said. One that apparently only took him when he was struck dumb at the sight of a dark-eyed beauty with a smile like the sun. He winced at himself.

Confound it.

"Did you have consumption?"

He well and truly coughed at that. "Consumption? Ah, no, no, it's nothing like that." He held his hands up, but Violet continued on as if he hadn't spoken.

"Because if it is we can put you in one of the southern-facing rooms for your health." Violet turned and made to go for the keys at the front of the boarding house with a worried look on her face.

"That won't be necessary. I'm quite fine."

She shook her head, giving him a pained look. "It wouldn't do to have your health put upon by your lodging conditions. I had no idea you were sickly, I—"

Julian's eyes widened, aghast. "I am not sickly."

How had this happened? *Sickly*. Of all the things this

woman thought of him while he went moon-eyed over her? He did his best to draw himself up, posture snapping into place as he worked to project an air of perfect health.

There were many things Julian wished Violet thought of him.

Manly? *Of course.*

Virile and in possession of strength of will? *Certainly.*

He'd settle for well-read and debonair, but sickly? *No.* Under no conditions did he want that to cross her mind when she looked at him, as she was now with her big brown eyes full of concern.

He'd made an ungodly mess of this. One errant growl and suddenly he had been stricken with consumption.

"But your cough," she said.

"Is...a tickle, nothing more." He inclined his head. "Please show me to the rooms. It's fine, Miss Shield."

She worried her bottom lip. That full, pink, plump lip that begged Julian to come closer. He stood still, feet planted where he was, and gave her a tight smile.

"If you're sure."

He moved to give her a gallant bow, more at home in a ballroom than the hall of Miss Hill's boarding house. "I am. You needn't make a fuss over me, Miss Shield."

She shook her head, looking unsure, but her posture had relaxed somewhat, and if Julian didn't know better he would swear that her cheeks were dusted a pretty pink.

Was she blushing? His heart sped up, pulse hammering against his chest. Had he made her blush?

Violet swallowed and met his eyes, and this time Julian knew it was he who had put that dusky color on her cheeks. That was dangerous knowledge, it was, but for whom Julian wasn't quite sure yet.

"But your sister and her husbands, they—"

"Are quite the handful, are they not?" he asked, turning away from Violet. It was enough that she was blushing as she was, face flushed more like a dewy-eyed debutante than the cook she'd proclaimed herself to be.

The worry melted from her face as she sent another one of her heart-stopping smiles his way, though he only glimpsed it from his periphery, turned as he was under the guise of not paying attention.

What a farce that was. If Julian could preserve these happy looks, these unguarded moments with this woman, he would never want for anything again.

It had been so very long since anyone but his family had treated him like this. Hadn't wanted anything from him. Gazed at him as soft-eyed as Violet was now, even when she didn't think he saw.

"They are," she confessed before turning to continue down the hallway. "I want to make sure you're comfortable here while you visit your sister. You don't know what a boon it's been to the town for your sister to come teach here."

"And I will be, Miss Shield. Of that I promise you. Consider me the same as any other boarder, please."

She nodded, falling into step beside him. "Then please, call me Violet."

Julian nearly stumbled over his own feet at the invitation, and when he turned a surprised look on her she shrugged. "No one calls me Miss Shield. I don't—well."

She paused and looked down at her feet. "That's for a lady."

"And what are you if not a lady?" Julian asked before he could stop himself. He was elated at her allowing him to speak to her on friendly terms, but the slight frown, the pinch in her brow, that little slump to her shoulders that reminded him of a wounded bird wouldn't allow him to enjoy the pleasure of saying her given name.

Violet's eyes moved away from his. "I just...I'm not a lady," she replied, her voice quiet in a way that Julian hated for the way she seemed to shrink in front of his very eyes. "What I mean to say is that I'm a working woman," she added with a laugh that sounded hollow.

"Working or not, it has no bearing on whether you are a lady. Believe me when I tell you I can spot a lady at a hundred paces. And you, Violet, are a lady of the first degree."

She laughed then, a real laugh that had his heart singing as loudly as the bells that rang in the New Year at Trinity Church.

"You say the strangest things, sir," she said when they came to stop in front of a door that Julian supposed was meant to be his for the duration of his stay.

He held a finger aloft and gave it a wag. "We can't have that."

"Have what?"

"If I am to call you by Violet, then you can't address me as sir or Mr. Baptiste. That's my father. You must," he said, then gave her his best beseeching look, "call me Julian."

"But I-I'm just the cook. I'm not, I mean, I'm no one."

Julian felt her words as surely as if he'd been caught

unawares at the weekend boxing club he frequented. It was sharp, cutting, and left him shaking his head.

"That is quite wrong," he told her. This woman was someone—could be someone to him—but he batted away that errant thought and continued speaking as if it hadn't come unbidden to him as easily as it had. "Jobs do not determine who a person is. What you are on the inside does. Everything else is just details, Violet. Please call me by my given name. I beg you."

Her eyes widened at the word *beg* and Julian wished he could rip it back from the air as soon as it fell from his lips, but he supposed what was done was done, so he forced himself to look unbothered by that little slip of the tongue.

"All right, si—er, Julian," Violet said, her voice soft and unsure as if she were testing the word out for herself.

He quite liked the sound of his name on her mouth but knew better than to reveal it.

He smiled at her then. "Thank you."

"Of course." She leaned closer as if she wanted to say more, but then leaned away again and held his keys out to him. "These are for your rooms. Breakfast is served between the hours of seven and eight and lunch is at noon, but I am happy to make you a bite whenever the mood strikes you. If you need anything at all just, well, please ask."

He took the keys from her and ignored the way her fingertips brushed his or the fact that the metal was still warm from her hand. Shoving it into the lock, he inclined his head.

"Thank you."

“You’re very welcome…” She paused, as if not trusting herself to say his name without incident. “Julian.” She took a step back and again smiled a smile that made him feel light and alive in a way that he hadn’t known in years. At that Julian said the only thing he trusted himself to say.

“Goodnight, Violet.”

CHAPTER 2

Julian had only meant to sit for a moment, which led him, after touring his rooms and finding them more than suitable, to close his eyes and relax.

As much as he loved his family, they were taxing on a man—as much as he loved Seylah, the baby girl had a habit of waking him repeatedly and at an hour entirely unsuitable for anyone not imbibing or gambling. And that meant Julian was one thing, and one thing only.

Exhausted.

He had no clue how his twin managed to care for her new daughter and still teach. Nor how her husbands were able to keep the peace in a town this close to the frontier, with the hours they kept. The men couldn't be sharing more than three hours of uninterrupted sleep between them. Julian supposed parenthood made one into sterner stuff, capable of rising to the challenges and intricacies of raising an infant.

Parents were indomitable, no question about it. But

Julian was not a parent, and therefore he needed sleep. Six to eight hours of uninterrupted sleep, to be precise, which was what he found despite only meaning to rest his eyes. The only thing that woke him was the brisk knock at his door before a woman's no-nonsense voice called out to him.

"Breakfast will be ready in five minutes, Mr. Baptiste."

He blinked and managed a semi-intelligible answer. A groan escaped his lips as he slid from the chair with an undignified thump onto the floor.

"Blast," he murmured, rubbing his eyes and rolling his shoulders, trying to regain feeling. Sleeping upright for an entire night was not meant for a man of 21.

"And with a bed right there," he sighed, rising to his feet and casting a forlorn look at the neatly made bed to the right. Shaking off the soreness from the night before, Julian hurried through his morning toiletries, a feat considering he didn't have another pair of clothing, but he would make do with what he had. His waistcoat was only mildly wrinkled.

He brushed the dust from his boots as well as he could given his five-minute warning—which had been delivered in a voice far sterner than Violet's lilting tone—and then scrubbed his face clean. With his overcoat hanging neatly, there was little else he could do but enter the dining room as casually as one could after falling asleep sitting upright and wearing yesterday's clothes.

Violet caught sight of him the second he hit the dining room entrance, and her eyes widened at seeing him in his rumpled clothing. Julian stifled a groan. It wasn't gentlemanly of him, he knew, to be wearing the previous day's garb, but there was no helping it, not with Seylah intent on torturing her household with sleep deprivation and sound-torture tactics.

"Good morning, Violet," he greeted her.

Her brown eyes were warm on him, though they were full of curiosity. "Good morning, s—" She caught herself and then said, "Julian," in a far lower tone.

"On a first-name basis already?" a woman asked as she entered the room in a sweep of skirts. She had a kind face and blue eyes that were bright and, Julian suspected, saw more than most people intended.

Violet blushed. "Well, I—"

"It was my doing," Julian supplied, giving the woman a smile. "It didn't make sense for us to be so formal."

She raised an eyebrow. "Oh no?"

Julian shook his head and pulled out the chair in front of him. "Certainly not. We are on the frontier, no? I had hoped to—"

"To what? Become intimately familiar with my cook?" She crossed her arms, pinning him beneath a steely gaze as she took a step forward. "We may be on the frontier, but I look after my employees, because they are my friends. Miss Shield is very dear to me, and I'll not have her being wooed and left heartbroken by sweet words from a man in a rumpled suit."

Julian smiled at her and unfurled the napkin in his lap. "Admirable. You must be Mrs. Hill."

"I am."

"Julie told me all about you."

Mrs. Hill faltered then and took a slight step back. "Julie?"

He hummed. "My twin. She sent me this way last night to procure a place to stay while I'm in town visiting. An uncle's duties are never done, you see." He gave her a conspiratorial wink, and Mrs. Hill cleared her throat.

"I didn't know. My apologies, Mr. Baptiste."

"There's nothing to apologize for, Mrs. Hill. I'm very happy to know that you have your friend's best interests at heart. I never intend—"

"It wasn't his doing. I told him I wasn't a lady," Violet interrupted.

Both Julian's and Mrs. Hill's eyes snapped to Violet, who stood holding a platter of toast. Mrs. Hill opened her mouth but Violet continued on.

"He was addressing me as Miss Shield, but that's—" She broke off, shaking her head. "That's for ladies. I told him not to."

"Violet..." Mrs. Hill frowned.

Violet lifted her chin in defiance. "And he did me a kindness by asking me to call him Julian. Don't go scaring off customers, Alice. He's been a complete gentleman."

Julian knew better than to say anything as the two women stared at each other, and after a moment of pause Mrs. Hill sighed and turned toward Julian with an apologetic smile.

"I should not have assumed the worst," she told him, her tone contrite.

Julian inclined his head. "You were right to do so. To be honest, I am happy you did. It's good that you keep your guard up, Mrs. Hill."

"Call me Alice," she said. "Please. Your sister will give

me an earful if she hears you calling me Mrs. Hill. Only people I abhor call me that."

"I'll keep that in mind if you rescind the invitation during my stay." Julian grinned, taking the coffee cup Violet handed him. "Thank you," he told her. Their fingers brushed, and the slight touch hit him stronger than he would ever publicly admit.

But that didn't mean Alice's too-sharp eyes didn't light upon it, a fact he was sure of when her eyebrows lifted. He anticipated a comment on the display but was saved from losing face by the entrance of another boarder.

"Is breakfast served, then?" asked a woman in her mid-forties. She had salt and pepper hair done up in a style Julian instantly recognized as the height of fashion. Alice had barely a second to answer before a slender young woman with flaming hair entered behind her with a similar coif and a dress that would be more at home in a parlor in New York than on the frontier.

Julian nearly swore when the young woman's eyes met his. Of course he would be sitting in the previous evening's attire in front of two haut monde women such as this. He didn't miss how their eyes, both the same shade of emerald green, moved over him, taking in his appearance before they shared a glance that Julian felt was both predatory and uninterested. How a look could be both he wasn't quite sure, but he was impressed and took note of it. He stood from his seat in response to their arrival.

"Ladies," he greeted them with a slight nod, "good morning."

"And a good morning to you too," the older of the pair replied, offering her hand out to him in a gesture more suited to a debutante at her coming-out than a grown woman with an adult daughter, but Julian smiled and played the part of suitor assigned to him. He took her hand and shook it before stepping back and clearing his throat.

"I am very happy to make your acquaintance..." The woman's voice trailed off, and she gave him a considering look.

"Ah, Julian Baptiste, of—"

"New York?" the younger woman finished, suddenly coming to life. She grasped the other woman's arm and gave it a shake. "Mother! He's the heir."

Julian cleared his throat. "I much prefer just 'Julian' to 'the heir,'" he told her with an easy smile that made her cheeks flush.

"Marissa," the woman he'd shaken hands with gasped in shock at her daughter.

"I meant no offense, sir," Marissa murmured, lowering her eyes, and Julian held out his hands.

"None taken. You will have to forgive me. I haven't had more than a sniff of coffee, which I find makes me very dry indeed." He gestured to the seats in front of the women. "May I?" he asked, stepping close and moving to pull back their chairs.

"We would be so grateful," the older woman gushed, already moving to the side for Julian to pull her chair out. "I am Sarah James, and this is my charming if excitable daughter Marissa James."

"My apologies." Marissa blushed as she settled into her chair and gave Julian a contrite look. "It's just that I've never met an heir, and we read all about you and your sister coming out west. I've never heard of anything more exciting in my life. I could never do something like that!"

"But you are here too," Julian pointed out, taking his seat across from the women.

"Well, yes, we are—but Mother and I don't have fancy—"

"What my daughter means to say is that we would find it quite hard to leave the comforts of New York for the Montana territory. As it is, we came from San Antonio and have missed it terribly since arriving, even if is nowhere near as cosmopolitan as New York." Sarah shot a narrow-eyed look at the younger woman.

"Ah, yes," Marissa agreed, folding her hands in her lap. "That is what I meant."

"The frontier has its charm," Julian replied, unfolding his napkin and picking up his cup of coffee. His eyes fell on Violet as she poured for the women and placed plates of fruit and steaming oats in front of them. "And a beauty that the city cannot hope to touch."

"It's a bit wild for my taste," Marissa said with a little laugh. "Things out here are just so..." She cleared her throat and leaned forward over the table. "Did you know that there are gangs of Sioux?"

Julian's eyebrow twitched at Marissa's aghast tone. "You mean the people native to this area?"

"And I heard about some truly scandalous relationships in town," she continued on, missing the pinched look on Julian's face.

"Oh?"

"Yes, that there was maybe a woman with two hus—"

"Marissa, that's enough," Sarah interrupted her

daughter and shoved a plate of biscuits at her. "Eat your breakfast."

"But there was—"

Sarah shook the plate viciously. "Eat. Your. Breakfast."

Marissa's mouth snapped shut and she took the plate with a muffled, "Thank you."

Julian sipped at his coffee and then shifted uncomfortably in the heavy silence that descended on the dining room without Marissa's chatter. He knew whom Marissa had heard about. The woman with the scandalous relationship was his sister, and he guessed that Sarah knew that, though her daughter did not.

"Will there be anything else?" Violet asked, hands clasped, watching the trio with open curiosity.

"That will be all, girl. Go," Sarah replied curtly with the special brand of high-handed dismissiveness that set Julian's teeth on edge.

Julian never tolerated it in New York, and he would not tolerate it now. He looked toward Violet to see her nodding and backing out of the room. Julian found he could not stomach the sight of her bowed head and ready acceptance of Sarah's lack of manners. To Julian, the woman was kind, warm, and her intelligence obvious though they had only just met the night before. And even if she hadn't been any of those things to Julian, she would have still deserved far better than this treatment.

"Violet—ah, Miss Shield." Julian pushed back his chair and got to his feet. "If you'll allow me to accompany you?"

Violet blinked at him. "I—what?"

"Accompany her?" Marissa whispered to her mother at

a volume more at home on stage at the theater than in the small dining room.

"Yes," Julian answered before Sarah could. "Miss Shield is a dear friend, and I have been remiss in my duties." He crossed the dining room to Violet, who looked at him with something akin to awe.

"Duties?" Sarah asked.

Julian hummed and offered his arm to Violet. "Indeed. Duties. Have a lovely breakfast, ladies," he told them with an exaggerated formal bow that made Violet giggle.

Julian's heart leapt into his throat at the sound.

It was beautiful.

Just like her. A lesser man might have offered the world to hear it again, and possibly even swoon in the process. But Julian was made of sterner stuff, and he survived the sound of it by increasing his speed, which he supposed was entirely logical.

One outran the things that threatened their resolve, didn't they?

His plan was foolproof. Or it might have been, if Violet hadn't struggled to keep up with him, which forced him to slow and offer her an apologetic look.

"I apologize," he said, taking his arm back and looking around the kitchen.

"You went very fast from there," Violet told him, turning toward the counter beside her. "Why?"

"I don't like rude people."

She looked over her shoulder at him. "They weren't rude to you."

"That doesn't mean they were not rude."

Her eyebrows shot up and she stared at him for a moment before she held out a small meat pie. "Eat this."

"Bless you. I was worried I had sentenced myself to begging Julie for sustenance. She cannot cook, despite her many other talents. I would have starved." He took the meat pie and bit into it with a happy sigh. "This is sensational. You made this?"

Violet nodded. "I did, but it's one of Alice's family recipes."

"How much is it?" Julian asked, reaching for his billfold, but Violet stopped him with a shake of his head.

"It's free." She paused and nodded back at the kitchen doorway toward the James ladies. "For what you did back there."

"I didn't do anything, but you..." He shook the meat pie at her. "You made this delectable treat. You have to take some kind of payment."

The corner of her mouth lifted in a smirk, and Julian felt his spirits rise with it. "You did more than you let on. We both know it."

He lifted a shoulder in a shrug in a mirror movement of her lips and took another bite. "Perhaps we do and perhaps we don't. I did what anyone should have done, which is leave."

"Not everyone would have left."

Julian finished eating his pie and set about trying to locate another. "I'm not everyone."

"I'm coming to see that," Violet said, handing him another pie and earning a grateful smile.

"Then that is all the thanks I need," he said, and

nodded toward the door. "Does that lead to the main street?"

"It does."

"Good woman. I'm off to see my dear sister and family. Perhaps procure a few of my things so I'm actually presentable." He gestured toward his rumpled attire and opened the door.

"Goodbye, Julian. Have a wonderful afternoon."

"My lady," Julian said, and because he was a fool, he gave Violet a sort of exaggerated bow, replete with a grand hand flourish. He wouldn't swoon over the woman, but he wasn't made of iron.

Her laughter followed him out into the morning air, and Julian headed toward the main thoroughfare with a bounce in his step that he would swear was due to the delicious meat pie—if anyone pressed him for information on the matter.

Humming tunelessly and without discretion, the notoriously tone-deaf Julian made his way down the bustling main street of Gold Sky. It was a small town, but it was prosperous and the people were accepting and kind—they had always treated his sister well, and that was all Julian really needed to know about the frontier town to consider it every bit as good as New York City. It was even better, in fact, because here he didn't have to worry that every conversation would be disingenuous at best.

There were far too many sly and eager individuals from all walks of life in New York City that either looked to trap or make use of him for his connections. The using he could understand, because it was simply the natural order of things. Who could fault one for trying to improve their station in life by every means available?

It was the trapping that he had a problem with.

When people tried to trap someone it was never for a good reason, and in Julian's case he had long ago learned that it was often done with malicious intent. His father had done an exceptional job at preparing him for the world that awaited him outside the doors of their home. People did not think as their father and mother did, and would not be able to see a person for their worth and character. They likely would be blinded by skin color.

It was ugly but true, and Julian was under no illusion that a man like himself would be free to move through the world as he did without the power of his name and money. The realization of just how precarious his situation in society was was both sobering and motivating.

Julian did all things with passion and dedication. He was tender-hearted, caring, and a notorious prankster with a penchant for spending far too much time dreaming—but those qualities were reserved for the few souls he trusted, which amounted to the members of his family, or more specifically, the women of his family. To his mother and Julie, he was carefree and light, all smiles and on the hunt for the next frivolity...but to everyone else?

To the world, he was a Baptiste man. His father had told him as much.

"The world will try and make you forget who and what you are. Weak people fear the strong. You are a Baptiste man, and that makes you a target. It is nothing new, but your journey will be harder than the rest of us."

"Why?" he had asked his father.

"Because the weakest people will never see you as their equals. And that means you will have to be the strongest Baptiste man of all."

He'd been all of nine years old, just a boy, when his father had sat him down for this lesson, a lesson meant to ensure Julian's success in the world. Yes, he had the protections of his name and wealth, but all of that would only serve him so much. The rest he would have to do on his own.

His path would be harder.

Baptiste men were strong. He would have to be stronger.

And so that was precisely what Julian had done. He learned business, became the best in his class at Columbia University, learned the art of conversation, cultivated those relationships which strengthened his place in the Four Hundred, and proved himself to be a shrewd businessman. He grew to understand the subtleties of power within society, and learned to wield them like a weapon in tandem with his business prowess.

Not only could he keep the company of royalty without faltering—they were cousins, after all—but he was capable of commanding a boardroom with all the confidence of a king. Because a misstep could and would cost him everything his family had built. And that he would not allow.

If there was a favorable angle, he would find it. Every dollar that passed through his hands multiplied, and soon his reputation as a lucrative investor with an eye for the golden goose was unparalleled.

Investing could be risky, but not for Julian.

In this regard he was perfect, which drew any and all serious business hopefuls, both new and old, to him like flies to honey. He steadily made a name for himself, more so with his recent spearheading of a new railway line from New York to the frontier. It would bring jobs, supplies, and the much needed infrastructure that westward expansion demanded. The fact that he now had an excuse to visit the frontier was just an added bonus to what he saw as a profitable investment.

It made his decision to stay behind after his parents returned to New York a sound one, even if he hadn't quite told his mother or sister the entirety of his motivations.

His family and the promise of good business were not the only reasons for his interest in staying in Gold Sky. Julian was not only interested—perhaps he was even a tad excited at the prospect. And that was because of one dark-eyed woman whose laughter had him spiraling back to his years as an untried youth.

Violet Shield.

The woman was gentle and kind, unassuming in her warmth, and Julian felt a need to be closer to her. She inspired the same feelings of protection and nurturing as his sister and mother, but with something less familial.

Violet made him want to do these things, not as a son or brother, but as a *man.*

The morning's events flashed before his eyes and suddenly the pastry in his mouth turned to ash.

Sarah James had called Violet *girl.* Julian detested it. Violet was a woman, one he was drawn to in ways that he had never allowed himself to be in New York City. Perhaps it was the need to constantly keep his armor up that had dissuaded him from calling on young ladies more than once, or paying them too much attention beyond the necessary niceties. It was hard to relax when he saw the shrewd look enter their eyes as they calculated his net worth, as they began to work out the quickest way to not his heart, but his name.

And his billfold.

He was a Baptiste man. He was stronger than the rest, wasn't he? For that reason he guarded himself, and his heart, from forming attachments beyond fleeting affairs, and most of those had been conducted in Europe where things were different for him. It was easier to blend in there, and one couldn't throw a stone without hitting a minor duke or rub elbows with a royal every time they turned around.

That made him not so special, so singular, in his appeal to women. Gold Sky was a little like Europe in the way that he could catch his breath and lower his defenses. Violet inspired that in him, with her easy acceptance and the free and guileless smiles she sent his way—and her laughter. It was infectious, and put a smile on *his* face, which was precisely how Forrest and William found him when they crossed paths in front of the schoolhouse.

"Morning, Julian," Forrest called to him with a cheery wave. He was sitting astride a chestnut mare and looking entirely at ease in a way that made Julian wish to expand his horsemanship mastery beyond sport to pure function.

He wondered if Violet liked to ride. Perhaps he could ask her, and…

Will cleared his throat and raised an eyebrow at the faraway look in Julian's eyes.

"Forrest. Will." He nodded at both men respectively and popped the last of the meat pie in his mouth. The grin on his face was uncontainable as he chewed, and he was glad to be on the frontier where manners were...*lax*.

"What's put a smile on your face?" Will asked, peering at him from the buckboard.

Julian shrugged. "It's a beautiful day. Can't a man smile and take in all of this fresh air? We've nothing like it in all of New York."

Will snorted. "Fresh air doesn't put a smile on a man's face like that."

Forrest laughed and leaned back in his saddle. "Agreed."

Julian waved them off and threw out his arms. "Until you've been oxygen-deprived you wouldn't know the biological renaissance I am experiencing."

"Where'd you get that food?" Will asked.

"Violet—er, the boarding house."

Will and Forrest exchanged a look. "What was that?" they asked in tandem.

"Was that the boarding house, or were you maybe naming a particularly pretty cook?" Forrest grinned.

Julian was proud that his face gave away nothing. "I meant the boarding house, but now that you mention it, there is a lovely cook there."

"Believe her name is Violet," Will pointed out, flicking the reins and nudging the buckboard into motion. "She's real pretty. Smart and sweet too. Likes to read."

"That so?" Julian asked.

Forrest nodded. "Been in town for a few years. Came

this way via California. Except she's got no plans on leavin'. Alice is the closest thing she has to family."

"They did seem close at breakfast," Julian replied, keeping his tone even. He trusted and liked his brother-in-laws because Julie had chosen them, but that didn't mean he was keen on showing his hand this early.

"She's a fan of art. Likes to draw, from what I know," Forrest continued.

"Paint too," Will added. "You'll thank us later." He smirked one last time before he snapped the reins and rolled off in the direction of town.

"Thank you?" Julian tried.

Forrest urged his horse forward and only laughed at Julian on his way past. "Mark our words. You'll thank us. Let us know when you get a hankering for knowledge."

Julian saluted them both. "You have my sincere future thanks, though I'm not sure what for…" His voice trailed off, and he gave them a quizzical look that only made Forrest laugh harder as the pair headed into town. Julian tried not to notice how the sound of the men's laughter rang in his ears long after they had vanished from sight.

CHAPTER 3

"Give her here," Julian said, holding out his arms to his mother, who stood cooing over her granddaughter. The two ladies had set up court on the settee in the parlor, Seylah gurgling happily at her grandmother as Manon bounced her in her lap.

"And why would I do that?" Manon asked with a raised eyebrow. "The two of us are quite enjoying ourselves."

"Because I am her uncle and it is my birthright," he replied, continuing forward with arms outstretched. When Manon looked fit to protest he added, "I was away last night, and I suspect you've been monopolizing her."

"She prefers me. You all know it."

"Sharing is a mark of maturity. You taught me that."

Manon's mouth pursed, and she sighed as she finally relented. "Well, come on then, take your turn with my little angel."

"*Our* little angel." Julian grinned down at her and cradled the baby close. Seylah didn't fuss and immediately began reaching for Julian's lapels.

Manon rose from the settee and waved a hand at him. "Minor details."

"Did you let anyone hold Julie or me? You must have been a terror to Father when we were small." Julian looked up at his mother to see her giving him a chagrined look.

"I was...very hands-on."

Julian made a note to tell Julie they owed their father a fine whiskey for surviving their childhoods in one piece. "That's putting it mildly. You're incorrigible."

"I believe the term is maternal," Manon corrected, coming to stand beside him and tapping a finger on Seylah's pert nose.

"I stand by my statement."

"You are your father's son."

"That I am," Julian said, looking up from his niece and kissing his mother's cheek. "I secured lodging at Mrs. Hill's boarding house for my stay."

Manon tickled Seylah's feet. "Oh, is that where you were last night? We were worried, but Forrest and Will were certain all was well."

"I fell asleep sitting upright in a chair. I only meant to rest my eyes, but..." He gave Seylah a mock scowl. "This lovely banshee has been keeping terrible hours, and I am feeling the effects."

"Babies do have that effect on the general population. Those without the maternal instinct," Manon informed him with a smug smile.

"I'll not refute you, though I feel it is a blanket statement. The other men are in fighting form, leaving me the weak link."

"That's because they are fathers and husbands," Manon said, turning away and walking toward the parlor windows. "There is a certain change a man goes through when those milestones occur."

"Then I am woefully lacking."

"Only because you care to be," Manon said, turning away from the windows and looking back at her son.

Julian hummed. "I don't know if that's the case," he lied, not meeting his mother's eyes. It was so much easier to stare down into the wide, innocent eyes of Seylah, mostly because she was distracted by anything colorful or moving, which suited Julian.

"We both know it is." Manon smiled at him and clasped her hands behind her back. "But maybe things can be different with a little time away from New York."

"What do you mean?"

She shrugged in a gesture so reminiscent of his twin that Julian forgot whom he was speaking to for a moment. "I mean that the city makes you different. Harder."

"I'm as docile as a lamb. You know this. I don't know what you—"

Manon held up a hand. "Don't lie to me, sweetheart. I know it makes you more closed off. Turns you into a different man—but here you can open up and let people see you."

Julian's jaw clenched. "Mother…"

"You deserve to be seen," she told him simply.

"I'm seen plenty. I am…" He cleared his throat and bounced his niece, pressing a kiss to Seylah's forehead. "I am fine."

"You are not fine. That's one of the reasons I was so

happy to come visit Julie, so overjoyed when you took a break from work and joined us. How happy I am that you're staying behind."

Julian nodded but said nothing. She didn't know he had brought his work with him. That he probably always would take his work with him.

"It's been refreshing to be here. A break will be nice."

"I think so too," Manon agreed, and then crossed the room back to him. "I love you, sweetheart. You make me so proud everyday with all of your hard work, but please don't forget to let yourself remember that you deserve a good life, too."

"My life *is* good. Excellent, in fact. I have everything I want."

"Except for someone to love. Someone of your own, a home of your own." She looked down at her clasped hands and sighed before glancing back up at him with shining eyes. "It's okay if that home is not in New York. Your father and I will understand."

He swallowed and hitched Seylah up to his shoulder so he could slip an arm around his mother's shoulders. "I know, *maman*. Thank you."

She turned into him and wrapped her arms around him. Though she was small, there was no mistaking the strength in his mother's embrace, and some of the tension in Julian's body leaked out at her touch. For so long, his family had been enough of a home, the only tether he needed to keep himself grounded. But her words gave form to the feeling that had been sitting heavy on his chest as of late.

"I love you, Julian."

A home of his own.

Someone of his own.

He took in a shuddering breath and squeezed his eyes shut as he rocked Seylah and hugged his mother. This was his family, his home, but for the first time Julian allowed himself to dream that he could have so much more, and in a place more wild and beautiful than any he had ever known before. For it was in those wild and open spaces that a person could think, could evolve and grow into whomever they were meant to be.

"I love you too, *maman.*"

IT WAS JUST after lunch when Julian had gotten his things moved to Mrs. Hill's boarding house and put away. His stomach growled, and he set off in the direction of the café down the street. He might have sought out Violet in hopes of pilfering a few more meat pies for the occasion, but he didn't trust himself around the woman.

Not after his conversation with his mother.

The whole thing left him feeling both off-center and grounded. A curious sensation. Where his emotions usually functioned like a carefully controlled flame, Violet set him ablaze like a wildfire. And that was precisely why, after Julian dressed in fresh attire, he slipped out of the boarding house with the intent of not seeing Violet.

He turned his head and squinted into the afternoon sun. All around him people hurried by on business, horses whinnied, and wagon wheels creaked, adding to the din of chatter all around him. Yet for all of the activity it felt like

Julian was in his own world. A world where everything moved slower, or not at all, depending on how Julian looked at it. He preferred to think of the world moving in slow motion as a side effect of hunger—not Violet, or the fact that seeing his sister's happy home made him want the same for himself.

It was all just the doing of a light breakfast and a nonexistent lunch. Nothing that a hot meal couldn't fix.

He crossed the street and saw himself to an empty table. The tantalizing smells wafting from the kitchen had his stomach agreeing with his assertion that he was only hungry and nothing more. A woman emerged from the back and flashed him a bright smile.

"Are you Mr. Baptiste?" she asked, practically bouncing on her toes.

Julian smiled at the woman. It was plain to see that she was friendly, her features an open book, and he instantly liked her. "I am...but you are?"

"I'm Lily Rhodes. Ah, my husband is the barkeep at the saloon in town, but we run this café as well. We are so happy to have your family in town, and we just adore Julie."

He inclined his head. "Any friend of my sister is a friend to me. I'm pleased to meet you, Lily."

She beamed at him. "What can I get you for lunch? Though I didn't think to see you here, since you are staying at Alice's."

He nodded. "I am," he said, and gave her a questioning look. "What do you mean, you didn't think you would see me?"

She held out a menu to him. "Well, Violet is a

wonderful cook. We hardly ever see any of the guests from the boarding house because of it. It's the first choice for diners in town, but the boarders get preference, which doesn't bother me none because I know how divine her cooking is."

"She is a wonderful cook," Julian agreed, taking the menu from Lily. He scanned through the offerings and saw that while it was simple—chicken, smoked trout, potatoes, and fresh bread—it was all good and hearty food, perfect for the frontier. "But as a newcomer, it would be remiss of me not to sample all the fare in town."

"Well, whatever the reason, we are happy you are here, though I don't expect to see you regularly once you've had a dinner from our Violet."

Our Violet.

The words stirred that heavy longing in his chest that Julian was not yet accustomed to feeling. He needed to eat.

He gave her the smile he reserved for meeting debutantes. The smile was meant to distract, to derail a conversation when it ventured far too close to sensitive topics. "Then let us make the most of our time together, shall we?"

Lily blushed at the smile and Julian knew he had chosen the right tack to change the subject of conversation from Violet and her cooking. "What would you like?"

"The chicken and potatoes. I would love some of the biscuits as well."

Lily beamed. "Of course! I'll have that out in a jiff."

"Ah, er, thank you!" Julian called out to the woman as she spun on her heel and rushed toward the kitchen.

He leaned back in his seat and surveyed the rest of the room, happy to see that it was busy. There were people of every class at nearly every table, all of them enjoying their meals and spending their money, which was good for a frontier town like Gold Sky. When people had extra money to spend on niceties like a lunch out, then the economy was good. It was when places like the café were only populated by the rich that one worried. That meant the cash was gone, which told Julian that there were no more opportunities for growth.

Gold Sky, from the looks of the busy town and full dining room, was anything but. Reaching into his breast pocket, he pulled out the notebook he carried with him and began to go over the notes on the business venture he had thought to explore in Gold Sky.

A new railroad depot.

The location for a new line was perfect. Gold Sky was on the edge of the frontier, but close enough to Butte City that it was a smart choice for a depot. A depot that could serve as a point of connection for the lines already established farther west. If he positioned himself just right, he would be able to direct supplies and new citizens on their journey west.

Gold Sky was ripe for such an endeavor, and while his colleagues were still back east considering the best way to go about building and launching the necessary infrastructure, Julian had made the leap and arrived in Gold Sky well ahead of the would-be rail tycoons. Theirs was just a dream, something men liked to wax poetic about in smoke-filled drawing rooms over too many glasses of brandy, but to Julian it was a reality so close he could touch it.

Some men dreamed, but Julian acted.

He expected he might have ended up in the frontier town even without the allure of his sister and family pulling him west.

He shifted in his seat, attention drawn to the figures he had estimated for the initial stages of building the railroad depot. He would need a carpenter and other skilled tradesmen. He had heard the name Stark mentioned more than once since he had arrived, and made a note to stop by the man's shop after lunch. From there, he would visit the bank and have his accounts put in order from New York.

All in all, his day was beginning to fill with tasks, and Julian relaxed. If he was busy doing then he wouldn't be busy thinking, or giving excessive and flourish-riddled bows to beautiful women who made him dream.

He was feeling much better and in control of himself when his lunch arrived, and was more than happy with the food Lily set in front of him. It was flavorful, fresh, and generous in portion. Far better than he would have anticipated this far away from any major city, and it was only when he was halfway through his meal that he paused and glanced out the window to the boarding house.

If this wasn't as good as Violet's cooking he wondered what, other than the meat pies he had sampled that morning, was on the menu. He could see customers lined up at the door, and it made perfect sense given the meal in front of him was delicious. He took another bite and continued to look out the window, watching the hopeful diners. Violet's cooking was well-known and profitable, which he estimated gave her a measure of power in town.

Respect was owed to her, if Lily's bragging on her was anything to go by, but then why had she folded under Sarah James's high-handedness with her that morning? He was certain Alice Hill would have taken on the woman from Texas with just the same fire as she had given him if she had only known.

And that begged a very important question.

Why had Violet kept her mouth shut? Why hadn't she told Mrs. Hill?

Julian pursed his lips and looked back at his meal. Here he had gone to the café hoping to escape thoughts of Violet, but now she intruded on him and drove him to daydream. He snapped open the journal and forced himself to stare at the lines inked with numbers and tasks until they swam in front of his eyes. There was nothing like hard work to keep one's thoughts from straying away from the task at hand, which for him was business.

It was always business.

Business was safe. Business he understood.

He set off from his lunch as determined as any man could be, and refused to look toward the boarding house on his way past. The walk to Stark's Carpentry was short, which meant he had very little time to rein in his thoughts.

Stark proved to be an interesting character, an equal mix of mad inventor and creative genius with a sprinkling of skilled woodworker. He was offbeat and colorful in a way that Julian found refreshing, if only for the fact that he could tell Stark was earnest and genuinely interested in helping Julian in his plans to bring a rail to town.

"This would be good for business," Stark said, tapping his chin and looking thoughtful. "More people means more business for me. And in any case we could use some new blood around here."

"Oh?" Julian asked, hiding a grin at the carpenter's wry tone.

"It was getting a little too tame around here before your family showed up. My mind is running rampant with excitement at what other gems of personality we are missing out on, being this far out on the frontier."

"So then you'll help me make the necessary contacts and locate supplies?"

"Thirty-Five percent cut?" Stark asked, and Julian glowed with admiration. He could respect a like-minded businessman when he met one.

He held out his hand, offering the other man a handshake. "Consider it done, partner."

Stark clasped his hand and winked at him. "The deal is struck, partner. Gold Sky is in for renaissance, and we will be at the front of it. Truly exciting times."

Now Julian ambled along, his heart and spirit full of that particular sense of exhilaration that business success brought with it. His accounts at the banks had been set to rights and it had been a wonder that the bank manager hadn't passed out when he received word from New York verifying Julian's financial details.

The funds were made available on credit and Julian intended to begin making use of them immediately.

Stark had given him a list of contacts and references

for the builders, labor, and supplies necessary for the project, and there wasn't a moment to waste. Julian patted his breast pocket where his journal resided. All that precious information recorded in its pages made the little book Julian's most prized possession. He would guard the information with his life, though he suspected there would be little occasion for that considering his brother-in-laws were the area's lawmen.

He breathed in, pausing where he stood at the cross-roads of town. The town square and chapel were to the right of him, and in the distance he could see the boarding house. Within its walls he knew that Violet awaited him, and his heart sped up at the thought.

He wanted to go forward but he didn't move, feet rooted to the spot as he turned over what would happen if he let himself go to Mrs. Hill's boarding house.

He would not go straight to his rooms. He would be drawn into conversation with Violet, he would spend time with her, and they would both enjoy it.

That dream would feel more like reality, and Julian would be left wanting more of it, which would leave him confused.

He turned the other way and headed for the masonry.

Business was safe. Business he understood.

CHAPTER 4

"Will you be having breakfast today?" Violet's voice made Julian freeze with one hand on the doorknob. He'd been about to leave the boarding house, intent on getting his day started as early as possible, which may or may not have had something to do with avoiding a certain cook. He'd been at the boarding house for all of three days, and had managed to be absent for all meals save for that first almost-breakfast.

Even with his back to her he could hear the hopefulness in Violet's question, and he could imagine what she looked like now, staring at him with wide brown eyes and a soft smile. He could see it plainly, perhaps because he had thought of Violet frequently, turning over their brief conversation in his mind like a treasured possession.

It was infatuation, he told himself. Nothing more.

He turned to look at her, fully prepared for his heart to flip-flop in his chest, and was instantly hit with a wave of longing so heavy it almost made him stagger. He'd wanted to look at her for days now, but hadn't allowed himself the indulgence.

Violet wore a pale blue dress that worked to emphasize her brown eyes in a way that made it a challenge to not maintain eye contact for longer than was polite. Her raven hair was pulled up and away from her face, and a freshly starched apron rounded out the picture. To some, it was a plain work outfit, but Julian knew the woman would have held his attention even in a room full of debutantes wearing the season's latest fashions.

He let himself look his fill, and the smile he gave her happened so swiftly that it shocked them both.

"Sorry?" he tried when he realized he hadn't responded.

"Breakfast?" Violet cleared her throat and clasped her hands in front of her. "I set a place for you, but you've been rising earlier than I anticipated. Or is something the..."

She paused and seemed to think twice about the words she spoke before saying, "I trust your stay is meeting your standards of comfort? Do you have any cooking requests?"

There was worry in her eyes, and her fingers twisted in her apron as she awaited his answer. Julian almost swore when he realized it had crossed her mind that her cooking might be the reason for his hasty departures every morning.

"Oh, yes, of course," he rushed to say. "Your cooking and the accommodations here are second to none."

She frowned, raising her eyes to his. "Then why are you—" Again she stopped herself and shook her head.

"Why am I what?" Julian asked when she didn't go on speaking.

"Nothing," she said, giving him a quick smile that he noticed didn't reach her eyes.

His heart clenched in a way that told him this was more than a passing fancy. He wanted to get to know Violet, to see what was important to her, and from what he had gathered her cooking was very important to her—so important it was driving her to ask after his absence.

"You don't have to guard your words with me, Violet," he said, letting go of the doorknob and taking a step closer to her. "In fact. I wish you wouldn't."

She bit her bottom lip, and then her eyes slid over to meet his gaze. "Lily says you've been in every day this week, so I thought…well, I thought perhaps you didn't enjoy the fare here."

He sighed and gave her an apologetic smile. "No, not at all. Lily's cooking is wonderful, but yours is exceptional. My hours have just been rather erratic with my new little undertaking, and I haven't been able to make your dining hours."

"Undertaking?"

"Yes, I mean to bring a railroad through town."

Her eyes widened. "That's not a little undertaking, Julian."

He grinned at her. "I suppose it isn't, but it also means I've been distracted as of late—scattered, if you will. Meals at my sister's or the café are proving to be the best fit at the moment."

She blushed scarlet. "Of course, that makes sense. I just—I'm sorry for not—" She waved a hand with a wince. "I should have known you were busy with something very important."

"Meals are important," he replied. "Thank you for asking after me."

"Of course. I wanted to make sure you weren't having to inconvenience yourself if I wasn't providing food you agreed with."

In wooing a woman, one must know a woman's heart and mind. Cooking was, Julian could see, firmly present in both places for Violet. And while his logic told him this was a passing fancy, his heart refused to budge on the matter. Which was precisely how he found himself offering his arm to her and nodding at the dining room behind them.

"And I thank you for your concern, Violet. You said my place is set?"

She swallowed, looking down at his arm, and Julian knew he wasn't alone in recognizing the spark between them. That was more gratifying than learning the lumber shipment he expected would be available right when he was ready to begin construction.

"It is."

"Then please lead the way, and forgive my errant attendance. You can expect to see me for lunch and supper today."

'You musn't put effort in on my account."

"Your account?" He raised an eyebrow and looked down at her. "My reasons are not entirely noble. I have a penchant for gluttony, and if I am able to scratch that itch with your cooking, then why not? Besides, my sister has gotten it into her mind that she will master cooking this summer, and her meals are...lacking."

Violet winced. "She's trying to cook again?"

"Ah, so you've heard?"

"Everyone in town knows about her pies."

"Those are manageable now," he told her with a shake of his head. "Or, rather, I can manage to keep them down. God bless her husbands."

Violet laughed, fingers tightening slightly on the arm she still held as they stepped through the dining room. "There is a lid for every pot, and in her case two lids. The three of them were made for one another."

"The three of whom?" a voice asked, and Julian's gaze snapped to the table to see that Sarah and Marissa James were already seated and serving themselves.

Violet's eyes shifted to Julian before she said, "No one, ma'am."

"Were you just talking about the triad marriage I heard about at the mercantile yesterday?" Marissa asked. "And the lawmen, of all people, with the teacher! How absolutely scandalous is that?"

"Isn't your sister the teacher?" Sarah asked, looking at Julian with a raised eyebrow.

"So she is," Julian said with a bland smile. "You'll never guess who my brothers-in-law are."

The older woman's eyes widened. He could tell she was calculating what to say next, estimating the payoff versus the possible penalties of how she expressed herself on his sister's marriage. Meanwhile, her daughter, blissfully unaware, slathered jam on her biscuit with a giggle.

"I would have never suspected such salacious

behavior from a teacher. I thought they were all supposed to be rather rigid. But two husbands? That's just—"

"Just fine," Sarah said, cutting in with a smile, and Julian had to repress his bemused expression. So she had chosen honey rather than vinegar. He made note to watch the woman for a motive, but kept his face impassive as he continued to assess the situation.

"I think as much," he agreed, but offered the two women nothing else. A swift kick from Sarah cut Marissa's comments short, and Julian let out a relieved sigh, though he was granted little time for recovery.

"Well, don't the two of you look fit for a ball?" she observed, taking in the way Violet's hand still rested on his forearm. Violet stiffened at the comment and let go of him, stepping away so fast Julian was surprised she didn't pinwheel into the sideboard.

"Tell me, have you ever been to a ball?" she asked Violet. "Do they let people like you attend?"

Julian balked at Marissa's words and he squared his shoulders, reaching to take back Violet's hand. The way they spoke to her was improper, not to be tolerated, but when he moved toward Violet she only gave him a quick shake of his head. Her dark eyes told him everything she wasn't saying.

It's all right. Stop.

His fists clenched, because it was not all right.

"I expect she hasn't set foot in one if she wasn't working. Isn't that right?" Sarah crossed her arms, green eyes going cold as they landed on Violet, and Julian's lips pursed into a thin line. He didn't like the way the woman looked at Violet. And he didn't much care for her daughter's comments.

Violet shook her head. "No, I haven't, Mrs. James." She turned to Julian but avoided looking at him. Even so, the sight of her pleading eyes staring at him burned into his mind. "Is there anything I can get you for breakfast?"

"No," he murmured, and gave her a quick shake of his head, suppressing the urge to tell Violet that unless she had a way of providing him with new breakfast company there was nothing that could be done to improve his dining experience.

But that he wouldn't do, not with her silently begging him to stay quiet.

He would respect her wishes, though that didn't mean he wouldn't do what he could to inform Alice of today's events. He did not think she would take kindly to how the women treated Violet.

He cleared his throat and glanced over at the pair, who watched them with rapt attention. As much as he wanted to make another quick exit, there was no way to do it without raising Violet's suspicions concerning his absence from the boarding house meals. Or leaving her alone with only the women for morning company.

He would stay, if only to act as a buffer.

"Thank you. Everything looks delicious," Julian told her, careful to keep his voice light and his best smile trained on her. She didn't deserve anything less than his best, not with Sarah and Marissa watching. She nodded at him and then left the room on her heel without a second look.

Julian crossed to his seat and prepared himself for

enduring the necessary pleasantries that a gentleman was expected to extend over breakfast, even if his dining companions were not of his choosing, when a quick *ahem* made the three diners turn toward the doorway Violet had just vanished through.

Alice Hill stood there, wearing a severe look on her face.

Her blue eyes moved over the room before they came to land on Sarah and Marissa.

Julian swallowed and thanked his fortune that her look was clearly not directed at him.

"What did you say to Violet?" she asked in a clipped tone.

Sarah tossed her head. "I don't know what you're talking about. Who is Violet?"

"Miss Shield," Julian replied, sipping his coffee.

"The cook?" Marissa asked.

"Oh, well, who—" Sarah began, but her voice cut off when Alice continued.

"Yes," Alice said, stalking into the room, "the cook. The cook, who has a name. The cook, who just left this room like it was on fire."

Julian forced his face to stay collected as he watched Alice's anger bloom and fill the room. The woman was electric, and he wouldn't be surprised if she were to reveal herself as an incognito Valkyrie.

Sarah looked uncomfortable under the full weight of Alice's attention. "Yes, about that—" she began, but Alice kept speaking.

"I will ask you once more, Mrs. James. And keep in mind that if you do not answer me truthfully, you will be asked to leave my establishment. What did you say to Violet?"

Marissa made a choking sound at Alice's words, but her mother tossed her head again and stood from the table. "If you wish to quarrel over a servant, then I have no wish to be present at your establishment. There are finer places in town for us to take our money to."

Alice crossed her arms. "Then, by all means, please exercise your rights and vacate the premises immediately."

"Is she serious, Mama?" Marissa whispered, watching the scene with wide eyes.

"Quite," Alice replied, stepping to the side as a sputtering Sarah swept toward the dining room door in a flurry of skirts and curses so colorful that Julian was impressed.

He leaned back in his chair, content to watch the whole affair unfold in front of him like the latest vaudeville theater production. It was certainly full of dramatics and energy.

When the women left for their rooms, Alice sighed and fell into a dining room chair with a groan.

"Those horrible women."

Julian nodded. "They are very...undesirable."

"I debated on kicking them out earlier this week, but Violet wouldn't have it," she told him, and Julian looked at her in surprise.

"Why not? Why would she do that?"

"Because she wanted us to have their money. Because Violet cares more about this place than she does herself.

Because she never kicks up a fuss and works hard for the ones she loves."

"She does seem that particular sort of woman."

"She is. The very best," Alice said. "I shouldn't have listened to her. I should have sent them away from the very first when I saw how they treated her."

"I was meaning to bring that to your attention after breakfast." He drummed his fingers on the table and leaned back in his chair. "But..." His voice trailed off and he threw up his hands.

"But it's my business," Alice said, meeting his eyes with a shake of her head. "It shouldn't be on you to protect Violet. That is on my shoulders, as her employer and friend."

Julian nodded in agreement, but it was hard for him to shake the feeling that he should have done more. "Even still..."

Her mouth pressed into a thin line. "Even still, nothing. You're just like Julie, thinkin' you can fix everything for everyone, but you couldn't in this instance. It's a delicate thing, we both know it."

"I suppose," Julian grumbled. The sound of a slamming door and raised women's voices made him look toward the door with interest. Alice only sighed and rolled her eyes at the racket.

"Two squawking hens, the pair of them," she told him, turning in her seat to watch Sarah marching forward and dragging her daughter along behind. Marissa struggled to keep up while pulling a trunk.

"Mm," Julian hummed, and had to cover his mouth

with his hand when Sarah paused in the doorway and shook a finger at Alice.

"Shame on you!" she yelled, face turning as red as her hair.

"Yes, shame on me for protecting my friends," Alice said, looking unbothered at the yelling woman. "Good day, Mrs. James."

"And you!" Sarah turned to point at Julian. "You are a gentleman from a fine family! How can you let us be turned out like this?"

"He has no power here." Alice stood from the table and shook a finger at Sarah. "This is my boarding house, not Mr. Baptiste's. If I want you gone, then you will go. Now go!"

Sarah's eyes shot wide and she jerked back as if she had been slapped. "I never," she sputtered, but made a beeline for the front door all the same when Alice took a step toward her.

"I'll wring that woman's neck like a chicken if I see her again," Alice seethed as the door slammed shut. "I'm going to check on Violet," she said, bustling toward the doorway, but she paused and looked at Julian. "Do me a favor, for Violet?"

"Anything," Julian said before he could stop himself. Alice beamed at him and then pointed at the table.

"Be a dear and eat as much as you can? As in everything? I don't care if you have to fill your pockets, but get as much of that food down as you can. Violet does get a case of melancholy when her food goes uneaten."

Julian saluted her. "I will do my citizen's duty to keep Violet's feelings intact."

"Of that I have no doubt." Alice grinned at him. "I thank you for aiding me in my efforts to keep Violet's spirits up. It's up to me, as I am the only family she has, and that is the way it is, at least until…" Her voice trailed off, and she looked away with a frown.

"Until what?" Julian asked.

"Until she marries," Alice sighed and looked down at her hands. The image of Violet with another man, a faceless man as it were, happy and thriving, struck Julian between the eyes before he could stop it, and he cleared his throat.

"Ah, yes, that. Marriage."

"Ah, yes, that," she replied with a chagrined smile. "Though I think I've had the most brilliant idea on the matter."

"Mrs. Hill?" Julian tilted his head to the side and tried to make sense of the eager look in the woman's eyes. "What are you meaning to do?"

"You'll see," she told him, already dancing out of the room with a laugh. "You'll all see! It's just the thing. Just wait!"

Julian stared after her as she dashed from the room, vanishing faster than Sarah James and her hapless daughter had moments before. The woman was on a mission, an ambitious one at that, one focused entirely on Violet. Julian couldn't quite figure out what she meant to achieve with her plan, so he turned his thoughts to calculating how many meat pies could one make off with if one's suit pockets were optimized to maximum capacity.

CHAPTER 5

Julian spent the rest of his day getting to know Gold Sky's mayor and local businessmen. Now that he knew the plan was entirely within his means to execute, the finer points of business required attention, and that meant hours and hours of face-to-face contact with Gold Sky's most influential citizens.

Without their support the undertaking would be impossible, even with his considerable means. Julian would not be able to secure the necessary land from the township on his own.

He knew the best way to a person's support was through their pockets, and at times, their hearts. The men and women of Gold Sky proved no different than anyone else he had met in New York City or abroad. Everyone was motivated by the promise of prosperity and security, after all. But while Julian called it relationship-building, or cultivating connections, Anthony Stark referred to it as *schmoozing and boozing*, a term Julian couldn't say was wrong.

As such, when he returned to the boarding house that evening after a particularly fruitful schmoozing and boozing session, Julian felt relaxed and looser than he had in days. All the unpleasantness of the morning was far behind him, but the moment he entered the boarding house it all came back in a rush. The establishment was a flurry of activity with the influx of eager diners filling the dining table and parlor with chatter and laughter.

He paused in the doorway and took in the boarding house with new eyes. It was electric. Positively buzzing with energy.

And it was all because of Violet's cooking. Though he would argue that it was the woman and not her cooking that brought Gold Sky residents for dinner.

His eyes fell on Violet as she exited the kitchen and made her way to the dining room, a platter of pastries in hand, and he didn't miss how her body jerked when she caught sight of him. Her warm brown eyes widened and a pretty blush colored her cheeks, and Julian knew she was surprised but pleased to see him for dinner.

It brought him no small amount of pleasure to put the shy smile on her face, and after a beat she started forward. His heart began to thump in his chest with all the force of a runaway steam engine as she approached, and he felt his feet begin to move in a mirror of her steps.

She smiled at him as they came closer. "I'm happy you —" she began, but her words cut off when a man hurried out of the dining room, a large bouquet of flowers in his hands.

He stepped in front of Julian and dropped into a low bow in front of Violet. "Miss Shield," the man exclaimed and then looked up, thrusting the flowers at her. "These are for you."

"Alex?" Violet hopped back from the man and blinked at him. "What are you doing?"

"Making my intentions known."

"What?" Violet gasped as he continued to wave the flowers at her.

"Well, I, uh," the man stammered, and Julian felt a surge of pity for him. Coming up with one's motivations, let alone romantic intentions, when standing upright was troublesome enough, let alone when holding a right-triangle posture.

"Your ad..." he said, trailing off when Violet made no move to come closer.

"My ad what, Alex? I don't have an ad for anything."

Alex looked up at her then, and Julian didn't miss how the man lost all color in his cheeks. "You don't?"

She shook her head no, eyes flicking to meet Julian's over Alex's bent form. "No, I most certainly do not."

Alex righted himself and reached into his breast pocket. "Oh, Lord above, I cannot have read it wrong. I read it three dozen times since this morning when it was printed. It says you're—"

"That I'm what?"

"Looking for a husband."

The platter of desserts slipped from Violet's hands. "What?" she cried, her hands moving to clutch at her chest. "You can't be serious."

Julian made as undignified a sound as any and shook

his head. "A husband?" he asked, a touch more alarmed than he liked. He cleared his throat and did his best to hold his tongue while Violet processed Alex's words.

"Give it here," Violet ordered, reaching out a hand and pointing at the newspaper clipping Alex held in front of him, looking at it with increasing confusion.

"Erm, yes, okay," he stammered, giving her the slip of paper. He clutched the bouquet and gave Julian a sidelong look. "I got here first, so don't try any funny business," he told Julian, shaking the oversized bouquet at him like a sword.

Julian batted away the flowers with a frown. "I believe it's Violet's choice, not who arrives first."

The man's eyes narrowed and he jabbed Julian in the chest with the flowers, sending a spray of petals flying. "And she'll choose me. Just because you are high society doesn't mean you are a better choice."

"A better choice for what?" Julian asked, dodging another jab from the flowers and giving Violet a concerned look. "Are you all right?"

She shook her head. "I feel like I'm losing my bearings," she whispered, a hand going to her forehead.

"What is it?" Julian shouldered his way past Alex and held out a hand to her. "May I?" he asked, gesturing at the paper she clutched. Wordlessly she handed the clipping over to him.

Julian dropped his eyes to the clipping and saw that it was indeed an advert. A short one, but what it lacked in length, it made up for in impact.

Make haste, men of Gold Sky.

Young, accomplished, skilled cook seeking well-suited husband.

All interested applicants should begin courting Violet Shield ASAP.

Can be found at Mrs. Hill's boarding house.

"It's as he says," Violet groaned.

"Who would do this?" Julian asked her, shooting a glare over his shoulder when Alex edged closer. "Back off, you cad."

Alex was aghast. "I am not a cad. I am trying to court her. The ad says to do so. And to make haste in the endeavor!"

"Is this what haste is to you? Does it look like she wishes to be courted by you?" Julian jerked his chin over at Violet, who stood with her arms wrapped around herself.

"Well, I haven't a clue," Alex replied. "I've never courted a woman."

"Allow me to do you a service by explaining that women do not behave as she currently is when the man is welcome."

When Alex sighed and looked ready to dismiss Julian's words, he crossed his arms and stepped in front of the other man with a scowl.

"You'll go no further. I don't care how many times you swing those flowers at me. They'll be down to the stem by the end of it."

Alex's mouth pursed. "Very well, but if I lose out on this deal because of your interference, then I—"

"Then you'll what?" Julian asked, voice low and quiet,

but unmistakable even with the chatter coming from the next room.

Alex balked and took a hasty step away. "Well, I don't rightly know quite yet."

"Then perhaps take some time to gather your thoughts and get back to me on the matter, hmm?"

Alex drew himself up. Julian knew the other man was angry but was uncertain how far he was willing to go to run him off. That uncertainty was enough to send him running—Julian could see it in the man's eyes as he scoffed and slunk out of the boarding house.

Julian held his imposing posture until he was certain Alex was gone, and only then did he turn toward Violet. She leaned against a wall, a hand braced on it while the other covered her mouth as she bent over.

If Julian wasn't mistaken, she looked as if she were about to retch.

"Do you need water?" he asked, taking a hesitant step toward her.

"Yes," she rasped, and then shook her head, lifting her eyes to his. "No. I mean, I don't know. I feel like I need something far stronger than water."

"I'll fetch you whatever you like."

"You've done enough just by sending Alex away. Thank you."

He waved a hand. "A man has no business forcing his attentions on a woman. Anyone would have done the same."

"Even so, I appreciate your kindness, Julian. I've already taken too much of it."

"You cannot take too much of something freely given."

She pushed herself away from the wall and blinked at him. "There you go again," she said in a voice so soft it made him think of butter melting in the sun, of the sticky sweetness left on one's lips after a summer treat.

"Who was he?" he asked.

"No one of consequence. A banker."

His heart soared at that dismissal, so he ventured a quick, "Who wrote the letter?"

Her face darkened. "There is only one person who would have done this to me."

"Who?"

"Alice."

He winced, mind flashing to the memory of Alice rushing from the dining room that morning with a plan that would 'be just the thing' for Violet's situation. It seemed that, rather than let Violet's life run its natural course, Alice had sought to speed up the effects with a little newspaper advertisement.

"That would be very unfortunate, but…"

"What would be unfortunate?" Alice asked, poking her head out from the dining room and casting a suspicious look at the two of them. "Can anyone tell me why there are flower petals all over the hall?" she asked, pointing at the scattered petals that had come loose in Julian's encounter with the weaponized bouquet.

Violet narrowed her eyes, the softness she had been directing at Julian melting away to reveal a fire that made Alice's earlier anger at Sarah James pale in comparison. "What have you done, Alice?"

"What? I haven't done a thing. I've been in the parlor

playing whist, like any god-fearing frontierswoman, and—"

"*Make haste, men of Gold Sky?*" Violet bit out, throwing her arms wide, and Alice stopped short with a little laugh.

"Ah, yes, that."

"*That.*" Violet stalked forward. "That's all you have to say for yourself, putting an advertisement calling for suitors—"

"Not suitors, but a husband," Alice corrected, walking backward into the hallway. "That is an entirely different thing, you know."

"How so?"

"Suitors are for fun. A husband is family."

"And I have all the family I need in you," Violet insisted.

"But what happens when I'm not here anymore?" Alice asked, crossing her arms. "I won't be around forever. I've told you and Peter this countless times. That boy is going to drive me into an early grave anyhow, and that means I need to see you off as well as I can."

A heavy silence settled over the hallway and Violet took in a ragged breath. Her eyes shone bright with unshed tears. "Alice, no."

Alice scoffed. "Alice, yes."

Julian laughed at the two women and then shrank under the weight of Violet's ire. "And that is my cue to make a hasty exit." He nodded at them and skirted toward the dining room. "I'll just grab a bite and be on my way, ladies."

Violet cleared her throat. "Goodnight, Julian. Thank you again."

Alice winked. "Talk soon, Julian."

Julian faltered in his steps and raised an eyebrow, puzzled at the amused smile on the woman's face. "Ah, of course."

Violet shook a finger at Alice. "Don't you dare bring him into this." She gave him an apologetic smile. "Julian, please enjoy your dinner."

He nodded at her and, not willing to risk another sharp look from either woman, kept his mouth shut and his steps determined on his way to the packed dining room.

Upon entrance he saw that it was arranged quite differently than it was for the mornings. Gone was the one elegant breakfast table, and in its place sat a serving sideboard laden with food. Two servers hurried about, refreshing drinks and clearing away plates from the six smaller tables occupying the rest of the room. The diners seemed blissfully unaware of the drama taking place only feet away in the hallway.

Through the doorway at the end of the dining room Julian could see a card game in the cozy parlor, and he debated where to best focus his attention, but his rumbling stomach told him where to indulge himself.

"Food it is," he murmured, taking a plate from a server and filling it as quickly as was allowed in mixed company. Glancing around, he spied an empty seat at a table with three other men. Thankfully, they saw his plight and waved him over.

"Thank you," he said when he pulled out the seat, and sank into it with a grateful sigh.

"Not a problem, young sir," a man with a long grey

beard and a wizened face told him. “Place is jam packed tonight on account of the big news.”

Julian unfolded his napkin and picked up his fork and knife. “Oh, what news is that?” he asked, perking up at the prospect of new information. Seeking to bring the railway to Gold Sky meant it was now his business to be as well-informed and connected as he could.

“Why, the news about Violet, of course,” the man sitting next to him, a big blond man, told him with a nod. “Wore my best clothes tonight for it, I did.”

The other man at the table, a youth of no more than fifteen years, nodded along with the others and ran a hand over what looked like a coif made possible by the liberal application of pomade. It was then that Julian truly looked at the men and saw they were all scrubbed clean of any dirt, their skin pink and raw, clothes neat, pressed and freshly laundered, shoes shining bright under the light of the dining room.

“I see.” Julian took a bite of his dinner and chanced a glance around the table as they all began to extol Violet’s many virtues.

“She’s beautiful,” the youngest sighed with a moon-eyed look.

“She can make a meal out of anything,” the blonde said, patting his stomach with a sigh. “Can you imagine it?”

“I heard she’s a sure hand with a horse, too. I’m sure children would be easily managed,” the older man told them all.

Julian frowned. These men were here for Violet, or rather, Alice’s ad. She did not have value to them as a person, as a woman, but rather for her skills, which he supposed was a frontier frame of mind. He didn't like it in the least.

"There she is." The youth pointed a finger at the dining room entrance, and Julian turned to see a stunned Violet standing in the doorway with a fresh platter of desserts in hand.

A hush fell over the tables, which Julian finally noticed were packed with only male citizens. Violet must have noticed the same, because he watched her face turn bright red. She swallowed and made it all of two steps into the dining room before a man appeared at her side and offered to take the platter for her.

Violet murmured her thanks and looked prepared to endure the company of the men gathered, but when an entire table leapt to their feet and began presenting her with flowers, her resolve vanished like a puff of smoke and she whirled away, intent on fleeing the dining room.

The only thing that stopped her escape was Alice, who appeared in front of her and caught her arm. The other woman turned her about and flashed the room a bright smile.

"We are so happy all of you came tonight," Alice exclaimed, guiding Violet further into the room. "You all, no doubt, understand that Violet is a lady of extreme quality and elegance."

A murmur of agreement rippled through the crowd, and Violet paled, looking as if she wished to be anywhere but in the crowded dining room.

"Thank you for coming." Violet's voice was weak and Julian couldn't help but notice that she struggled for her next words. He knew what it was like to be the center of attention in a crowded room, and that it was daunting even when one was used to it. Violet must be drowning under the weight of so many eyes.

"Now then." Alice clapped her hands and pointed at a seat someone else currently sat in. "Give her that seat and let's all spend a bit of time getting to know one another, hmm?"

The man in the seat nearly fell to the floor in his scramble to present it to Violet, but she didn't move toward it until Alice nudged her forward. She glanced back at Alice and bit her lip. An encouraging nod made Violet move forward on heavy feet, and Julian felt a wave of regret for the woman.

If Alex's earlier approach and the men at Julian's table were any indication of Violet's night, then she was in for a very long one indeed. But with a determined tilt of her chin and squared shoulders, she walked forward and took the seat. It might not be what she had wanted, but she seemed determined to see it through in spite of her earlier misgivings.

It would be so much easier for her to hide from the entire affair, but she had chosen to exercise the only polite avenue available to her given the circumstances.

Julian felt a measure of admiration for the woman.

"You'll all want to take a number if you hope to speak with her tonight," Alice said, coming to their table and holding out a roll of tickets. Julian raised an eyebrow as she handed out tickets to the men at his table.

"You don't want one?" she asked when he didn't reach for a ticket.

He shook his head. "No thank you, Alice."

"Julian, I should have expected as much."

"And why is that?" he asked, cutting into his meal with exaggerated slowness.

She shrugged, handing a ticket to the man beside him. "You just don't seem the sort to utilize an advert to find a wife."

"My sister did, though, once upon a time."

"So she did, but you are a different sort altogether, Julian Baptiste. Don't think I don't see it."

He grinned at her. "I thank you for noticing my differences from my beloved twin, but even so, that isn't why I don't want a ticket."

"Then what is it?" she asked, and the men at the table nodded along, their attention diverting from Violet for a moment to look at him curiously.

"Because Violet didn't choose this," he told her, taking another bite of his food.

Alice's lips pursed as he chewed, and she sighed. "That's because the girl doesn't know how hard the world will be without family by her side later on. This is prudent."

"Even still, she did not choose it. I cannot take part, knowing that."

She perked up. "Then, if it were her choosing...you would?"

Julian froze, fork halfway to his mouth. He had underestimated Alice's line of questioning. "If it were," he said, clearing his throat, and setting down his fork. "If she chose it, then that would be a different matter entirely." Alice's eyes brightened in victory, so he took in a deep breath and went on before she could say a word. "However, she did not, so the point is moot."

Alice rolled her eyes. "So you say, Julian. So you say, but now I know different." She took a step back from him and waved her fingers in parting. "Enjoy your dinner. And gentlemen, I shall be by to collect your tickets and escort you to speak with our fair Violet when it is your turn. Ta!"

And with that, Alice turned away in a swirl of skirts and moved to the next table, offering tickets to eager hands. Julian kept his eyes on his plate and didn't allow himself to look up at Violet, not once, not even when he heard her laugh.

If he did, he might make the mistake of forgetting that this was not her doing and wonder why exactly he hadn't claimed the entire ream of tickets for himself.

~

THE FLURRY of the previous evening was nowhere to be found by the time breakfast was served the next day. He entered the room half-expecting to see it full of ill-advised suitors, but not a scrap of poorly written poetry or even a flower petal remained from the dinner's excitement.

"Curious," he murmured, turning around to survey the dining room. It had been put back to rights, the long table once more in its place and breakfast laid out for one. Boarding house breakfast hours occurring a solid hour before the dining room was open to the public proved a blessing now that Sarah and Marissa James were gone. The quiet was refreshing after the fracas he'd sat through at dinner—though he supposed he got off far easier than Violet had fared.

She'd been a regular belle of the ball, albeit a reluctant one.

"Startling, isn't it?" Violet asked, walking in beside him, a coffee pot in her hands. She glanced back at him when he jerked in surprise at her appearance.

"Well, yes," he admitted, pulling out his seat and sitting down. "It was...lively last night."

"That's putting it mildly."

"Will you choose any of them?"

Violet gave him a shocked look. "No, of course not. Why would you ask that?"

"Because you sat and met them all. Alice gave out all the tickets she had," he reminded her.

She poured him a cup of coffee and let out a weary sigh. "I've learned that it's far better to go with whatever plan Alice has hatched rather than fight her on it. The more you dig in your heels, the more she fights to get her way."

"Is that so?" Julian asked.

"Quite," she replied. "Ask anyone in Gold Sky and they'll tell you the truth about how Alice Hill gets when she's taken an idea to mind. It's hopeless."

"Well, with that kind of attitude, it is." Julian sipped from his cup and then nodded at the seat across from him. "Sit down for a moment?"

Violet hesitated, her fingers flexing on the coffee pot before she let out a long sigh. "I suppose I can take a moment to sit."

"You wouldn't make me eat alone, now would you?"

Julian asked, unfolding his napkin across his lap with a grin. "A breakfast partner would enhance my stay by untold amounts."

Violet laughed. "Oh, is that so? I suppose you'll have me eating too, if I sit?"

"You're onto me. Allow me," he told her, reaching for the serving dish of fruit beside him and gesturing at the empty plate in front of her. The corner of Violet's lips turned up as she handed him the plate and took it back with a murmured thanks before she began dishing potatoes out to the both of them.

"What's the occasion for wanting to have breakfast?"

"I enjoy your company," he told her matter-of-factly. "I haven't been present enough lately, and given the turn of events I suppose this may be the only hour I'll be able to steal with you. You are the most popular woman in town, after all."

"I wouldn't go that far," she said, pouring herself a cup of coffee. "It's just a simple advert by Alice."

"It's an advert for a husband, so there's nothing simple about that."

She sipped her coffee and shrugged. "That depends on who you ask." Her voice was even in tone, but Julian detected a waver that had him looking up at her in curiosity. There was a note of despondency to Violet's words that he didn't understand.

"Why do you say that?" he pressed.

"Who would want to marry me? In earnest."

He raised an eyebrow at her and gestured around himself with both hands. "This entire dining room was filled to the rafters with men who were eager for the honor of being the man who calls you wife. Do you not remember that?"

She shook her head. "That's not—they don't mean it."

"And why not?"

Violet bit her lip and looked up at him, her brown eyes meeting his with an unblinking stare. "Those men didn't know me. Not the real me. They know I can cook, but everyone does. That's my job. All I am to them is a hot meal and someone to raise a brood with. Nothing more. My life may not be much, but it is mine. I am free to come and go as I please, and I'll not tie myself to a man who sees me as an extra pair of hands around the house at the price of my freedom."

"Meaning?"

"Meaning that men fancy they can tell a woman what to do, how to think and act. A man who does not love the woman he marries will care little of what she wants for herself, and that is not the life I want. I want my freedom, precious little that it is."

Julian blinked at her words. They hit him over the head like an anvil, and he suddenly saw the world through Violet's eyes. It wasn't a place full of opportunity, but one hemmed in by circumstance and gender. It was sobering, and he sighed, considering her words. "That...is reasonable."

She blinked at him, her fork hitting his plate with a clatter. "It is?"

He nodded. "Certainly. I abhor anyone telling me how to live. Why should you be expected to like it?"

"Well, because—because I'm a woman."

He waved a hand. "Pah. Julie is a woman, a lady even,

but that has never stopped her from disliking authority. She's practically made a business of shirking it since she arrived on the frontier."

She grinned. "I have heard that. Witnessed it firsthand, in fact."

"Then you know precisely why I understand what you mean." He scrubbed a hand over his face and asked, "What will you do if you don't intend on taking a fiancé?"

Violet drummed her fingers on the table, a thoughtful look on her face. "I hadn't quite worked that detail of my plan out."

"So there's a plan, hmm?"

"Well, so to speak, there is."

Julian leaned forward on the table, all thoughts of manners and where gentlemen should put elbows when dining in the company of a lady evaporating at the prospect of enjoying a conversation with Violet. "Care to tell me your plan? I may be able to help."

She looked at him in surprise. "You would help me?"

"Of course. I consider it my duty, as a gentleman, to aid any lady in need of assistance. They practically make us swear an oath on it when they discharge us from university."

She raised an eyebrow. "Oh they do, do they?"

"They make us swear on a pile of cravats and cherished timepieces."

Violet laughed, a full-bodied laugh that Julian instantly took to. It was warm and rich, like her smiles, and poured so freely from her that his mind instantly skipped to how he might make her laugh again in the future.

Any woman who laughed like that should be encouraged with impunity. He'd always been a wondrous enabler. Julie would testify to that.

Violet grinned at him, her cheeks flushed and a giggle on her lips. "I supposed I would be delinquent if I did not take your offered help."

He gave her a serious look, steepled his fingers together, and rested his chin against his hands. "Very, Miss Shield. One shouldn't ignore available assistance when it is readily provided. Now then, tell me this plan of yours. What does step one entail?"

"Step one is just what you saw last night," she explained, running a hand through her hair. "I planned to hold off Alice by meeting the men and politely hearing them out but, honestly, I hadn't made it much further than that. I had rather hoped Alice would tire of this little scheme and turn her attention elsewhere."

"Mrs. Hill seems far too shrewd and focused a businesswoman to let an opportunity like this slip through her fingers."

Violet winced. "I know."

"So then what? We know Mrs. Hill will not let go of the chance to see you happily and advantageously married off. Is there some way we can point her attention away from you?"

"I have been thinking hard on that. I know she means well. That she is doing this because she truly believes it to be the best thing for me—and that will make dissuading her so much harder. We are often blinded when it comes to those we love."

"Have you tried speaking with her in earnest? She will listen if you tell her your heart like you told me."

She sighed, eyes dropping to the plate in front of her. "Alice feels responsible for me. I have no one but her. My family...my family died two winters ago when I was nineteen. We had only just arrived in town. We came from California and Papa wasn't the best with planning, which meant our travel was delayed in the mountains. We were supposed to have been here at the start of summer. Plenty of time to find lodging and work. To be secure, safe, and warm when winter came—but that didn't happen. We came in the middle of a winter storm, my parents took ill, and both passed from pneumonia. I was fortunate enough to survive it. Alice took me in and cared for me when everyone else thought I would die too. She asked me if I wanted to stay with her, seeing as I had no one, and she was so kind to me, so I did. When I was well enough I began working for her as a cook to earn my place and to hopefully repay her for what she did for me."

The dining room was quiet. The only sound was the ticking of the grandfather clock in the foyer, and Julian's heart broke with each tick. Violet sniffled, a hand coming up to dab at her eyes, but save for that small gesture she remained straight-backed and lifted her chin to look him in the eyes. "I owe much to Alice Hill, and she believes she is doing me a kindness in this moment, as she did then. Th-this situation is not one that can be easily done away with a simple conversation."

Julian could understand that. He was indebted to countless teachers and mentors, people who had seen something in him and taught him how to nurture and grow his raw talent into something formidable. It was a tricky thing when one needed to step away from those who had led and cared for them, and that was under normal circumstances. Violet's was more intricate than that, and he did not envy her position. He reached across the table and put a hand on hers. "It will come out all right in the end. You'll see."

She gave him a bitter smile. "I only hope it doesn't see me married to a man I did not choose."

"No, never that. She would never want that for you," Julian rushed to explain, but Violet continued on.

"Or a man who did not choose me."

That stopped him cold. For all the reasons Violet had listed to him, for the harsh way frontier life had about it that prioritized function, skill, and usefulness above beauty and love. His sister had come away with a great fortune in finding love, and doubly so with her husbands, but who knew if fate would smile as kindly on Violet?

He felt sick at the thought, but gave her a bright smile. He'd learned long ago to keep his true emotions close to the cuff. It was far easier that way—easier to help others keep calm if he presented a controlled version of himself. Now would be no different.

"That will not happen. I give my word."

Violet's eyes widened. "How can you say that? I thought you said they made gentlemen swear on cravats...that seems a lofty promise to make without being able to keep it."

"How do you know what kind of promises I can and cannot keep?" he asked, crossing his arms and leaning back in his chair. He met her gaze boldly, all thoughts of propriety gone. He'd touched her hand moments before, hadn't he? What was a few stolen moments of staring into her deep brown and ocher eyes if not permissible and a touch less scandalous? Flouting what was proper and what was not was allowable and entirely worth it, if only to make her blush as prettily as she did.

She swallowed hard and surprised him when she leaned forward, her elbows landing on the table with a light thud, and reached for his hand. Her palm was up, fingers splayed out and reaching for him. Instantly Julian moved, interlacing their fingers tightly.

"It will be alright," he told her, rubbing her knuckles with a thumb. "I swear it."

"I believe you," she whispered, eyes on their joined hands. She looked up at him and smiled. "I believe you."

Her hand squeezed his. It was just a touch, but it was for him, and that was far more than he could have ever asked of her.

CHAPTER 6

"What are you doing up at this hour?"

Violet's head jerked up from where she was bent over the table, a sketchpad in front of her and an assortment of crayons, a box of watercolors, and graphite pencils spread around her.

She blinked at him owlishly and gestured with a pencil. "I couldn't sleep."

"So you…" His voice trailed off as he stepped closer, giving the drawing in front of her a curious look. "You're an artist."

"I draw," she said simply with a shake of your head.

"May I see?"

She bit her bottom lip, teeth wiggling her lip nervously for a moment before she gave a slight incline of her head, and pushed away from the table so that he might see what she worked on. It was a single sheet of paper, but if Julian hadn't known better he would have considered it a little bit of magic.

Sunlight, bright and shining, warmed the landscape

Julian instantly identified as Montana. Cliffs steep and dark shadowed a coursing river, and a shadowy figure of a woman leaned close to the water. Her face was turned away, hands out at her sides, but there was no mistaking the figure. It was Violet. And though it was but a rough sketch of her person Julian could sense the freedom in the pencil lines.

She was turned away from any that might view her, her head angled toward the dark line of trees and underbrush that stretched on as far as the eye could see. It was there, he knew, that Violet had in mind to head. What awaited her there no one could see, not even she, but Julian suspected that was the allure of it all.

The unknown, while frightening, meant escape...a chance to begin anew. But from what, Julian didn't quite know yet.

He glanced down at the drawing and was once more shocked at the skill in Violet's scene. The paper beneath her hands wasn't simply the work of someone who couldn't sleep—it was alive.

"You're incredibly talented," he told her, nodding at the scene.

She smiled thinly at him. "It's a hobby."

"Nothing more?"

When she gave a quick shake of her head, he nodded at the counter behind her. "May I join you? I was going to make myself a cup of tea."

"No, please," she said, gesturing at the seat across from her, "sit. I can fix the tea." She went to push herself up from the table, but Julian waved her off.

He grinned at her and wiggled his fingers. "I've all my

fingers. I can manage tea for the both of us, Violet." When she looked fit to protest he raised an eyebrow. "Unless you are intimating that I lack the necessary skills?"

She blushed and picked up a brush again. "You uttered the words, Julian. Not I."

"So I did." He didn't miss the sly smirk from Violet, and he laughed while he busied himself setting out the necessities for a proper midnight tea. Milk, sugar, and maybe a treat or two made their way onto a tray while water boiled.

"What has you up at this hour?" Violet asked. She had resumed her sketching, an eraser in one hand as she smudged the cliffs, adding shadows here and there.

Julian shrugged and stretched his arms overhead. "I suppose the usual, for anyone our age."

"Which is?"

"The future," he admitted, the words tumbling out of his mouth faster than he was aware.

Violet turned in her seat and gave him a curious look. "The future? But...but why?"

Julian met her eyes and saw confusion—but most of all surprise. He understood the look. It was one that he had given himself many a morning as of late, when he awoke to repeat what felt like the same day. Each one seemed to follow the same cycle, the same circle of people to speak with, to impress and rub elbows with, the same faces at the same eateries and playhouses.

The same, the same, the same.

It was stifling. By the time Julie had asked them all to visit Gold Sky, Julian could scarcely breathe. He had surprised his parents by declaring he would accompany them out West, especially considering the journey would remove him from the Four Hundred's social roster. He would be missed at dances and trips to the coast, his mother had reminded him. However would he find a woman who suited him if he whiled away his hours in a frontier town?

His father, on the other hand, wholly supported Julian's break from the city and the haut monde. They were "infinitely spirit-crushing," according to his father, and a bit of adventure beyond a mezzanine or poker table would do Julian good.

Julian couldn't have packed fast enough. Adventure, a change of pace and scenery, even at the risk of robbery—he was happy to leave New York. Anything to break the routine and remind him that he was free to be whoever and whatever he wished.

Adventure.

That one word set his heart racing, and it was like he was a boy again. The years of being careful in his actions and speech, always watching his back, keeping his distance from others...all of that could be put on hold in his venture westward. Gold Sky was a time to let his defenses down—a gift he hadn't indulged in since boyhood.

And along the way he had met Violet. So unexpected, but welcome in her appearance, with a smile that reminded him why he had been desperate to escape New York's social scene.

She expected nothing of him but offered her friendship freely. Julian wanted more of that honesty in his life, and cherished the special kind he had found in Violet, even if the woman had no clue of what she meant to him, or how quickly she had come to occupy such a place.

He removed the now screaming tea kettle and concentrated on pouring it into the porcelain teapot. "The future is often a scary thing."

"Well, yes, but why would it be scary for you?" Her meaning was clear. She meant for someone in possession of such an advantageous place in life. How could he, with the resources and means to live however he chose, be frightened of the future?

"Because I am never sure who I can trust."

Her mouth dropped open. A colored pencil hit the table with a clatter. "But your family…" she said weakly.

"Is my family. But outside of them, the world is a precarious and greedy place."

She swallowed and looked down at the drawing in front of her with a furrowed brow. "Yes, it is."

Julian picked up the tray in front of him and started for the table, searching for an empty space to set down their midnight tea. "Freedom is precarious if you choose the wrong confidant."

Violet scrambled to clear away a space for the tray, eyes still trained away from him and on the pencils in her hands. "I never thought of it like that. I just assumed…"

"Assumed what?" he asked, taking a seat next to her.

"That life was easier with money and a pedigree," she answered.

His hands went still around the teacup he had begun preparing. "Most people often do think such a thing, but alas." He resumed the tea preparation and placed her steaming cup next to her.

"Thank you," she murmured, taking the cup with a dip of her chin.

"Of course. I may or may not have pilfered a few treats, but I think the cook would excuse it just this once."

She smiled and sipped her tea. "Just this once, but don't tell the proprietress of this establishment."

"Oh? She's a real stickler for rules?"

"Rules with an iron fist. We would never hear the end of it, but I promise to keep silent on the matter as long as you brought a lemon curd with you."

Julian grinned and pushed the plate toward her. "Well, we must count our blessings, because it just so happens I did."

Violet hummed, taking the pastry with a bright smile. "Then you can count on my silence. I assure you that I will not breathe a word of your filching tendencies."

Julian opened his mouth retort but stopped short when he caught sight of a pile of letters on the seat beside him. Violet's name, written across the top letter, was hard to miss, as was the crude penmanship. She stopped chewing when she noticed Julian glancing at the stack of letters.

"I apologize. I didn't mean to snoop," he said, sitting straight in his chair and giving her a chagrined smile.

She waved her hand and took another bite of her curd. "It's nearly impossible to miss that tower of letters."

He gave the pile another assessing look. "May I ask what are they from?"

"The advert Alice placed."

"The inquiry for a groom?"

"The one and the same," she replied, shoving the rest of her tart into her mouth with a savage jerk of her hand.

"There seem to be dozens," Julian observed.

"Forty-three, to be exact," she told him, and he choked on his tea.

"In addition to last night's ticket event?"

"Mm, it's been quite a bit of excitement, to be sure."

He nodded at the letters. "What do you mean to do with the lot of them?"

"Answer them, I suppose."

"Each and every last one?"

She gave him a pained look. "I see no other way around it. Alice would find out and, well, the sooner I select a groom, the sooner this will end."

"You mean to see it through, do you?"

Violet was silent for a moment before she began to gather up the art supplies in front of her. "I do."

"But why?"

"She isn't wrong. Alice I mean. She means well, and though the way she has gone about it is...aggressive, her point that I need a family of my own, a husband to—to make life easier in her absence wouldn't be a bad thing to consider."

"You would marry a stranger?"

She set her notebook to the side and positioned her collection of supplies neatly beside it. "It wouldn't be the first time anyone has done such a thing. Why, I even know of three people who experienced very happy results. I only pray to be half so fortunate as they are."

There was a note of envy in Violet's voice that Julian understood all too well. They both knew she meant his sister and her husbands. The triad's love was the real thing, a shining light of adoration that Julian too craved for his own.

He pointed at the stack of letters that threatened to topple over. "In that case, shall we?"

She looked at him in confusion. "Shall we what?"

"Read them. If you intend to take a husband, then we should take care that he is the best of the bunch, should we not?"

"You would help me do that?" she asked in surprise.

Julian felt like his heart had cracked open at the wide-eyed look she sent his way.

He would do that for her. Even if it pained him to do so.

"I would," he told her, "as it's what friends do."

Four midnights later...

"I don't know how much more I have in me," Violet told Julian, slipping into the seat across from him. It was the fourth night that week in which they had engaged in their new midnight ritual. "They all seem to be getting progressively worse and more incoherent, but it could be that we have been at this every night this week."

Julian hummed and took another fortifying sip of coffee. Tea had been dismissed in favor of a beverage in possession of more stamina. It was only a matter of time before they moved on to whiskey.

"It could be, or it could be that we have lost untold

amounts of intelligence deciphering exactly how these suitors aim to make an honest woman of you."

Violet gave a snort. "A true testament of willpower on your part to stay the course with me. You don't have to keep at this, Julian."

"What do you mean?"

"I mean that I would understand if you wanted your evenings, and your precious sleep, in lieu of this." She gestured at the letter-covered table. There were three piles: desirable, somewhat civil, and decidedly debauched.

So far there were far more debauched than not.

It had been slow going once the pair of them realized that most of the hopeful husbands, while eager for a woman's company, had little idea how to honor or cherish a wife. A good deal of the letters contained demands of three square meals, of a supper piping hot and expected on the table before they returned home, of a little missus happy to get to the business of having a family, and the more children the better. There were thoughts on how she should style her hair, what clothes would be considered "acceptable," and exactly how she was to conduct herself as a wife. Some of the thoughts on behavior focused on the day-to-day schedule, with each and every hour allotted its own task. And then there were those men who dared to write of proclivities particular to the bedroom.

Julian made quick work of filing those away in the debauched pile—a pile he took great pleasure in burning each night. But no matter how many letters he burned, more turned up the next day, and those forty-three letters from the first night turned out to be a paltry sum, as the number of missives steadily increased with each and every day.

And for all the letters, both debauched and not, there was one unsettling trend—there was little talk of a life outside of the household, or how Violet's talents might be employed. It troubled him that Violet's spirit might be traded in for what Julian considered a small life. It was small for the sheer reason that it was not what Violet wanted for herself—it was a lop-sided affair, and Julian knew it was doomed from the start. There were far too few letters in the desirables pile for him to feel optimistic about their endeavor to find Violet an eligible bachelor to wed.

"I would be woefully remiss in my duties as your friend if I were to abandon you now to this task," he told her, shoving another letter into the debauched pile. "I'll not leave you now."

She smiled and leaned back in her chair, fingers going to rub at her temples. "It is...good of you to stay the course after nearly a week. I had hoped we would have a more positive group of suitors by now."

"That makes two of us. I am thoroughly disgusted by my sex as a whole. I fight the urge to issue dueling missives and apologize profusely to you with each and every one."

"You would duel for me?"

"Of course."

The answer came too quickly and too easily said for it to be anything but true. They both knew it, and a blanket of silence fell upon them as Julian immediately set about ripping open a new letter in a bid to avoid the startled look on Violet's face. She was surprised by his admission, he could feel it in the weight of her stare as he unfurled the latest letter he held. He cleared his throat and strove to appear nonchalant.

"Of course I would. That is what friends do." He raised his eyes to look at her and saw the subtle color in her cheeks. The way she lowered her head slightly at his words.

A thought hit him with the force of a locomotive.

What if she wanted him to defend her, but not as friends? Yet—if not friends, then what did she care for him to defend her as?

"Yes, that's right. Friends," she said, giving him a tight smile that didn't quite reach her eyes.

Julian sat up straighter in his chair. Perhaps he *was* reading this entirely wrong. Did she not want him to act as a friend?

He looked down at the letter in his hands, something about boasting a large farm in the Washington territory, and he thrust it into the debauched pile. The thought of her going so far away from him made his stomach turn.

"Well, given the current state of our prospects, I do not want you to lose heart."

"Oh?" she asked, slumping forward and toying with the edge of an unopened letter.

Julian shook his head. "No, Violet. There is someone out there for you. I know it."

"And what kind of person would that be? So far we have only found entreaties for a housekeeper and cook, nothing more. No tenderness, no compassion. All of it is work and drudgery, and that I have plenty enough as is.

But at least here I am compensated for it." She frowned at the stack of letters in front of her. "It's no use, Julian."

"Ah, ah, ah, giving up is unbecoming, Violet." She shot him a withering look he felt down to his toes, but he managed a casual smile. "What I mean to say is that we must simply change our methods, not the expectation." He reached for a blank sheet of paper and pencil. "Now then, what is your perfect partner?"

"The perfect partner does not exist," Violet told him with another downturn of her lips. "These letters are proof."

Julian nodded along with her frustrated words and licked the pencil tip, readying himself to make a list of nothing but the very best qualities. "Then humor me, darling."

When she didn't immediately answer he looked at her and saw her blushing furiously, and he wondered what it was that left her speechless. "Violet?"

"Hmm?" She clasped her hands tightly on the table in front of her. "What was that?"

"Humor me." Julian gestured at the paper in front of him with his pencil. "If you were able to pick your perfect partner, what would they be like?"

"Right, right. *That.* Well, they would have to be kind."

He wrote down the word *kind* but gave her a pointed look. "Kind is a bit...well, you know..."

Violet crossed her arms over her chest. "A bit what?" she asked with a look that could only be interpreted as defensive.

He grinned at her indignant tone. "Boring. Kind is boring, Violet."

She sniffed. "I happen to find kindness essential to attraction, Julian."

"I am not saying that kindness is not desirable, but anyone can be kind. What I'm asking for are the attributes suited to your desires. That is the heart of the matter."

"Oh, is it?"

"Entirely," he told her, tapping his pencil against his chin as he thought. "Now, for you I envision someone of import. A very well-known person, with the influence to garner the respect you deserve."

"I, ah, respect?" She gave him such a quizzical look that Julian almost groaned in frustration.

"Yes, respect. You deserve it." He quickly wrote down the words *influence and respect* and then continued on. "Next, he would have to be open-minded and supportive of your talent at drawing and sketching."

Violet nodded in agreement. "That would be…agreeable."

Her voice was still tentative, but Julian could see her warming to the idea. It mattered not that the man in question did not exist, so long as they knew what she desired.

"And also able to understand that you require the freedom to do as you please. This means he would see you as a partner, not as property."

She perked up. "Yes, write that down. I am not property. I am a woman."

Julian wrote *woman, not property* and tilted the paper to show her. Violet clapped in approval and then said, "I'd like him to be funny as well. A light heart would be more fitting than a very serious man. I don't think I'd be suited to somber."

"Noted."

"And I want someone who likes to travel. There is so much to see and so little time! I want time without children, so someone amenable to that as well."

Julian's pencil flew as he tried to keep up with Violet's growing list.

"And if he were to have interesting eyes, I would find that very agreeable."

He frowned, still writing out the last bit concerning children. "Interesting? What do you mean?"

"Like yours."

His pencil went still.

Like his.

"Mine?" he asked, looking up to see that her blush had returned and now her cheeks were scarlet.

She clasped her hands and ducked her head. "Yes, ah, you have very fine eyes."

"And what would you call them besides interesting?" he asked. "For your list, I mean." He held up the pencil to show he was intent on documenting her answer.

Though, for all his play at innocence, Julian indulged the need he had to be close to her. To have her look upon him plainly, for the simple reason that it allowed him the same.

"They are, well, nice," she said, earning a smirk from Julian, who turned his chair to face her so that they were nearly toe-to-toe.

"And?" he continued, giving her an encouraging smile.

Violet's gaze dropped to his mouth for a moment before she cleared her throat and looked back up at his face.

She sucked in a breath, but leaned forward so that she could assess his eyes as he asked. "They are—light but...not. They look the way sunlight hitting whiskey in a crystal glass might."

That stopped him cold. Julian had always considered his eyes to be brown, perhaps a lighter brown than usual, but never had it crossed his mind that his eyes resembled whiskey in the sunlight. "Oh," he said.

She nodded at him, leaning closer, her hands leaving the armrests of her chair. "You have thick lashes that catch the sun as well, like smoke around your eyes. Very handsome."

His pulse quickened at her admission. "I'll add that to the list. Handsome?"

"It would...help," she whispered, her gaze moving over his face so thoroughly he could swear he felt her touch, though her hands hovered in the scant space between them. "There's also green in your eyes."

"Green?"

"Just a touch," she told him, lifting a finger to gesture at her own eyes, "near the center. The combination is lovely."

"No one has ever used the word lovely to describe me," he told her, finding himself leaning forward in his own chair. It was as if gravity had been turned on its side and Julian was powerless to fight the force that urged him forward. His fingertips brushed hers and he started, realizing that he had been reaching for her as well. His fingers twitched, but he made no move to pull his hand back.

"Then they are not paying attention as they should," Violet said, licking her lips. There was no denying how close the pair of them were now. The tips of her boots slid across the toes of his shoes and nudged his instep. The gentle brush of her skirts against his knees was enough to make him forget himself. It was the only reason for how close they were, how they kept coming closer still.

And how Julian found that he wanted to stop none of it.

Not with her mouth so close to his that her breath fanned his skin and made him want to lean just a bit closer and press his mouth to hers.

Her mouth would be soft and welcoming. He would touch her, taking her hand in his, giving into so much more than a simple brush of fingers. He would touch her hair as he deepened the kiss, and he would make her moan his name and kiss her still until she clung to him, asking him for more, the hunt for a groom entirely forgotten as they enjoyed each other.

Except that...except that they were meant to find her a groom. Not kiss.

If they kissed, then the entirety of their hunt was for naught. What would there be for Violet, for him, if they kissed and their entire friendship was suddenly changed?

By god, what was he doing?

He jerked back with a nervous laugh and snatched up the paper. "I'll add that to the list. Very thorough, Violet. Excellent work."

She blinked at him as if waking from a dream, and her mouth snapped shut with an audible click. "Thank you," she murmured, voice catching in her throat. "That will prove useful, I'm sure." She rose from the table and began to put away their cups and plates. "Shall we call it a night?"

He nodded, gathering up the debauched pile and smiling at her in what he hoped was an entirely platonic way. "I'll just dispose of these. Just a moment and I'll help you with all of this." He nodded at the letter-strewn table.

"Oh no, please. I'll manage it. I have some baking I'd like to set up now, given the hour."

"What time is it?" he asked, reaching for his pocket watch, and he blanched, seeing that it was a quarter after three. "I hadn't realized it was such a late hour."

"Or early, depending on how one thinks of it." Violet put the dishes in the sink and began to fill it with water. "Go on—I'll see you at breakfast?"

"Of course." He hesitated in the doorway. "Are you sure I cannot be of help?"

"You are already doing your part by ridding us of those letters. I'll be just fine. Right as rain. Goodnight, Julian."

"Goodnight, Violet."

He turned and walked toward his suite. The almost-kiss spun in his mind, but unfolded in an entirely different way. In this version, he did close that space. He kissed her slowly and thoroughly, tasting her lips in an unhurried manner before telling her that the hunt for a groom was over.

Over, because he himself would fill the role.

He glanced down at the list of attributes he still clutched in one hand.

Kind

Influence and respect
Open-minded
Woman, not property
Freedom
Light-hearted
Eyes like mine

He swallowed hard.

Eyes like mine

She had nearly kissed him. Had he not stopped it, interrupted the tender moment, there was no doubt in his mind that Violet would have given him that precious kiss he was now sure would haunt him till morning.

Eyes like his.

He'd been utterly wrong in his early assessment that the man in question did not exist. Because he did. And Violet already knew the man she wished to marry—at least, according to the list they had crafted.

That man was known to her. That man was in Gold Sky. That man cared a great deal for her.

That man was Julian.

CHAPTER 7

It was a bright and sunny day in Gold Sky, the kind that made one want to shirk their duties and spend what could be considered productive hours lounging beside a lake or sprawled beneath the boughs of a tree with a book or a glass of port in hand.

Julian had never allowed himself such a luxury in New York, but he may have been inclined to do so on the frontier if he had not acquired company for the afternoon by accident. He glanced at the woman on his arm and gave her as warm a smile as he could manage.

Marissa James.

Julian had been strolling through Gold Sky, contemplating whether or not to work more on his plans for a railroad depot or if he would choose to simply relax, when the woman had approached him with a smile and an eager hello. Though he wasn't the fondest of her mother he had no firm reason to avoid the girl, so he did his best to be cordial.

And that was how they ended up walking arm-in-arm through town.

"It's a beautiful day, don't you think?" she asked, turning her emerald eyes on him with a little too much flutter of her eyelashes.

Ah, yes. The coquettish behavior from the lady on his arm was a hindrance to an otherwise pleasant walk, but it was nothing he wouldn't or couldn't handle with politeness.

"It certainly is." He gave her a reassuring smile and turned toward the center of town. "I had been thinking of how best to spend it myself before we met."

"Would you care for a picnic?" she asked with hope in her eyes that Julian found he didn't have the strength of will to reject.

"That would...be nice," he managed to get out.

Marissa wasted no time in procuring a picnic basket. Curiously, Sarah had just happened to be passing by with a fully stocked basket—the handoff couldn't have been more seamless than if they had rehearsed it a thousand times before.

Julian suddenly wished he hadn't agreed to the outing. A picnic with Marissa was one thing, but being caught up in Sarah's machinations was an entirely different matter altogether.

He didn't care for it, but it was plain to see that Marissa was just as much caught as he was. He couldn't begrudge her, and worked to keep their outing as pleasant as possible.

What was more, Julian suspected Violet had been the one to prepare the lunch offerings. His suspicions were confirmed when he asked as much and she gave him a puzzled, "Well, yes, but I ordered it all."

He nodded absentmindedly, his thoughts already leaving the picnic and landing squarely on the hands that had prepared the lunch of chicken, salad, fruit, and cheese. It was simple but delicious, and paired with the bright sunlight and perfect spot beneath a shady tree close to the town square it had the makings of a perfect lunch.

Or, it did, if his dining partner had happened to be the woman who had made the meal.

He tried to keep his face schooled into polite interest as Marissa told him of her trip out west from Texas. He asked how she found Gold Sky, and what she thought of her plans to make the move permanent, which were respectively: agreeable enough, and hopeful although she didn't think her mother was of the same opinion. Julian listened politely and attentively. Despite her mother's meddling and scheming, Marissa retained the youthful naïveté that Julian rarely observed surviving the first season for debutantes. But somehow the young woman was still sincere in her smiles and words.

Curious how she had managed that.

Julian leaned back on his hands, giving Marissa an assessing look that wasn't nearly as covert as he had assumed, even for Marissa.

"What is it?" she asked, taking a bite of her lunch.

Damn. He would have to use more finesse in his musings, especially with a woman who plainly spoke her mind. It was refreshing, but could also prove...difficult.

"Ah, nothing," he said with a shake of his head. "I was reflecting on the weather."

She wrinkled her nose. "The weather? It looks perfectly sunny." She looked up at the sky and then gestured with an arm. "See how sunny and lovely it is?"

Julian's eyes moved along the length of Marissa's hand, but it wasn't into the perfectly blue sky that Julian looked. Instead, his eyes landed on the cerulean blue of Violet's skirts. She headed toward them, furiously drawing in her sketchbook, her eyes lifting periodically to ensure that she did not walk into a passing horse or misstep from the boardwalk.

"I do," Julian murmured, not entirely sure what Marissa had said, but vaguely knowing it had to do with the blue of Violet's clothing. What was it again?

"I've never seen a sky so blue."

There it was. The sky.

"Quite nice," he agreed.

"I think it is the loveliest sight I've been gifted with on my journey west."

Julian's eyes followed Violet as she drew closer to them. The curve of her smile made his breath catch, a flash of white teeth as she grinned down at the image she drew.

"It *is* lovely," he breathed.

Violet was now mere yards away, and Julian wondered if he would be able to catch her eye. Perhaps he could walk her to her destination, or offer her a place at the picnic? It was a fine day, after all...

Marissa let out a peal of laughter, and the sound of it jolted Julian from his reverie. "Oh you say the sweetest things," she giggled, as if he had spoken an endearment to her and not...well, not the sky.

"I—ah, the sky is lovely," he said again, taking careful pains to emphasize the subject of his sentence.

Marissa scooted closer to him, and Julian forgot his earlier admiration of her guilelessness. "So it is, but that isn't the only thing I feel you have on your mind, Julian."

"I have no idea what you—"

"It's Violet, isn't it?" she asked with excited eyes. She reached out and slapped his arm. "I knew it earlier when you inquired after who had made the picnic."

"That isn't—" He cleared his throat and then lowered his voice. "What makes you say that?" He looked up and nearly choked on his tongue when he saw Violet was no longer smiling or oblivious to their presence. She had slowed to a standstill, her hands clutching at the sketchpad, that smiling mouth no longer curved but instead pressed into a thin line.

"She's looking this way. Do you suppose we ought to make her jealous?"

Julian jerked away from Marissa as if she had struck him. "No, that is not the way to a lady's heart."

She tapped her chin. "Then I suspect I have missed many an opportunity, and it explains much."

That caught Julian's attention. What did the young woman mean by that statement? He went to ask, but she nudged him again and nodded at Violet. "Go speak to her."

"What am I to say?"

"That you enjoyed the picnic."

"One that I had with another lady?" he asked, giving her a raised eyebrow. Her smile faded.

"I hadn't thought of that when Mother put me up to this."

She swallowed hard and gave him a worried look. "I'm sorry. I've made a mess of things again, haven't I?" Her eyes shone suddenly with unshed tears, and Julian held his hands up.

"Oh dear, please." He reached out to pat her shoulder. "I beg of you, do not cry."

"I just..." She sniffled and Julian thrust his handkerchief into her hand. "I never manage to do things right. No matter how hard I try."

"There, there, it cannot be all that bad." He patted her shoulder again and Marissa threw her arms around him so tightly the air left his lungs. "All is not lost…" he managed to choke out.

"You do not know my sins, Julian. My life is...it is over." Her voice was low, far more somber than he had ever seen from the smiling woman, and Julian frowned.

"Whatever they are, they are only one moment in your life," he told her, wrapping his arms around her and giving her a genuine hug. "I promise you the storm will pass and you will still be standing."

Marissa lifted her tear-stained face to his. "You are a true gentleman."

He patted her arm and fished out another handkerchief to hand to her. "Thank you, Marissa."

"I am so dreadfully sorry that I made a mess of things between you and Violet," she told him.

"There's no mess," he assured her, but the quick shake of her head had him confused.

"But there is. Look." She nodded over his shoulder, and Julian turned his head just in time to catch a glare from Violet before she turned on her heel and strode off in the direction she had just come from, her sketchbook tucked under one arm. She offered no smile or pleasantries to anyone as she walked.

Julian knew that look: the set of a woman's shoulders bent on not paying heed or mind to a particularly aggravating sight. He knew it well from his sister and mother. And he saw it now in Violet.

"She thinks we are on an unchaperoned outing. That you are courting me."

He sighed, looking down at the picnic spread. "It would appear that way."

"I will tell her myself. I will fix this. You will see." Marissa sprang to her feet and dusted off her skirts. "I promise. Your kindness will not go unpaid."

"What kindness?" he asked, rising from his seat and doing his best to follow after Marissa. He stopped short and turned back toward the forgotten picnic. Someone had to pack it up, and it appeared from Marissa's quick departure that it would be him.

"The kindness of reminding me I am worthy of such tenderness." Marissa smiled at him and then held up a finger. "I shall set it all to rights. Mark my words!"

Julian scrambled to shove their plates into the basket and keep sight of the redhead as she barreled away. "Set what to rights?"

And then there, in front of god and every citizen of Gold Sky, Marissa let loose his secret for all to know.

"You and Violet, of course!"

Julian blanched, his face becoming the most unattractive shade of mottled red, which proved bothersome as gentlemen were not known to blush as easily and as deeply as Marissa had drawn from him.

"I have no idea what the lady means," he said to a passing couple, who gave him a snort in reply.

"What a day," he sighed, yanking the picnic basket firmly against his hip and shaking his head. It was rare that he was caught so unawares by a person, much less a lady. Julian supposed he had underestimated her if she was able to elicit such a reaction from him.

Giving himself a firm mental shake, he forced his thoughts to the more pressing matter at hand.

Marissa was right. Violet had seen the picnic. He would need to make the true spirit of their outing known to her.

Never mind that it was perfectly normal for him to be seen out in public with an unattached woman like Marissa, and not that he owed an explanation to a woman he only considered a friend—but she had made the lunch. Shouldn't she understand exactly why it had been ordered?

Even as Julian walked hastily through the streets of Gold Sky, assuring himself that his reasoning was entirely plausible, perhaps demanded by proper courtesy even, he knew his excuses were...precarious at best.

His grip tightened on the picnic basket handle. He supposed it was thin. Oh, damn it all. It was *laughable*—but he marched forward, undeterred in his hunt for Violet.

He had to find her at once.

His feet hit the steps of the boarding house and he shouldered his way in the front as gracefully as one could expect with a picnic basket for two under one arm.

He would find her and make her see that it had only been a friendly outing. That whatever nonsense Marissa spouted was pure fiction.

Julian swallowed hard as his legs ate up the polished hardwood that spanned the front door to the kitchen where Violet most likely was. He did not think of her like that...but he was adamant that she know what her food had been prepared for.

She must know.

Understand that he...that he...

Julian skidded to a stop in front of the kitchen door.

That he what?

The question hung like a weight on him, and the uncertainty of what he wanted to say to Violet felt heavy on his tongue. He took a step back from the kitchen door.

What was he doing, barging into the boarding house lugging the picnic basket with him?

He glanced down at the offending object and wished it gone.

A footfall from the other side of the kitchen door made him scramble back, desperately searching the hall for a hiding place—whether it was for the basket or himself he couldn't be sure.

"Julian?"

Violet stood in the doorway, giving him a confused look at catching him scrambling to try and shove the basket behind a potted parlor palm.

He swallowed hard and straightened. "Hello, Violet."

"What are you doing?" she asked, looking at the picnic

basket in his hands. He didn't miss the way her eyes narrowed slightly. Why hadn't he abandoned the basket before entering the boarding house?

He glanced down at the offending basket and moved it behind his back with a shrug of one shoulder.

"Ah, checking the soil in this plant," he lied.

"I didn't know you had a green thumb."

"There's much you haven't learned about me."

"Yes," Violet's eyes moved to where he held the basket and her lips pressed into a thin line. "I expect that is true."

He winced and cleared his throat. He was nothing if not willing to handle less than desirable situations head-on when it came to business, so why should he be made of weaker stuff when it came to people? "Violet, I know that—"

The front door banged open behind him with a crash and a barely muffled curse.

"Violet!"

Marissa's sharp greeting made Julian want to moan and sink into the floor. Of course she had happened upon them just at this time, despite her earlier start.

"I've been looking for you!" Marissa rushed up in a rustle of skirts and breathlessness. She stopped short when she noticed Julian and then jerked her head back to look at Violet. "I've interrupted, haven't I?" she asked fretfully.

"No, you haven't interrupted anything in the slightest." Violet turned her eyes away from Julian, and he felt the chill of it despite the summer heat.

"But I have," Marissa insisted, biting her lip and looking at Julian. "I'm very sorry."

Violet started and gave the younger woman an assessing look. "What are you apologizing for?"

Marissa clasped her hands in front of her. "I meant to set it all straight, and now I've made an even bigger mess of it. I'm always doing that, you know. Mama says there's no hope for me."

"I wouldn't listen to your mother on matters such as that," Julian replied smoothly and gave the woman a kind smile. "It's all right, Marissa. I was just explaining to Violet about our picnic."

Marissa bobbed her head. "Yes, it was lovely." She paused and looked meaningfully at Violet. "But it was only a friendly occasion. He was quite forced into it as well."

Julian looked at her in surprise. "I would not say—"

"You were. But you were too much a gentleman to refuse the invitation." She tipped her head to Violet. "And you should be made aware of such a fact."

Violet stiffened, but a blush dusted her cheeks. "I do not see why that would be of import to me."

"I may not be fluent in the art of subtlety or social graces but even I know that's a lie."

Julian laughed at Marissa's frank words, while Violet spluttered, "Wh-what are you intimating?"

Marissa stepped back and looked between them with what Julian supposed was a smug smile. "We both know quite what I mean to say."

This time it was Julian who protested. "I do not believe that is true."

"The sooner you are both able to admit it, admit you

have romantic feelings for one another, the happier you will be."

Violet and Julian uttered a shared gasp that had both of them shuffling back from one another at a speed so great their shoes slid across the polished wood floors. Neither stopped until Violet was ensconced in the refuge of the kitchen and Julian firmly seated on the settee in the parlor.

Marissa watched the couple's rapid retreat without surprise, sighing mournfully through the entire ordeal, and only then did she turn on her heel and leave the boarding house as quickly as she came.

Romantic feelings, she had said.

The words ricocheted off the walls and floor until they landed in Julian's lap, and the man found that he had not a ghost of a prayer on how to deal with Marissa's observation. He suspected Violet was as unprepared as he, and not for the first time that day he was left feeling as though he had underestimated the younger James. It was a misstep he could not and would not repeat if he hoped to survive his stay in Gold Sky.

CHAPTER 8

Violet monopolized Julian's thoughts for most of the afternoon, and it wasn't just in relation to her predicament with Gold Sky suitors. In fact, while Julian wasn't surprised he was thinking about the woman, he had never dreamed it would be in connection to the new railway endeavor's current obstacle.

A map.

Or lack thereof.

Julian wasn't familiar with the expanse of the Montana Territory, and Stark's knowledge only went as far as his shop. This meant a proper and exhaustive map would be a necessity if they hoped to avoid a misstep.

"We had a mapmaker. Decent one, I guess, but he went back home," Stark told him as they looked over the woefully lacking maps of the area.

Julian tapped a finger on a section of the map that was practically blank, save for a single trail. "If he's decent, then why is this area nonexistent? And where is home?"

"I said he was *decent,* which is relative for the area,"

Stark offered with a frown, and then added, "Home is Ireland."

Julian groaned, rubbing his temples. "So then we are lacking a mapmaker."

"Unless we can locate a new cartographer...we do have a fair amount of newcomers to town, and Butte City is nearby. We can look for talent there." Stark rubbed his chin. "Plus, there's Violet Shield to consider. I don't know why it took this long for me to think of it."

"Violet?" Julian croaked in surprise.

Had he given away more than he intended despite his public protests that he did not want any part in Alice's husband hunt for Violet? That hadn't stopped him from lending her his help in secret, or giving her an almost-kiss.

His face flushed at the memory of how close she had been, how she had described his eyes as fine, how she had added them to her list of hopes for a husband. He cleared his throat and turned away from Stark, not wanting to give the man any cause for suspicion.

"What about Violet?

"The thing about Violet," the carpenter said, striding forward and turning around to face Julian, "is that she has proven to be quite talented and clever."

"She is," Julian conceded, wondering where Stark was going with his train of thought, which was thankfully not related to the topic of Julian and Violet together. Or how soft Violet's lips appeared to be at indecent morning hours.

"It might be worthwhile to commission her talent for the map."

"She knows cartography?" Julian asked. "I thought she was mostly skilled in sketching."

The other man raised an eyebrow at Julian's words. "How do know she's an artist?"

Julian's heart sped up at the assessing look in Stark's shrewd gaze. The damnable man was sharp, a quality Julian valued highly in a business partner, but for once he wished the carpenter was a tad less astute. "Ah, my brothers-in-laws imparted the knowledge. Everyone knows it, or so I had thought?"

Stark nodded. "True. It's impossible to not know about her talent. And she is quite talented at cartography, though she leans more toward the artistic side of her craft. Her father had a big name for it in California. That's one of the reasons her family came this way. He was supposed to be working on maps for the government, but..." Stark sighed and looked away. "Things don't always work out the way we intend."

"She told me about her parents. What happened, I mean."

"She told you herself?"

"She did," Julian said.

Stark looked at him, head tilting to the side. "That's surprising. She doesn't usually share that with anyone. I only know because I was here when it happened. We almost lost her too, but Alice willed that girl back from the dead. I've never seen anything like it. Peter and his mother didn't leave her side."

Violet's devotion to Alice was a given, if Stark's story was to be believed. Even if it had landed Violet in a sticky situation.

"Where is Peter?" Julian asked. "I keep hearing of him but I haven't seen him." Another level-headed person that knew how Alice thought might tip the scales to sway Alice to give up on finding Violet a husband.

"Away, attending medical school in Billings. He won't be able to help you rein his mother in, I'm afraid."

"How do you mean?"

"I saw the advert too, you know."

"Ah, yes, well—"

"I've also seen the way you look at Violet. Plain to see you've been spendin' time together."

Julian cleared his throat and stuck his hands in his pockets. "I have no idea what you mean." He walked the length of Stark's woodworking shop and stopped in front of the windows. "She's a nice woman. Pleasant to speak to, sharp-minded, amiable in spirit, and now I know she's a talent with cartography.

Stark hummed but said nothing.

"And that means I am invested in ensuring that the woman doesn't find herself chained to a man who would stifle her talent," Julian continued, his mind flying to the stack of debauched letters he had taken to burning each and every night of the past week. It didn't matter that they had nearly kissed—what was important was her stack of prospects was painfully thin.

Stark was right in his assessment that he had been spending his free time with Violet, but that was neither here nor there.

"Of course, clearly—that would really put a damper on our plans, would it not?"

"Truly," Julian agreed.

"And what kind of businessman would you be if you did not see to the security and well-being of a future employee?"

Julian whirled back around. "That's exactly what I think."

"If I were you, do you know what I would do?" Stark pressed, fixing Julian with a serious look.

"What?"

"I would march right over there and secure her for myself!"

"That's a wonderf—" Julian snapped his mouth shut and swallowed the words that almost came out. "What do you mean, secure?" he asked with narrowed eyes.

"Hire," Stark replied with too much wide-eyed innocence to be natural. "What else could I mean?"

"Nothing. Nothing at all," he said, forcing away the knowledge that Violet's list pointed to him as a possible suitor.

He was meant to employ her, be her friend, not marry her.

"But I *am* right. Let's have the record show that." Stark drew a line through the air with a chuffed expression on his face, and then pointed at the door. "If I were you, I'd make haste for Violet and get her on the payroll. If we have that in writing, then it won't matter what her boorish future husband has to say."

Julian swallowed hard. "Boorish?" He didn't like the sound of that. Why would the man Violet wed be boorish?

Images of letters burning in a fire made his stomach clench. Stark was right—he was painfully right.

Stark nodded. "Of course, boorish. You have met the

men here, yes? They are not like you and me. They do not value critical thinking and an independent spirit. They'll crush that flower underfoot if they manage to wed her. Not to mention let loose their more...amorous needs."

"Must you—" Julian stopped and sighed, hands going to his hips. "Must you say it like that?"

"Yes, I must, because it's the truth." Stark's face was somber, and Julian couldn't argue, because in his heart he knew it was true. He had sat beside her and read the evidence of it. It was a fact that Violet's future husband, should she choose from the offerings, would be...*difficult.*

Still, he tried to maintain a brave face. "That doesn't mean—"

"Doesn't mean what? That you have an easy solution to Violet's problem?"

Julian frowned. "And what solution is that?" He narrowed his eyes and watched Stark closely as the other man beamed and strode up to him.

"Employment, my good man. What else?"

"She's already gainfully employed by Mrs. Hill," Julian pointed out.

"That doesn't mean her employment as a cook is utilizing her talents to the fullest. She is meant to be a cartographer. It's in her blood." He let out a long, drawn-out sigh and added, "And there's the matter of her keeping some measure of independence once she's wed. The men in Gold Sky mean well, but they are simpler."

"I could...see that."

"So you will speak with her, then?" Stark asked, turning to look at him hopefully. There was an earnestness in the man's gaze that pushed Julian to nod.

He could tell that he cared for Violet, was genuinely concerned for the woman's well-being, and for that reason he said, "I'll speak with her."

Stark clapped him on the back and gave him an approving smile. "Good man. I believe she's at the mercantile, picking up a shipment for Alice."

"You mean for me to speak with her this instant?"

"Of course—as we speak, she is toiling away. You, sir, are going to secure her future independence and our business venture. What a blessed day indeed." Stark hustled him toward the front door.

"Tomorrow would be just as—"

"No time like the present. Early bird gets the worm," Stark insisted, throwing open the door and all but tossing Julian out of the wood shop. "I'll be here, eagerly awaiting your return. And remember, you are going to make her so very happy with the offer."

Julian froze and swallowed hard. Her earlier words swam in his mind.

A man who does not love the woman he marries will care little of what she wants for herself, and that is not the life I want.

His heart clenched, and Julian found himself in motion before he could think better of it. "I'll return shortly," he called out to Stark as he set off toward the mercantile.

I want my freedom, precious little that it is.

Stark was right, Violet would be overjoyed at the offer, at the possibility of having a secure and dependable outlet for her creativity and talent. It would be a bastion of peace in the worst-case scenario that she ended up married by Mrs. Hill's scheme.

Married to a boorish man. Julian's lip curled at that. Violet deserved more than the bare minimum when it came to marriage and a happy life, especially given the loss of her parents. The hardship of going through life alone was enough to steal Julian's breath and leave him determined to offer her what he could.

A job.

A way to hold on to her freedom, even if she did marry.

He clenched his jaw, teeth grinding painfully at the thought. Why did Alice Hill ever put this foolhardy plan upon Violet at all? Even if the woman meant well for her charge, it was infuriating, to say the least. Julian continued to stride down the street, each step fueling his resentment at the circumstances until he was all but charging down the busy road.

The only destination that existed to him was the mercantile. The only person that mattered at that moment was her.

Violet.

He nodded stiffly at a group of shoppers exiting the building and then slipped inside, eyes scanning the room, looking for a familiar head of dark hair. He frowned when he didn't see her and pushed further into the store.

Hadn't Stark said she was here?

He rounded an aisle and was about to start forward when he heard hushed voices to his right. He stifled a groan and kept moving; lowered voices usually indicated gossip, and he had learned to pay no mind to gossip.

And he might have made good on ignoring the excited whispers if he hadn't picked up mention of Violet's name.

"Can you believe how desperate? It's absolutely shameful."

"A woman like her, thinking she can marry her way out of her situation, is laughable."

Julian's skin prickled and his blood turned boiling at the words.

"There was an event there last night. Men bought tickets to talk with her. Can you believe it?"

"You know, when Marissa and I stayed at the boarding house, we noticed the most lewd behavior by the little chit. Selling tickets for her company is within her loose character. She's nothing more than a prostitute."

Julian stifled a groan, recognizing Sarah James's voice. It was no surprise the woman was eager to join in on the gossip surrounding Violet.

A gasp went up from another woman. "I thought she was a cook, not *that* kind of woman."

Julian bristled at the intonation, the meaning put behind what kind of woman Violet was. It was one thing to listen to her insistence that she was not a lady, and quite another to hear from this group of women who didn't know Violet in the slightest. There was no way they did if they were speaking about her in such a manner.

"I think you'll be surprised just what kind of lady she is, which is not one at all. I suspect she trades favors to the male boarders at Mrs. Hill's," Sarah James continued.

"Favors?" a voice gasped, and Julian could practically imagine the women all shuffling forward, their eyes dancing with glee as they drank up the lies Sarah James spun.

Julian shook his head and squared his shoulders. He

had to say something, had to stop the gossip going on just a few feet away. This was not harmless. These words had power to destroy, especially for a woman with no family at her back. This gossip could ruin Violet's present and future, could take away any prospects or hope of her ever leaving Alice's for a life of her own.

If anyone believed the women's gossip, these kind of words could steal her freedom as surely as any overbearing and narrow-minded husband would ever be able to. Even more so, if she were left with no job prospects saving cooking at the boarding house.

And for what? Bored women seeking a bit of entertainment?

No, it could not stand.

Julian rounded the corner, fully prepared to tell the women precisely what he thought of their repugnant behavior, but stopped so suddenly he nearly tripped over his feet when he saw that he was not the only one who had joined the women in the aisle. Instead of just the now silent group of five women who had been dragging Violet's name through the mud, the object of their ire had made an appearance.

Violet stood at the opposite end of the row, her eyes wide, clutching at the basket in her hands. Her mouth opened and closed a few times but nothing came out, and a blush colored her cheeks. Julian's heart lurched into his throat and he tamped down the urge to push past the women and go to her.

That would help no one, least of all Violet, in light of the women's words. He would have to choose a more prudent way of smoothing over the situation. Something logical, even-keeled, and deliberately done.

"Violet," he greeted her, eyes fixed on her face as he willed enough care and warmth into his voice to tell her that it would be all right. Despite what she had heard, he would help as much as he could, and that included offering his support and name. It would go a long way in Gold Sky to have his influence on her side, and he was not above using it to remedy any damage done by the public gossip.

All of that made sense, and would be the way to handle things in such a predicament, so when all ideas of prudent behavior flew from his mind and he made his way to Violet's side no one was shocked more than himself.

He held a hand out to her, offered her as elegant a bow as any ballroom had ever witnessed from him, and smiled warmly at her.

Violet's hand hit his and she looked shocked at the gesture. "Julian." That one word was a breathy utterance and slipped from her lips so quickly that it shocked them both.

"Good afternoon, dear." He dropped a kiss on the back of her hand, fully aware of the women now watching them in shock. They were, no doubt, committing every everything said and done between the couple to memory so that word of it would be all over town by supper, which made Julian's next utterance all the more important. There was only one way left to play his hand, only one avenue left to him if Violet's reputation and standing in town could be saved.

Ironically enough, it would be through marriage. But

Julian had never anticipated that said marriage would be to him.

"What are you doing?" she whispered at the brush of his lips on her bare skin.

"Greeting my fiancée, of course."

CHAPTER 9

"Your what?" Sarah James's eyes were as wide and round as a pair of porcelain saucers at Julian's declaration.

"My fiancée," he said again, for all to hear. Mostly the women gathered in the aisle, but he supposed it was good to get the word out and circulating among the townsfolk.

"Julian, you can't," Violet started, her fingers tightening on his.

He gave her a quick look. "I can," he murmured to her and then tucked her hand into the crook of his arm. "And I am."

"But it isn't proper," she whispered, giving him a reproachful look that he could only hope the gathered women interpreted as a swoon.

If they meant to sell their arrangement then it was going to be doubly hard with her frowning at him thusly.

He smiled sweetly at her. "It's entirely proper for a fiancé to escort their intended in broad daylight."

"But we aren't—"

"Going to be on time for our appointment with Stark. We can just make it, but only if we leave now." He stressed the word *now* in the hopes that Violet would understand the importance of beating a hasty retreat. The longer they stayed here engaging in conversation with Sarah James and her gathered ladies, the greater their chances of being discovered in their lie.

The lie wasn't necessarily theirs. Not quite yet, and he almost winced at that, but managed to school his features into a mask of calm. Though the lie wasn't technically theirs to share, it had been done out of necessity.

Dire necessity.

If Violet supposed her freedom to be precious little now, she had no idea just how much smaller it could get under the influence of the gossip Sarah James had been spewing.

"Our...appointment?" she asked, looking down at her hand tucked into his elbow and then back up at him, realization slowly dawning in her eyes.

He nodded, maneuvering her toward the door. "Yes, our appointment. We must hurry, though. Stark is a busy man and all."

"I—yes, of course." She set the basket she'd been carrying down on the shelf next to her and moved with him toward the door. Only when they were what Julian deemed a good distance from the women did he turn back to them and give them a look.

"Good day, ladies," he offered with a perfunctory nod. They all stared, some with their hands clutching their chest or skirts, but all with wide eyes and open mouths at the sight of him and Violet together.

"Mr. Baptiste, wait a second, if you please," Sarah James called out suddenly, snapping out of her daze and rushing forward in a swish of skirts. "Do you mean to say that you answered the advert for...for *her?*" Her tone wasn't only unkind, it was full of disbelief, and he pulled Violet's hand closer at the sound. Violet colored at that and dropped her head.

"I did," he answered calmly, though he fought back a wave of frustration when he met Sarah's cruel eyes. She looked at where his hand rested on Violet's and sneered.

"But a man of your standing and good reputation has no need for a connection, let alone an intimate bond such as marriage, to a woman like—"

"Like what?" Julian challenged, his voice holding an edge this time that he had not used before despite her many missteps in his presence, and Sarah James took a hesitant step back from them.

She swallowed hard but nevertheless continued on, "She's a servant."

"As was my mother," Julian replied, arching an eyebrow. "For knowing much about my reputation and family, you seem to have forgotten where she came from. Who she was before the war."

Her mouth snapped shut and for once Sarah looked abashed. "I meant no disrespect to your mother."

"There is no shame with working with one's hands. It is a far nobler way to earn one's bread than what many of those you consider in possession of 'good reputation' do. There's also no shame in wanting a better future, or someone to share that with," Julian said, and leveled a stern gaze at the women, who looked anywhere but at them.

Sarah James nodded but said nothing other than a murmured, "Of course." She inclined her head when Julian gave them another departing nod. She looked properly chastened and stepped back, head bowed and eyes averted, though if it were simply an act or if she truly felt the sting of his reproach he didn't know.

What she did when his back was turned he did not concern himself with, as all of his focus was solely on Violet. The woman was stiff as a board next to him and blushing furiously as they walked out of the mercantile. Her lips were pressed into a thin line and she kept glancing at him as they walked, but she didn't make a sound.

"I'll explain it all. Just—" He pressed his fingers to the bridge of his nose and breathed heavily. "Just let us get behind closed doors."

Violet's fingers tightened on his arm and she nodded once, just a slight nod of her head, before she looked away again.

Julian cursed silently the second her eyes moved away from his. What did it mean that she was so quiet? Julie would have been kicking up a fuss and giving him hell, but save for the tight clutch of her hand on his sleeve Violet showed no reaction.

When Stark's workshop came into view Julian blinked in surprise. He had used it as an excuse but hadn't truly meant to go there—in truth, he had simply been walking blindly as he worried over Violet's reaction to his public declaration of their betrothal.

"I thought it would be best to stick with your story," Violet said softly, and nudged him forward with another squeeze on his arm.

So she hadn't simply been clutching him but had guided him here while he had been unaware. He licked his lips and cautiously looked down at where her hand rested on the crook of his arm, her fingers tight on his sleeve, the pressure comforting and so unassuming that he hadn't even paid it mind.

But he supposed much of Violet's life was like that: she was comfort and stability, a steady hand in a way, even when no one noticed her as she guided them along.

"Julian?"

"Ah, pardon?" He gave himself a shake and jerked his gaze back up to meet her curious eyes.

"Are you feeling well?" she asked, worrying her bottom lip.

"Quite," he assured her, and then nodded at the workshop. "Shall we?"

She nodded and fell into step beside him, remaining silent until they were inside the workshop. Only when the door swung shut did she come alive. If Julian had any misgivings about Violet's quiet acceptance of her fate and demure nature, it was all put to rights as she glared at him.

"What do you think you're doing?" she asked with a stamp of her foot.

"Saving your reputation," he growled, surprising her enough that she was silent for a moment before he saw the fire in her eyes rekindle.

"I don't care a wit for my reputation where vipers like Sarah James and the rest are concerned!"

He crossed his arms. "You say that now, but you would sing another tune entirely if the woman gained any footing with her accusations against you."

Violet snorted and whirled away, dark hair flying over her shoulder. "Accusations? This is not a witch hunt, Julian. Those went out of fashion quite some time ago."

This time it was Julian's turn to snort. "You truly have no idea how close you came to losing everything today, do you?" he asked, and when she looked back at him with angry eyes and not a hint of caution he knew it was true. For all her ham-fisted manners and insistence that Violet marry, it appeared Alice Hill had sheltered Violet from much of the world, including the precarious position of single women.

"I was in danger of losing nothing but my temper," she told him.

He shook his head and blew out a sigh. "That—that is not so, Violet. If that woman, viper or not, had convinced anyone of her thoughts on you being a prostitute, the freedom you cherish would have vanished as surely as any poor match would have taken it from you."

Violet shook her head. "That's not true," she said, but her voice was softer now, and there was a waver in her words that hadn't been present moments before. "No one would believe her."

"People believe what is convenient. People believe what makes them feel higher than another person."

"That makes no sense."

"If you fancy yourself not a lady for the sheer reason

that you are a cook, what would happen in this town if they treated you thusly?"

"They already do..." Her voice trailed off and she looked at him then with understanding.

"Who would you believe if you were of the mind to raise yourself up by standing on another's back?"

She shook her head. "But it would be a lie."

"Lies are easy to swallow, Violet."

Violet's shoulders sagged and she raised her hands to her hair, fingers tugging on the dark locks. "But it isn't true. It isn't right."

"Small minds rarely care about what's right when there's an easier way. It's the way the world works. I hate it as much as you but...I did what I did today to stop it."

"I would have really..." She swallowed hard and looked away, but Julian knew that if he saw her he would see resignation on her face. She understood now the gravity of what had nearly happened. She must. "I would have lost it all because of that woman?"

He nodded, dark eyes somber. "Yes, that could have happened if the wrong people had believed her. Even still..."

"Even still what?"

He gestured between them with a finger. "Things are still tenuous. I put her in her place, so she won't press the issue, but it would be best to let this settle before you do anything rash."

She leaned back against a workbench and raised an eyebrow. "And what exactly do you think I would do?"

He remembered how she'd stamped her foot, and lifted a shoulder in a shrug. "That remains to be seen. But whatever it is, make sure it is prudent," he said, and the irony of his advice was not lost on him. He had acted with little forethought that afternoon—the only motivation for his actions had been to secure her safety, to offer her what protection he could, which regrettably had only been afforded through the idea of matrimony.

"Thank you," she told him, voice so small that he looked back at her in surprise. She wrapped her arms around herself and breathed deeply. "Thank you for what you did. If what you—" She shook her head and then frowned at the floor. "I know what you say is true. Sarah James could have ruined me. Couldn't she?"

He nodded. "Easily."

"Why would she do such a thing?"

Julian cleared his throat and looked away. He knew the reason for Sarah James's ire was twofold. The woman was small in spirit and sought to crush another like Violet beneath her boot to feel taller. But there was also the matter in which Julian played a part, and that was the reason he chose to disclose, even if it was the one he hated saying for the sheer fact that it showed his true feelings for Violet. And if he admitted those out loud, then he may just have to accept that he hadn't claimed to be her betrothed from the sheer goodness of his heart.

It had been in part because he wanted her for himself, and not as an employee as Stark had urged.

"Because I prefer you to Marissa."

Violet's eyes snapped up to his. "What?"

He walked forward until he stood in front of her. "It is not lost on me that her daughter is of marrying age. That she knows my family's pedigree, recognized me on sight, and showed distaste for you when it became apparent we were friendly. She felt slighted and is lashing out at you."

Violet's brows drew together in consternation. "But I did nothing wrong."

"No, you did not," Julian conceded.

"I was only doing my job."

"So you were."

She turned then, fixing a mournful stare on him. "And now... now people think we are to be married."

"We are," he said, taking a seat beside her. "But it doesn't—we don't have to follow through."

Violet went still. "What do you mean?"

"I mean, if we keep our wits about us and do not give Mrs. Hill a scrap of anything to go on, then I believe we can call off the engagement after a time and all will be returned to as it was." He gave her a kind smile and patted her hand. "This will all work out, you see. Do you agree to it?"

"Right then." She stood quickly and Julian frowned at seeing the momentary look of surprise on her face. It was so fleeting, like a flash in a pan, that he almost thought he imagined the expression of disappointment that crossed her features afterward. "Of course. I agree to this...arrangement you have offered me. The engagement is only for a time, until it no longer serves its purpose of keeping me from ruination. Not that I understand why I need saving."

Julian crossed his arms and nodded in agreement. "I understand your frustrations. You shouldn't need me to save you, but the world is imperfect. It is not fair, but..."

He cleared his throat and cautioned a look at her. "We have each other."

She had been pacing, taking small and quick steps around in a circle, her hands on her hips, and she froze at his statement. "We do?"

He nodded. "Yes. Partners in justice, or whatever it is that we are doing here, but I—*we* won't allow your future to be stolen."

"But what do you get out of it?" she asked, frowning in confusion.

"The satisfaction of knowing that a good person hasn't been trampled underfoot by someone selfish and careless. It is a kindness that was given to my mother once, and I can only try to repay it as I can."

"Your mother. Yes...I heard a bit about her and your family from Julie." She rocked back on her heels. "That makes sense. You love your family very much."

"I do. Family is important."

Her eyes clouded at that. It was like watching the moon block out the summer sun. She blinked quickly, turning away from him with a jerk. "Yes," she replied, voice soft and husky, "family is important. Thank you, Julian."

"Of course." He stood then and did his best not to notice how fragile she seemed at the barest mention of family.

If he were well and truly her fiancé he would cross the room and take her into his arms. He would gather her close and press a kiss to her temple, his hands warm and soothing on her face as he murmured sweet assurances that *he* was her family, that *he* would not leave her.

She would know that she was not alone, that she was cared for, wanted.

But since he was not, and they were only joined together by farce, he kept his gaze on the door ahead of him and crossed the room without a falter. He stopped in the doorway, one hand on the frame, eyes still focused on the wood in front of him lest he break in his resolve to honor their agreement.

"I will inform the newspaper of our new arrangement. I expect them to have the ad removed before the next publication and have the news of our engagement printed immediately."

She gave him a tight-lipped smile. "Thank you. I—well, that sounds prudent."

He nodded and opened the door, squinting into the bright sunlight. "Goodbye, Violet."

"Goodbye, Julian."

Her farewell followed him out into the afternoon, and Julian wished he could go back to her then, but blessedly his feet continued forward.

That did not mean that he wasn't entirely aware that he had left a piece of his heart at Violet's feet in Stark's workshop.

~

"Do you mean to tell me how you ended up engaged to Violet, or is that something you would like for us to figure out on our own?"

Julian looked up from the ledger in front of him. His sister stood with hands planted firmly on her hips, a glare on her face and her lips pursed in annoyance. Julian was used to being on the receiving end of such a look, especially when wielded by Julie, but never before had he seen the type of fire in her eyes as he did now.

He tilted his head to the side and considered his sister again. She'd always been sweet, kind-hearted and without any real malice behind her disapproving looks, but now was different. Now he could see that she not only disapproved of his sudden and no doubt surprising connection, and that there was metal behind said disapproval.

It seemed the frontier had changed his sister in more ways than he had realized.

"'On our own' is always more rewarding, is it not?" Julian asked, keeping his tone even while Julie's eyes flashed once more at him. She stomped further into the room.

"When you told me you were staying on for an undetermined amount of time, I never imagined that meant a marriage."

He held up a finger. "An engagement does not a marriage make, little sister."

"You're approximately three minutes older than me."

He smirked at her, unable to resist poking the bear that had seemingly taken his sister's place. "And all the difference it has made."

She scowled at him. "Oh, really? A difference, you say?"

Julian opened his mouth but Julie waved a finger at him. "Because for all of that difference you somehow ended up a mail-order groom. What was all the ruckus you kicked up when I told you of *my* plans?"

He leaned back in his chair. "I supported you after little more than a bit of fuss. Besides, this is different-"

"And precisely how is this different?" She arched an eyebrow and took to pacing the length of the parlor. "You're engaged to someone who had an advert for a spouse. If you think just because you're male that this is any diff—"

"Because it isn't real," Julian told her, his voice low.

Julie went stock still at his admission. The only sounds in the room for several seconds were the ticking of the grandfather clock and the swish of her skirts as she jerked around to stare at him with an open mouth.

She swallowed l and then asked, "What do you mean, not real?"

He steepled his hands and considered her for a moment as he tried to choose his words. Much had gone on during his stay at Mrs. Hill's boarding house. His easy friendship with Violet had caught him by surprise; his plans with Stark, who never seemed to be lacking when it came to encouraging the entire affair between Violet and himself; Sarah James's biting words.

It seemed like a lifetime since he had been able to share the finer details of his day with his twin, and he slumped forward after a moment.

"I mean to say just that. Things are not as they seem," he said, voice utterly despondent. Julie started at the tone and frowned, truly taking in the sight of her brother. Gone was the confident and collected, if also joking and playful, man. In his place was one with worries that weighed heavily on his spirit.

"Then explain it to me?" she asked, voice softer as she

approached the settee on which he sat and sank down beside him. She took his hand in hers. "I'm listening."

"Where to begin, dear sister?"

"I hear the beginning is often the best place in times like these."

He cracked a wry smile. "And what such times are these?"

"Well, I suspect any time that finds you the intended of a woman you scarcely know qualifies as 'times such as these.'"

"Ah, that." He held up a finger and wagged it at her. "I agree with your observation. And you are quite right, the beginning would prove the best place to start, and for that we must retrace my steps to the Fourth of July celebrations."

Julie nodded, settling back on the cushions of the settee. "The night you vanished."

"I didn't vanish, I simply rested my eyes and fell asleep. You make it sound like a magic act. Has anyone informed you the frontier has given you over to dramatics?"

She rolled her eyes and smirked. "I may know a man, or two, who agree with you. But no derailing me. As you were saying, your beginning lies on the Fourth of July. Then what?" she urged him on with an impatient wave of her hand, making Julian remember just how excitable she had been as a girl.

It was refreshing to see that lively spark return to her —something he knew was only possible because of her life in Gold Sky. Furthermore, it was a trait wholly encouraged by her husbands. Julian would be forever grateful to the men for bringing joy back into his sister's life.

Would Violet's husband be up to that task? Taking care to nurture and encourage her...give her the one thing she desired most, full rein over her life? He swallowed hard; the prospect of considering precisely what kind of man Violet would wed proved a far more difficult task than he had anticipated. It left a bitter taste in his mouth, and he raised himself from the settee, intent on the sideboard where a decanter of bourbon stood at the ready.

"I met Violet that night. I was...thoroughly charmed by her then," he admitted, pouring himself a measure of the amber liquid. Julie made a muffled sound he knew to be a squeal, but he dutifully ignored it in favor of sipping from his snifter. "She is smart, capable, witty...beautiful. A rare type of woman, to be sure."

"And that is when you decided to marry her?" Julie interrupted.

At this, he turned to face his twin. "That is not what happened. I simply thought her a favorable acquaintance I should like to know better for the duration of my stay at Mrs. Hill's boarding house."

"Then how did you end up that way?"

Julian took another sip of his glass and stared at his sister over the rim.

After a moment of silence she crossed her arms and leaned back with a sullen sigh. "Forgive my interruptions. Continue on, dear brother."

He chuckled at the put-out tone of his sister's voice, but continued after a moment. "That morning I witnessed the most abhorrent treatment of Violet by a woman who considered herself her better. That woman was ill-mannered and a creature of low culture to consider her beneath her for the sheer fact that she worked in service. I did not intervene then, though I wanted to. Mrs. Hill handled the matter."

"Alice is a very good woman. She would protect Violet with her life."

Julian would not argue, but he gave her a chagrined smile. "And that is the crux of the issue, Julie. Mrs. Hill flew into a fit over who would care for Violet when she was no longer able to. Who would provide her with security and standing, should anything befall herself."

"Oh dear. She's the one who put the ad up, isn't she?"

"She did, and while it was well-intentioned it brought a maelstrom of attention down on Violet that she was not equipped to handle. And I—" He cleared his throat and took another fortifying sip from his bourbon. "I could not sit idly by. Especially when her talent is instrumental to my new business venture."

Julie sent a puzzled look his way. "How is Violet going to help you with the railroad depot?"

"Stark tells me she is a talented cartographer. I know it to be true from seeing her wildlife sketches and portraiture. I hadn't thought it translated to a technical understanding of the land. Securing Violet's freedom from an overbearing and controlling husband is pivotal to obtaining complete and in-depth maps of the land. Maps that I will need if I hope to convince builders and investors that the depot and new line is viable for profit."

Julie's mouth fell open. "Do you mean to tell me that

you have taken her as your intended under the pretense of *business?*"

He pinched the bridge of his nose with his free hand. "Not entirely for the pretense of business, but—"

"Marriage is a sacred thing! And you—"

"Ensuring the success of the depot is crucial to the continued growth of this town you love. Violet's talent is a resource, and—"

"I'll not have you do this to yourself, or that poor woman!"

He started at that. "Poor woman? Is that truly what you think of the woman I would call wife?"

"She is not a resource to be used, or allocated like a faceless unit of raw material, Julian. Violet has feelings and a heart. A heart that I'll not have breaking for the sake of success."

"She understands the engagement is a farce, Julie." This he said through clenched teeth, because the aghast look on his sister's face affected him far more than the bourbon, and he took another healthy sip of his drink. "She is just as much a participant in this as I am. No one's heart is in danger of being broken."

His words felt hollow and false; his engagement to Violet was a dangerous game he played, but the currency proved to be his own heart, not Violet's. She understood why he was doing what he was doing, believed his words about what he was receiving in return for offering his aid.

And Julian hadn't lied. At least not intentionally.

He was doing it to repay a kindness done long ago for his mother, but there was the fact that it was wholly and entirely for Violet's sake and no other's.

"I'm sorry I drew my own conclusions." Julie rose from the settee. "Would you allow me the margin of error afforded of being the younger of us?"

He raised an eyebrow. "Did you not just protest that it was only three minutes?" he asked in a mimic of her annoyed tone.

She smiled warmly at him. "Ah, but what a world of difference those three minutes have made, dear brother."

Julian sighed and shook his head, but huffed out a laugh at hearing his own words. He held an arm out to her and Julie stepped in close to him.

"What will you both do? Even if you say she is a participant, there must be a time where you both come clean, before it goes too far."

"Before we wed, you mean."

"Well, yes, ideally before then. Anything else and things become a great deal more...*delicate.*"

Julian grinned at her word choice. "Do not worry. I understand the nature of such a thing. I've informed the paper of our new arrangement and have asked them to take her advert out of the next publication. I expect our engagement will have bought us a good deal of time to decide how and when to handle our next move as a couple."

Julie nodded along, squeezed his hand, and murmured her agreement; she, like her brother, was still, for all her time among the residents of Gold Sky, a stranger to the frontier way of life. It was a mindset that demanded action, that knew how fleeting life could be and that tomorrow was promised to no one. For that reason the residents of Gold Sky tried to love as frequently and as much as they were able to, to take their pleasures and victories when the opportunities presented themselves.

And it was in that willful spirit particular to frontier life that the Gold Sky periodical issued a special evening edition of its printing to joyfully and enthusiastically proclaim not an engagement between Julian and Violet, but a *wedding*.

A wedding scheduled for noon the next day.

This sent the townsfolk into a flurry of activity and planning that both Julian and his intended were ignorant of as they carried on with their evening duties, well away from the excited people of Gold Sky, who wished nothing more than to surprise the new couple with their offering of a cheery wedding meant to provide a happy start to their life as man and wife.

After all, there was no time like the present to begin a happy life.

CHAPTER 10

The morning was a sunny, cheerful occasion that should have presented itself as any other Sunday in Gold Sky. Or rather, Julian supposed that it should have when he awoke that morning and began his morning toiletries and grooming. He was in good spirits, better than good—splendid, he would dare say. His planning with Stark moved forward amiably, and funding looked favorable for the railway and depot, given they were able to show prospective investors just how lucrative crossing the West could, and would, be.

All that was needed to do such a thing was one expertly crafted map.

Luckily, he had procured just the talented fiancée to provide one such map. His fingers stilled on buttoning his waistcoat, and he frowned.

"Fiancée," he said in the empty room.

He cleared his throat, and after a moment repeated it a touch louder."Fiancée. This is my fiancée." He gestured in pantomime at the empty space beside him, as if introducing his partner to guests.

He swallowed hard and looked at the void beside him. In his mind's eye he could see Violet standing there beside him with her dark hair and eyes. Those thoughtful eyes that had flared to life in her arguments with him, those high cheekbones and full lips that tempted a man, and her skin, all of that tawny tan skin that led his mind to decidedly ungentlemanly scenarios.

He cleared his throat and pushed aside salacious ideas of what her skin would feel like under his hand, and allowed his play at an introduction to blossom into a full scene. Perhaps it was a ball, or some dinner he needed to attend. A veritable who's who of the Four Hundred. There would be gleaming floors of marble and low-lit rooms, finery and frippery in excess, but it didn't concern either of them.

Not when they would have had eyes for only each other.

They would make a fine couple. Each of them striking in their own way. Complimentary in their dark hair and shining smiles. No one would be able to look away from him as he stood proud and firm, an arm extended to Violet, her hand clasping him above his wrist as she surveyed the room with interest.

Perhaps she would lean close to him, her body pressed to his side, the warmth of her heating his skin through the silk of her dress.

All would envy their easy companionship—that particular connection only made possible by lust, caring, and true choice as they had selected the other of their own free will and not sought to make a profitable or smart match.

Except that...except that it wasn't true. Not a bit of it.

Violet hadn't chosen him.

Nor he her.

He cleared his throat then, unwilling to allow the daydream to continue a second more. It was dangerous to think such things when marriage was done via post and hastily made public declarations.

Theirs was a business transaction of sorts. He would not allow himself to press upon Violet, would not take more than she thought to give. And that meant he would be as good a mail-order groom as he could manage.

He only prayed he made it out a semblance of the man he had been at his arrival in town.

With a heavy sigh Julian continued dressing and exited his room, mind whirring. The newspaper had promised to run a new announcement informing the town of their intention to marry. He supposed he would be busy answering curious questions on his daily tour of Gold Sky, and he took in a fortifying breath as he walked down the hallway.

A clank of a spoon and an excited voice made him pause.

The boarding house had no others in residence than he, and the dining room was closed to the public for a solid hour before Mrs. Hill opened it to the public.

He glanced at his time piece and saw that it was not time for public dining hours. Could the eager citizens of Gold Sky have already infiltrated the boarding house?

Bracing himself, Julian entered the room and balked

the second his foot crossed the threshold. The dining table was set for breakfast as usual, and Violet was there, but she was not alone. It seemed the entirety of Gold Sky had packed themselves into the dining room and awaited him with happy smiles and cheers.

"Congratulations!" they yelled, throwing confetti and rice at Julian with such force he swore there would be bruises later.

Violet did not seem to share their jovial attitude, and in place of the flushed cheeks typical of a blushing bride-to-be was what Julian suspected to be an angry flush.

"Ah, thank you," he managed to croak out when another barrage of rice hit him square in the chest.

"Good morning," Violet gritted out, setting down a coffee carafe with a touch too much force.

"Good morning," he returned.

Rosemary Stanton burst from the crowd in an excited flurry of blonde hair and flapping hands. "We have a surprise for you, and we could not wait!"

"Oh, you do, do you?" Violet asked, and Julian had to bite back the laugh he nearly let out. There was nothing quite like the pretty cook when she was riled, and it seemed her dining room being taken over by the town was the quickest way to test her resolve.

"We do," Rosemary said, and winked at Violet. "When Julian brought your engagement announcement we could think of nothing but the good fortune!"

"How very...fortunate," Julian offered as Violet's glare intensified. "I am indebted to the speedy and solicitous attitude of the periodical's staff. You most of all," he said, nodding at Rosemary, who beamed.

"I am so happy to hear that, because we have gone and decided that the two of you young souls deserve the absolute best start Gold Sky has to offer."

Julian nodded, giving the woman a genuine smile. "Simply having you as friends is more than enough to—"

"And that is why we have not simply announced your engagement," she continued on excitedly.

"I, ah, you haven't?"

"No." Rosemary bounced on her toes. "What we have done is so much better!"

"What have you done?" Violet asked in a strained voice.

"Why, we've thrown you a surprise wedding, of course!" Rosemary exclaimed, throwing her arms wide.

"Oh, dear." Violet sagged against the table and instantly Julian moved, rushing to her side.

"Is she swooning?" Rosemary asked with an interested look on her face, and then snapped her fingers at a man Julian supposed was on the periodical payroll. "Quickly, I want it noted that Violet Shield swooned upon learning of her nuptials."

"Done in triplicate," the man replied, scribbling away on the pad in his hand.

"What do you mean, you are throwing us a surprise wedding?" Julian asked, pressing a glass of water into Violet's hands.

"This is far more than Alice would have done," Violet whispered. Her voice was somber, eyes panicking as she turned a baleful look on him. "I thought this was meant to —" she began, giving his arm a quick yank, but Rosemary was suddenly there and giving them both a cheery smile.

"Well, we couldn't let Alice have all the fun, now could we?" Rosemary asked with a little laugh, and gave her a swat on the arm.

"Ah, I suppose not," Julian murmured, his mind spinning through possible excuses he could utilize to head off Rosemary's plan. "When is the wedding exactly?"

"At noon!" She unfurled the newspaper he hadn't noticed tucked under her arm and tapped a finger on the front page, which boldly proclaimed the intended time for the ceremony across the front of the periodical.

Wedding of the century!

Today at noon.

Bring cheer and good will.

He gritted his teeth at the block letters. "Wedding of the century?"

"Well, for us it is. You're practically a prince," Rosemary informed him with a wiggle of her fingers. "Now then, you have been informed and our happy plans are underway! I suspect you have appropriate attire befitting a groom of your station, mail advert or not. But…" She turned her eyes on Violet, who looked as if she were trying to sink into the floor with a pained expression on her face. "You are another matter entirely. But not to worry! I will handle it."

"But I do not need a—"

"A plain gown. You must have the finest gown, and we shall make it so. I'll have word sent to Alice to meet us at the dressmaker's, hmm?" She turned to Julian and grabbed Violet's arm as she made a beeline for the door with the entourage of newspaper men trailing behind, furiously scribbling in their notebooks. "Go on then and ready yourself to see the finest bride to grace our humble town. When you next see us you will scarcely believe your good fortune at having such a lovely bride!"

"Julian!" Violet made a swipe for him, a real and truly panicked gesture that made him step forward to offer his aid in any way possible. But no sooner had he moved than Rosemary's triad of newspaper workers blocked the way with disapproving looks.

"Women need peace to shop."

"Do not test Miss Rosemary."

"It's bad luck to see the bride before the wedding."

Julian made an exasperated gesture. "But I've already seen her. How does that bode for wedding luck?" He looked over their shoulder to see Violet disappearing through the front door with a yelp, her arm firmly in Rosemary's grasp.

At that they were stumped, but when he tried to side-step them they moved along with him, blocking his way. "You had better not press your luck. We know you are lovesick, but it's only a handful of hours until your wedding."

He went still at that bit of unfortunate information. He looked at his timepiece and swallowed hard. It was now just seven, which left him a scant five hours to derail his own nuptials. If he hoped to make any headway in the matter he would need to stop dallying with the newspaper men, all of whom looked ready to hold him down if they so much as thought he was going to stop Rosemary from dressing Violet in a wedding costume.

"Ah, yes, of course. You're entirely right. I should be off

then," he said, jerking a thumb back toward his rooms. "Plenty of groom preparations to be made."

They gave him curt nods and claps on the shoulder that nearly sent him sprawling, but he continued forward until he was in the relative quiet of his suite. Only minutes had passed since he had stood in this very spot, anticipating nothing more than awkward small talk, but now here he was on the verge of matrimony.

He knew that life had a way of taking unexpected turns, but this was a different variety of chaos than he was accustomed to.

A proper wedding? Him a husband and...Violet his wife?

Things were entirely out of hand.

He took a quick step back toward the door but froze at the murmur of voices he heard. There was no way he could risk exiting the premises through the gathered crowd of excited townspeople, lest they decide to hold the wedding then and there.

No, that would not do.

He spun in a circle and snapped his fingers when his eyes lit upon the windows at the back of the boarding house. Just the break he needed to get loose and make his way to Julie's home. There he would be able to put things back in order, or at least come up with a battle plan to stop Rosemary's forward march to get him down the aisle.

He eased up the window and winced when it creaked, though he chided himself at his caution. It was not like they would know he made to get away...would they?

He bit his lip and shook his head, preferring not to answer the question, and climbed through the open window before landing lightly in the alley behind the building. Turning to look both ways, and happy to see that he was yet undiscovered in his escape plans, he skirted around the corner, careful to keep close to the buildings and alleys until he was on the open lane leading to his sister's homestead.

Only then did he stop to take in a shaky breath and lean forward, bracing his hands on his knees. He sucked in a deep breath and set off at a pace squarely between running and walking—he supposed it could be called an energetic walk.

Walk or not, Julian was sweating by the time he arrived at his sister's door. He raised a fist to knock but the door flew open before he could announce himself.

"You are to be married?" his mother asked with an arched eyebrow. Julian opened his mouth to answer, but she tutted and grabbed him by his lapel, yanking him inside before he could speak. "I knew this day would come, but I never expected to learn of it as I did."

"You saw the article?" he asked with a nervous laugh that his mother did not return.

She shook the paper at him. "This was no article. It was an entire front page spread."

"Things may have...escalated from the plan that I originally had."

"And what plan was that?"

"To help a friend."

Manon tossed the paper on the writing desk in front of her. "By doing what? Marrying her?"

"Well, yes, that is what I had intended to do."

"Julian!"

"But not as this newspaper says. I only meant to make it seem as if I were marrying her, you see."

Manon's eyes rolled heavenward. "My children will not rest until they have driven me to an early demise."

"I've done nothing of the sort. At least not intentionally."

"You have," she said. "My nerves cannot bear this."

"Would you care for smelling salts?" He turned, gesturing around the room. "Julie hoards them for just such an occasion. Claims Will and Forrest need them frequently with Seylah's arrival."

The corners of his mother's lips turned up. "It's for the best that they learn now how to manage difficult children," she replied, and Julian bit back the urge to roll his eyes.

Gentlemen didn't give into such things...at least not when confronted by their mothers concerning a surprise wedding. He winced.

A surprise wedding. How on earth had this happened?

He rubbed his temples at the thought that a wedding now hung over his neck as surely as a guillotine. Violet's stricken face danced through his mind, and he groaned. The poor woman had looked like she was on the verge of passing out, and with Rosemary's insistence on a wedding dress he could only pray that she hadn't made a mad dash for Butte City.

Though a hasty exit could be considered a prudent action to take, given how enthusiastically Gold Sky had taken to the news of their engagement.

"I meant well," he said after another moment, and

shook his head. "The woman, Violet, was in a precarious position."

"Precarious? How?"

"Her character was under assault by a mean-spirited sort. She's a cook, no family, and her employer already had designs to see her favorably married."

"That would explain the advert."

"I came to know Violet during my time at the boarding house. She's kind, amiable, light in spirit—"

Julian stopped when he saw interest spark in his mother's eyes. She was an astute woman, and he cursed himself for speaking without thinking. "She is intelligent. I hope to employ her talent in my investment plans," he said, in a brusque tone reserved for business transactions rather than matters of the heart.

"Ah, the railway depot." Manon tapped her chin thoughtfully and gave him a sidelong look. "And your only interest in the lady is because of her talent and intelligence?"

At her dubious look Julian decided to give into rolling his eyes, and did so with a pointed look at her that had her grinning.

"I know what you're attempting, mother."

"Which is?"

"Hoping to ferret out if I have true romantic feelings for Violet."

"And do you?" she asked, to which Julian only managed a thin-lipped smile and a half shrug. "Answer me, Julian." Manon crossed to his side and gave him a sharp poke that made him jump in shock.

"Are you poking me?" he gasped, clutching his side and

trying to hop away from his mother, but she closed the gap between them, poking him once more.

"You're lucky I haven't taken to using a stick on you," she replied, giving him another sharp jab of her finger. "Now, dear, answer your mother. Do you have romantic feelings for this intelligent, kind, amiable, and no doubt beautiful woman?"

Julian balked at her words, but couldn't stop the flash of Violet's dark brown eyes from appearing in his mind's eye. "Who said anything about her being beautiful?"

"You did, with your reaction," she replied, and when she made to jab him again he skirted around the settee with an exasperated sigh.

"*Maman*, you are being unreasonable."

"I am not. I am well within my parental rights to know the why and how of my only son meaning to marry in a few hours' time to a woman that I have never met."

"You never met Julie's husbands, and there are two of them. I should think my situation slightly less shocking as it concerns only one unknown spouse."

Manon waved her hands. "Pah! Nonsense—do you care for the girl?"

"As...a friend."

"Then why are you so flustered at the mention of her beauty?"

"I am flustered because I am going to be married," Julian insisted. "If I do not marry her, then...then..."

"Then what?" Manon asked, her voice gentle.

His eyes drifted closed and he sighed, shoulders sagging in defeat. "Then someone else will."

"Oh, Julian." His mother's voice was soft, and Julian

knew if he looked at her he would see compassionate understanding on her face. She would give him a look that revealed he had hid none of the feelings he had for Violet from anyone, least of all his mother.

"What am I to do with you?" she sighed, coming to lay a gentle hand on his cheek.

He gave a quick head shake. "I'm not sure there is much to do about me," he told her with a rueful grin. "And, given the circumstances, I have little concern for myself at the moment."

"Why is that?"

"Violet is my priority. This entire marriage plot was not her doing, and I thought—I merely meant to offer her assistance, not speed the process along. She must be beside herself."

"There are worse fates than being married to you," she replied, earning a raised eyebrow from her son.

"But it is not of her choosing."

"Are you so sure on that matter, or is it merely your opinion?"

That stopped him cold. He hadn't considered that Violet might actually want him, might care to be his wife or even desire to tie herself to him in a way not strictly in the terms of employment.

"Well, I..." His voice trailed off and he swallowed hard, trying to understand the moments he had shared with Violet. He knew he wasn't the only one affected by their time together, and there was no mistaking the blush in the woman's cheeks, the way her breath hitched when he came close, or how their conversation only seemed to pull them closer, urge them to touch, and asked them to seek one another out in a room, if only by way of stolen glances.

Surely all of that had to mean something.

But even so...Julian gave himself a stern shake and raised a hand to cover his mother's. "It is not so simple, *maman*."

"And why not?" She turned her fingers up and tugged his hand close to her. "You are a good man, Julian. Any woman would be proud to be your wife."

"That does not exclude the fact that she has not *chosen* me. If I am to marry, I would prefer it to be on the grounds that my bride has chosen me. I do not wish to be forced on any woman, and I will not steal Violet's future from her for the sake of my own...attraction."

His mother looked down at their hands, her expression thoughtful for a moment before she straightened and looked back up at him, making Julian instinctively step back, but her hold on him did not falter. She tightened her fingers and pulled him back to her.

"Why are you looking at me like that?"

"Because I have had the most brilliant idea, my darling boy."

"*Maman*," Julian groaned, unable to stop the exasperation from leaking into his tone. He knew the bright light in her eyes, the way she had become energized, her small frame practically vibrating—she meant to take action. But what it would be and if he would be able to survive it were still questions Julian held his breath over. "Please do not—"

"Don't *maman* me with that look on your face. Please nothing, Julian." She gave his hand a shake and continued on as if he hadn't interjected. "Now then, if your concern is that Violet has not chosen you, then we can fix it, easily so."

"And how do we go about doing that?" he asked, not willing to risk her wrath now that she had seemingly hit her stride.

She released his hand and began to pace, her hands moving through the air as she spoke.

"*We* do nothing. But *I* will take care of it. Leave it to me to see that true romance prevails."

Julian nearly swallowed his tongue at her enthusiastic news. "*Maman*! This is no love match, it is not like Papa and you. We are linked together on purely business matters, and this—"

"Pah. If I know you, and I hope that I do as your mother, then I am fairly certain the woman who has caught your attention feels the same way. Given that I have the perfect plan—"

"Scheme, you mean," Julian interrupted, hands going to his hips as he watched his mother practically hop around the space like an over-energetic bird.

"—To properly discern the young lady's feelings on the matter and put this whole matter to bed entirely."

"And how do you propose to do that?"

"I slip in while the blushing bride is getting ready and ask her. Very simply and plainly make your feelings known. If she returns them, then she goes through with the entire thing and marries you—but if not, I will help the woman make a hasty exit. Your papa and I intended to leave for New York tomorrow. She can come with us. I'll offer her whatever means she needs to make the trip safely and begin anew."

Julian's mouth dropped open. "You would do that for her?"

"For you," she corrected with a gentle smile. "I would. I know your heart was in the right. You wanted to help. I understand that as surely as I do her precarious position. I would do this a thousand times over. Leave it to me."

He swallowed and looked away, not wanting her to see the hope her words had stirred in him. All of this could be made right. Violet would be off on her own journey to New York, with his parents offering the help required to make a new start.

She would have her freedom, her life, and her choices readily available to her.

That would be the choice she would make. It had to be.

And for that reason, Julian nodded and agreed with his mother's latest scheme. "Very well, *Maman*."

Her eyes widened and she went still, though there was no mistaking the glee in her voice. "Do you truly mean it?"

He nodded once more. "Yes. Carry it out. Ask Violet what she would like from all of this. I will carry out my end of it all and await her at the altar. That way no one will know anything to be amiss. If she comes, we will marry, and if not, I will dutifully play the part of the jilted groom."

Manon darted forward and pressed a kiss to his cheek. "It will all work out, darling. You will see it!" She whirled away and grabbed a shawl on her way out of the room. "All will be put to rights," she continued on as she hurried down the hall, the door slamming shut behind her as she set off for town.

Once she was gone Julian slumped back down onto the settee, the weight of the morning and the impending wedding crushing him. He sucked in a steadying breath and worked on calming his breathing even as his heart thundered on.

"No reason to get cold feet now," he muttered quietly.

Violet would choose her future. He would not be married, on account of there not being a wedding. No wedding night or any nights to follow.

He should be relaxing, not feeling the flutter of nervousness that made his skin prickle and his palms sweat.

She would choose freedom. Not him.

He knew it.

He could not and would not begrudge her that which he knew was most precious to her—her future and her freedom. He wished it to be everything she had ever hoped for, even if it was without him.

The thought pained him more than he cared to admit, but there was no helping it. With a weary sigh he rose from the settee and set out for the boarding house.

He had a wedding ceremony to dress for, even if there would be no bride.

CHAPTER 11

All his life, Julian Baptiste had been raised to have an assertive, confident, and unshakable spirit. His was a demeanor carefully cultivated by countless hours of practice in the face of the Four Hundred, or those who wished nothing more than to discover a chink in the Baptiste family's armor. For years that armor had been stalwart and impenetrable.

Julian had always thought it would remain so.

Little did he know how quickly being jilted at one's own wedding before an entire frontier town could act as the dagger neatly slipping between armor plates.

Julian swallowed hard and glanced around, aware of the fine sheen of sweat on his brow. There wasn't an empty seat in the small white clapboard chapel. If there had been adequate space, Julian was convinced there would have been Gold Sky residents among the rafters.

Precious little relief it provided, but with the entirety of the community's watchful eyes on him he would take what comfort he could find. He shifted and avoided tugging at the collar of his suit, which was now suddenly too close for comfort. He resisted...but only just.

Pastor Bruce shifted beside him and glanced at his pocket watch. "Violet isn't the sort to be late to such an...engagement," the man said, and Julian gritted his teeth together.

"No, she's not," he replied. But that was when she didn't have a husband to jilt and a new life to start.

"Do you reckon she's all right? Should we send someone along to look in on her?"

"No, I suspect everything is going to plan."

Pastor Bruce frowned, undeterred. "What if she's fallen ill?"

Julian folded his hands in front of him and gave the man as kindly a look as he could manage. "I assure you, Violet's health is in perfect condition."

The man shook his head. "I know Violet. This isn't normal for her. I'm going to have one of the ladies here look in on her and—"

"No!" Julian raised both hands, startling both the pastor and those in the first row of pews, who now looked at them in curiosity. "I mean, I assure you she will be along. You know how brides are. Nerves and the like."

Pastor Bruce gave Julian an assessing look. "If you say so…" His voice trailed off and Julian gave him as winning a look as he could manage, though the facade of the patient groom wore thin. He resisted the urge to check his own time piece to see how much longer he needed to play his designated part.

If she were going with his parents, then he expected either Julie or his mother would come to deliver the news that Violet would not go through with the wedding. There would undoubtedly be questions and concerns that he would have to field while Violet prepared for her departure to New York for her new life.

He only prayed that she would find the city agreeable —that she wouldn't hesitate to ask his parents for assistance if she needed it.

Perhaps he would see her there. It would be the most pleasant reunion of ex-fiancés, society could ever hope to see. It would be good to see her and ensure that she was happy with her new—

"She's beautiful!" a voice exclaimed, halting Julian's thoughts in their tracks.

He looked up to see the doors of the chapel had opened to reveal a vision of white. An absolute goddess of matrimony stood there, swathed in lace, the light of the bright afternoon bathing her in gold, which served to make her look even more ethereal.

"Like a princess."

"Is that Violet? It can't be."

"Exquisite."

The townspeople's murmurs tumbled over one another until they were nothing but background noise— and then, finally, quiet. All of it faded away until all that remained was Violet.

At her side was Alice. The woman was dressed in blue and wore a happy smile on her face as they continued walking down the aisle, their arms linked. Julian's heart swelled at the sight of the women and the way Alice's hand rested on Violet's arm. There was support there. Family and warmth. The very things lian hoped to offer Violet. He would be eternally grateful to the woman for giving her heart so freely to Violet.

"Speechless, hmm?" Pastor Bruce nudged him, and Julian started. His mouth, which had been gaping at his first sight of Violet, snapped shut with a click, and he nodded.

"She's lovely," he said simply, watching her move toward him. She gazed at him and he saw there was uncertainty in her eyes, but there was something else, a new look of bright energy that made it impossible for him to look anywhere else but at her dark eyes.

Julian's hands clenched at his sides as he steadied himself, forcing himself to be still as he awaited the women.

He could be patient. She had chosen him, after all. She had come against all odds, this was—he was—of her own choosing.

When she met his gaze he was unable to contain the warm smile on his face. Julian felt like he had been shot through with sunshine at the sight of her dark eyes staring back into his unwaveringly. Violet returned his smile with one of her own, shyer and smaller but welcoming nonetheless, and his heart soared at the expression.

She had truly meant this. Meant to find herself swathed in yards of white lace and pearls, standing in front of him and all of Gold Sky.

Alice fussed at her side once more before pressing a quick kiss to her cheek and reaching for Julian's hand. It took everything in him to spring to action and divert his

Julie waved her hands. "Who can say what is normal or proper these days?"

He laughed at that. "True. You would know, after all. How are things in the Wickes-Barnes household since my leave of absence?"

She brightened and bounced on her toes. "Oh, it's perfect. Seylah is healthy and strong and the time with *Maman* and Papa has been so good. I didn't want them to miss this time with her. It seems like she grows every day."

"She'll be walking and talking before you know it."

"I know. Will positively hates it."

"Oh?"

She crossed her arms and nodded across the square at the dance floor, where her husband Will stood, oblivious to the fast-paced music or the twirling dancers around him as he swayed in place with Seylah in his arms. "He wishes she would stay a baby forever, I think. He would watch her every second if he could."

Julian nodded, watching Will's tender expression as he looked down at his daughter. Children had never been a thought for Julian. A wife, let alone a family, had always been a distant concern for him. Yes, he would like both, but before his time in Gold Sky he had envisioned it at a much later date.

But now...now things were different. Now, he was married. Children would be a matter to discuss with Violet, assuming she was interested in a family.

Whatever it was that she desired, he would give her. He would spend each and every day showing her that choosing him in lieu of a new life alone was not a mistake.

Her happiness was his new mission.

And Julie had been correct in her point that he had never seen Violet in the company of strangers or particularly enjoying social settings, especially one as large as this. She would be ready to leave, whether a proper amount of time had passed or not.

It was their reception, after all.

He turned and pressed a kiss to his sister's cheek. "I'll see you tomorrow when *Maman* and Papa leave for New York. But for now, I have a bride to find, rescue, and abscond with."

Her eyes twinkled merrily in the light of the party. "How positively scandalous. Enjoy yourself, brother!"

Julian gave her an exaggerated bow before he turned and strode away into the crowd, his eyes scanning for the swath of white lace and silk that could only be Violet. Thankfully his search was brief and he found her at the edge of the dance floor, looking mortified.

"A dance is all I ask," a man he didn't recognize said, extending a hand toward her.

"I would rather not," Violet replied, moving to step back from him, but the man stepped closer, blocking her way.

"It's rude for a bride to refuse a dance on her wedding day," he said, an edge creeping into his voice. The sound made Julian's blood heat so suddenly he was scarcely aware of moving until he found himself blocking the man's hand with his body.

"And it's rude for a gentleman to force his attention on a woman, regardless of the occasion." He glared at the man and watched as the leer that had just been directed at his wife slipped away to reveal wide eyes.

"I was only trying to be friendly," he said, stepping back so quickly he nearly stumbled.

"Your efforts are dismissed," Julian replied, crossing his arms. "Unless, of course, you wish for me to be the one returning them in my wife's stead?"

The man had the grace to color. "No, that's not necessary."

"Then we thank you for attending our ceremony." He nodded at the man before he turned toward Violet and offered her his arm. "Are you ready to leave?"

"Quite," she replied, taking his arms with a shaky grip. "I couldn't find you…" Her voice trailed off as she glanced over at the man still standing a few feet away from them.

He touched her cheek gently, bringing her attention to him.

"I'm sorry for leaving you. I thought...I thought you might want time to enjoy the celebration on your own."

She shook her head and leaned against him as they walked. "No, I'm not one for parties."

"So Julie informed me." She smiled at that and Julian stroked her hand. "I only have my rooms at the boarding house, but I can procure other lodging if—"

"No, the boarding house is fine," she told him, suddenly looking shy, and Julian fought the urge to kiss her then as he had before.

This was not the moment for passion. Tonight would require patience and gentleness.

"Then let us be off from here for somewhere quieter?" he asked as they walked.

Violet ducked her head and nodded, pressing closer still to his side. He saw she had retreated into herself now, and he knew it would take time and tenderness to draw her back out as she had been during their vows.

Violet's demeanor more than suited Julian, because he had all the time in the world to get to know his bride.

Tonight was just the first of many for them.

CHAPTER 12

Julian closed the door behind them. Silence filled the room, save for the rustle of Violet's skirts and the click of the door's lock sliding home. He paused, eyes trained on the wood in front of him, and did his best to keep his breath even and steady.

In and out.

He closed his eyes, willing his pulse to slow to a reasonable speed. It would not do for him to lose his bearings and swoon like a lovestruck newlywed. His eyes popped open at the thought and he stood up straight, because he supposed he *was* a lovestruck newlywed.

The pair of them were. He and Violet.

Warmth spread through him at the mere thought of his new bride. If he were feeling this...anxious, then what emotions must she be wrestling with?

"Julian?"

Violet's voice roused him from his thoughts. He turned to face her, grateful that he had managed to keep his breath regulated and his voice steady when he spoke.

"You came," he said. "To the wedding, I mean."

She nodded, eyes roving the room for a second before they came back to meet his. "I did," she whispered.

He moved toward her then, the world ceasing to exist outside of her beautiful dark eyes. He could stare at her all day, had done his best not to in the days before, but now?

Now she was his wife, and he was free to gaze upon her as often as he liked.

That alone was enough to stir a heat in his belly that made him both lightheaded and anxious with unspent energy.

A curious mix.

"I did," she said again, surprising him when she moved forward to meet him. "I needed to."

"Why?" Julian asked. When her eyes widened in surprise he didn't miss the flash of pain that he saw in them. He had hurt her with his question. He winced, and instantly reached for her, his hands gentle on her sides. "I didn't mean it like that."

She nodded but looked away.

"I mean, why would you trade the chance at your freedom...one not beholden to anyone for a life with me?"

Her hands twisted in her skirts, fingers bunching the ivory material before she let it go. "I feel affection toward you."

"But Violet..." He gentled his tone and met her eyes unwaveringly when she looked back to him. "We are now married. That is quite a leap to make on the beginnings of affection."

"Your sister married—" Her voice broke off before she

shook her head and pressed on. "Your sister married two men after exchanging nothing but correspondence."

"But that was over the course of a year," he told her, suddenly feeling wild and desperate to understand exactly what she had agreed to with him. They were married and it was not, could not, be in name only. There was a fire in him that she ignited, a joy she brought upon him when she entered the room or spoke his name. He had to have her as his wife, *properly*. " I feel they knew quite a bit more concerning the arrangement and motivations. What you—"

"Those men, Will and Forrest, we know they are good men. She knows that now, that they love and cherish her. Honor her and their vows. But Julie didn't know that. Not then. Anyone can pick up a pen and pretend to be whomever they wish, but with you…"

"With me what?" Julian pressed. He forced himself to stay where he was and not cross the space between them, madc his hands stay behind his back rather than touch Violet like he yearned to do. It didn't matter if she had swooned in his arms a scant hour before, or that their passionate kiss still burned his lips, the ghost of it doing more for his health than any tonic.

"With you, I know," she said simply.

"Know what, Violet?"

"That above it all, you, Julian Baptiste, are a good man."

Her words stunned him, made his heart stutter in his chest before he felt the air in his lungs leave in a whoosh.

But Violet was not done speaking. "I know that you have my best interest at heart, that you genuinely care for me. No man willing to set me free, send me on my way with his money and his family, would ever be capable of—of hurting me."

He reached for her then, his hands coming forward to brush over the backs of her hands, which still twisted in her skirt. "Violet. Darling."

"And that you are someone I would want to have on my side," she whispered, giving him a lopsided smile as she turned her hands palm-up to thread her fingers with his. Her touch was hesitant, gentle in the way she explored his skin. "I could think of no one else I would want to go through life with more than a man like you, Julian."

"I want that too, so very much, Violet." He drew her closer to him and brushed her hair back from her face. "You will not regret choosing me as your family."

She leaned into his touch with a soft sigh. "I know." She moved her body closer to his, the heat of her warming him as she pressed herself against him until they were flush. "I know," she whispered when he only groaned.

"You're lovely," he murmured, rubbing a thumb across her cheek and placing a gentle kiss on her lips. "Let me take care of you?"

Her eyes, which had been drifting closed, popped open and fixed him with a questioning look. "Take care of me?"

He kissed her again, this time with more heat and pressure, their mouths moving together for a long moment before he pulled back. "Yes, darling," he told her, lips ghosting against hers as he spoke. "Will you give me the honor of taking care of you tonight?"

Violet raised her hands to his chest, fingertips trailing

over the material of his suit, burning a path across his skin despite the layers of cloth that separated them. He swore he could feel her touch on him, feel it etching into his skin, and he nearly stopped breathing when she pressed her palm flat, resting it over his heart.

"As my husband?" she whispered, the desire in her voice unmistakable.

She wanted him.

When she raised her eyes to his, the heat Julian saw made him groan aloud. He was a damnably lucky man to be wanted by Violet.

"Of course, darling." He leaned close, his lips brushing her cheek lightly before he whispered again, his voice husky, the timbre rich and low, "Do you want me, Violet?"

A light shudder went through her, her fingers twisting and tightening in the material of his suit. "I want you desperately."

That small admission, those few words, meant the world to him. He did not have to hide his affections from her any longer, from anyone that could look upon them and know from a glance that he had lost his heart to her.

They were man and wife—he was free to love her as he wanted.

Could touch her, finally, as he had wanted to for weeks.

And it mattered not that they were wed, but that she wanted him too, that she had told him to touch her, had whispered her ardor to him.

He turned her face to his and wasted no more time. He claimed her lips in a kiss that was unlike the one they shared in the chapel. Here, away from prying eyes, he kissed her tenderly, sweetly, and slowly. The world could fall down around them and he would not care, if only he were allowed to save this moment in his memories for the rest of his days. They kissed, touching gently and tentatively, breath syncing as one as they explored the other with care.

He placed his hand on top of hers and lifted it to his jaw, holding her hand against his skin. "You can touch me, Violet."

She blushed but did not look away from him. "I don't have much experience...there were a few men, but it wasn't like this."

"It was never like this for me either," he replied. Her eyes jumped back up to his and he saw surprise there. "No one has ever made me feel like this. I apologize for the excessive adulations, but I am entirely and wholly sincere in my feelings for you, Violet."

"I quite find that I enjoy your adulations."

He smiled then, dropping an arm to slip around her waist. "Then I am a very fortunate man."

She hummed, giving him a playful smile. "Indeed. You are an extremely fortunate man."

The lightness in her tone caused him to smile—*this* was his Violet. The woman he had grown fond of from spending time with, the woman who had seen him as a man rather than a means to an end. *She* was his

Violet.

His wife.

The thought made his heart squeeze, and he kissed her again, but this time his kiss was not chaste. It was all-consuming, hungry and wild.

"I'll do well not to forget my luck in the way of matrimony," he told her, trailing his lips down her neck, his mouth pressing along her jaw before it dipped lower to skim the line of her collarbone.

She trembled, hands clutching at his arms as she leaned into him. She tilted her neck to the side, a moan escaping her lips on her exhale.

"Julian," she breathed, and he found that he had never heard anything more exquisite. The sound set a fire raging in his blood, and he leaned down, pulling her up and into his embrace. He carried her across the room and set her down on the bed with care. He settled in front of her and lowered himself to his knees at her feet.

"I aim to have my name on your lips as often as I am able," he said, his voice husky. His hands pulled her foot into his lap but he stopped, fingers lightly touching the laces of her white leather boot. "May I?" he asked, giving the lace a gentle tug.

She licked her lips, hands tightening on the edge of the bed, giving him a quick nod. "Yes, please..."

He undid the laces and began to ease the boot off of her foot.

"....husband."

His hands stilled, the boot in one, her foot in the other. He swallowed past the lump in his throat. "Say it again?" he asked. "Please."

"Husband."

The title fell from her lips almost as soon as he made the request, and he warmed at the word.

He set her boot on the floor and started undoing the next. "You honor me."

She leaned forward, hands on the edge of the bed. She watched him intently as he set the second boot down beside them. Her stockinged feet touched the hardwood and at the gentle brush of his fingers she slid her leg closer to him.

"You can...I want you to continue." She ducked her chin, suddenly shy at the unwavering attention. "Please."

"Of course. Anything you wish."

He took hold of the leg she had nudged closer to him and lifted it back into his lap, fingers pushing up the hem of her gown. Higher and higher it went, and he scarcely thought he would be able to keep his breathing under control.

He managed, but only just.

Though he was glad to be securely on his knees rather than on his feet when his fingers found the top of her stockings. Carefully, he unrolled the material from one leg, and then the next. Only when he was finished with both did he allow himself a moment to run a warm palm along the length of exposed flesh.

"Will you allow me to put you first tonight?"

Her eyes fluttered closed at the question but she nodded. "Yes."

He gave her a gentle smile and lifted another hand to grasp her knee. "I will only go as far as you allow tonight. Your pleasure is first."

She returned his smile shyly. "Thank you."

He shook his head and lifted her skirts to her knees. "You have no reason to thank me. You deserve only good, Violet," he told her, his eyes moving over the tan skin of her legs. He caressed her gently and kissed the inside of her knee, his warm breathing fanning out across her skin and making her shiver beneath his touch.

"You are good," she told him, her eyes drifting closed as he kissed higher, hands bunching the fabric of her skirts at her thighs. He pressed closer to her, his shoulders pushing her legs further apart. He reached up a hand to her stomach and gently urged her back, his hand sliding higher as she slowly lay flat on the bed. He hooked a hand into the waistband of her drawers and she lifted her hips, helping him slip the bit of cotton and lace down her legs.

He kissed the tops of her now bare thighs, lips eagerly moving over each new exposed inch of soft skin. "You are so beautiful, darling," he murmured, lips moving lightly against her skin as he spoke.

His hands slid beneath her thighs and she let out a sigh at his touch, angling her hips closer to his when she felt the warmth of his breath on her now exposed skin. The tender parts of her were laid bare before him and he breathed in the warm scent that was entirely and wholly her.

He lowered his head when he saw that she lay flat against the bed, her chest rising and falling quickly, her breath coming shorter the longer he touched her without giving her the touch she desperately craved.

"Can I touch you?" He was almost caressing her now, but held himself back until she told him to go further. She had chosen him, but he would not take more than she wished to give, and he kissed the inside of her thigh as he waited for her answer.

"Yes," she choked out, her eyes squeezed shut and body tense.

He moved closer to her, slowly taking care that she was wholly aware of how close he was to finally tasting her. Her legs parted slightly, her heel pushing him closer as she wiggled her hips to draw nearer to him, and he almost groaned at the sight of his wife eagerly awaiting him.

He lowered his head and closed the space between them, his tongue lightly tracing the warm skin of her, and she let loose a sigh of pleasure when he laved his tongue over her folds.

The taste of her on his tongue was just as heady as he had anticipated and he tightened his grip on her thighs as he continued on. His tongue dipped inside of her, and he moved a hand to stroke that bundle of sensitive nerves he knew would bring her the utmost pleasure. Her moan and the gentle nudge of his heel against his side urged him on with fervor. He raised her leg over his shoulder with his free hand and focused on maintaining a steady rhythm for her to follow.

Oh, thi-this is good," she gasped, hands twisting in the bedsheets. "It feels—ah—good."

He glanced up her body to see that she had lifted her head and now stared down at him as he knelt before her. "Take your pleasure, darling" he urged her, meeting her eyes.

Only when she reached for him, her fingers grazing his forehead and urging him forward once more, did he lower his head and resume his ministrations.

Her nails scraped his scalp and made him moan against her skin, lips and tongue kissing and licking her until she writhed beneath him. He leaned closer, both hands now focused on pleasuring her as she began to move in time with his fingers as they pumped in and out of her. He increased the pressure of his touch until the focus of her pleasure mounted, and then snowballed, speeding up until she fell over the edge of ecstasy he had guided her toward.

Her body arched, legs squeezing tightly on either side of him, and the hand on his head pushed him close as she cried out her release.

"Julian," she sobbed, eyes squeezed shut.

He continued to touch her, gradually slowing his rhythm and easing her down from the high of her climax. Only when she shivered and relaxed beneath him did he release her.

She smiled, eyes still closed. "That was very good."

He chuckled and kissed her thigh. "You were lovely."

"You are an attentive lover." She opened her eyes when he rose to his feet and pulled her skirts down her legs.

"I have always endeavored to do my utmost," he replied, helping her sit up and setting to work undoing the buttons at the back of her gown.

"What are you doing?" she asked, giving him a curious look but not moving to stop him as the gown began to loosen on her body.

"Helping you undress. Ladies' garments offer far more resistance than one would think. If we wish to be in bed at a reasonable hour it will take the pair of us, I think." He pulled the dress open at the back, sliding it down her arms.

She shrugged out of it and nodded at him. "Fashion can be cumbersome."

The dress was now open, the bodice free of her arms and at her waist. She turned so that he could work on her corset ties.

"The sacrifices one makes for beauty. Though you are stunning in any garb." He gave her a smile when she blushed, and lowered his eyes to where the corset strings awaited him. "Now, this will be a true test of my skill, but I believe I am up to the task if—"

She leaned forward, catching his lips in a kiss that stole the words from him.

His eyes closed and he kissed her back, their mouths fitting together tenderly. She tilted her head, lips slanting to his with a moan of pleasure. Her arms went around him, fingers grazing his neck as she pulled him closer still.

His heart ached at the longing she poured into her touch. His wife was happy, content, and safe: he could sense it in the way she kissed him, in how her hands lit upon him, and he drank it down like a man dying of thirst. Whiskey amber met dark morena eyes and the pair looked intently at each other. The only sound other than their breath was the chiming of the grandfather clock ringing through the boarding house, declaring the late hour.

"You have given me better than good, Julian. You have given me wonderful," she told him, voice catching as she spoke. "Tonight has been perfect."

He caught her hands where they lay against the back of his neck and threaded their fingers together, then leaned forward, resting his forehead against hers. "And I shall seek to give you that for as long as I may. For as long as I draw breath, your nights will be filled with perfect," he promised, looking her in the eyes.

His words, sincerely spoken and heartfelt as they were, proved needless. There was no denying the deep emotion and connection between the newlyweds.

He hadn't needed to utter a single word for her to know the truth in his heart, nor did he require it of her. And when she kissed him once more, he counted the sweetness for what it was—a promise of what he offered, and the gift of earning her heart through all of it.

The pair had come together in the most unlikely manner. Yet for all that, Julian found immeasurable happiness in his circumstances. Julian Baptiste had excelled at every endeavor he set his hand to, and he would not fail now as a husband.

He would be a good husband to Violet.

Better than good, he wagered.

He would be perfect.

CHAPTER 13

The next morning when Julian awoke it was to the sleeping form of Violet beside him. He paused, lingering in the early morning light shining in through the window, and smiled at the woman in his bed. She was at peace in her sleep, the lines of her face smoothed away, and he savored the calm of her features. Violet so often hurried, thinking of the next duty to achieve in her day, that Julian wondered if sleep was the only time she slowed.

He pulled the quilt higher on her shoulder and sat up. Their marriage meant change, and significant change at that, for both of their lives, but Julian supposed Violet was due the largest shift in her day-to-day.

She would not be beholden to anyone she did not choose to work with...or serve. Her energy would be her own, her talents hers to employ as she saw fit. Her position would never again be precarious.

Julian would see to it.

He ran a finger through the dark hair that fanned out

across her pillow. The shiny black curls slid over his fingers, and he smiled when Violet shifted in her sleep, a hand reaching toward his side of the bed. Her fingers brushed his arm.

She raised her other arm over her head and gave a stretch reminiscent of a cat waking from a long sleep. "Good morning."

Julian smiled, reaching down to touch her fingers with his own. "Good morning. Did you sleep well?"

She nodded, sitting up slowly. "I did. I cannot remember the last time I slept so deeply."

It was true that she had slept soundly. The moment Julian had finished helping her dress and climb into bed she had drifted off, fast asleep long before he had joined her.

It had been soothing in a way Julian hadn't anticipated needing. Seeing Violet asleep and unbothered, safe, comfortable. He reached for her now and ran a hand along her cheek, cupping her face.

"I'm glad. You needed the rest."

She leaned into his touch, her head bumping into his shoulder as she did so. "I suppose you are right in that estimation. My life has been rather fast-paced. I don't think I noticed."

"It just means you are driven." He kissed her forehead. "There's nothing wrong with that, Violet."

She nodded, her head still pressed to him. Julian's fingers wandered from her cheek to her hair once more and he toyed with a lock, wrapping it around his finger before letting it slide free. He felt her relax against him, allowing him to support her weight as she did so.

The gesture was slight, but it pleased Julian immensely. She was relaxed and well-rested and Julian's thoughts turned to breakfast. Sustenance and all that.

"Would you like brea—" he began, but a sharp rap on the door interrupted him. The sudden sound made them both jerk out of the sleepy reverie they had been wrapped in.

"Breakfast!"

Alice's sing-song greeting from the hallway made Violet giggle, and Julian jerked a thumb at the closed door.

"Breakfast," they both said in unison with a knowing nod at each other.

"Just a second," Violet called out, already reaching for a dressing gown while Julian followed suit in a bid to make himself as presentable as one could expect the morning after their wedding night. When they were dressed in a semblance of normal attire Violet let Alice in, and the older woman grinned at the sight of the rumpled bed.

"Can I expect grandbabies soon?" she asked, cheerfully and willfully oblivious to the look on Violet's face.

Violet glanced toward Julian with horrified eyes, and he chuckled at her expression.

"I am entirely aware that you will not be returning as a full-time cook for me after your honeymoon has been seen to, which I expect would be at least through Sunday," Alice said, carrying on as if it were entirely commonplace to discuss such intimacies before a decent cup of coffee.

"Alice! If you please," Violet hissed.

"Life has a way of deciding those things," Julian said,

taking a seat at the breakfast table. "If my wife wishes for us to have children, then we shall."

"And if not?" Alice pressed.

Violet massaged her temples with a barely restrained growl.

"Then we shall not have them," he said, unfolding the napkin in front of him.

"You won't force it upon her?" Alice asked, clutching a pitcher of coffee in her hands and regarding Julian shrewdly.

He met her gaze with a calm smile and a shake of his head. "I wouldn't dare."

"You swear it?"

Violet wrung her hands at her sides, giving the woman an exasperated look. "Alice, please, this is—"

"I only want you to be happy," Alice said, turning to look at her.

"And he makes me happy." Violet's voice was soft, and her eyes shone with unshed tears. "And you will always be my family."

Alice nodded. "I would exact retribution if he made you unhappy." She turned toward Julian with a pointed finger. "Do you hear me?"

He inclined his head. "Yes ma'am." Retribution was never good in any form, and he didn't seek to know what Alice Hill's brand of it entailed.

"Good man," she said with an approving hum at Julian before she placed a heaping plate in front of him. She crushed Violet to her, and the women embraced for a moment before Alice stepped back and gave Violet a little shove into her seat.

"Eat your breakfast before it gets cold," she advised primly before bustling out of the suite as quickly as she'd arrived.

Julian was left staring after her with wide eyes, while Violet smiled happily after the other woman.

"What's wrong?" Violet asked when she saw the shell-shocked expression on Julian's face left in Alice's wake.

He dropped his eyes to his plate and picked up a fork. "She is a formidable woman," he said, cutting into his food and already working on contingency plans on the off-chance he incurred Alice's wrath.

Was he allowed to hire a guard? What were the rules on bodyguards when it came to an almost-mother-in-law?

"She only wants to see me happy."

"As she should." He looked up at her and gave her a smile. "You deserve to be happy…and I hope, ah—I hope I can make you happy. Now, and in the future."

Violet reached across the table, her hand touching his. "You do make me happy," she gently corrected.

Their eyes met over their breakfast plates and a shared smile warmed the space. A comfortable silence settled around them and they returned to their meal, which was pleasant. It was the most relaxed and enjoyable morning Julian could remember having, save the morning he met his niece Seylah.

Before long they were ready for the day, with the bulk of Violet's belongings having been brought to Julian's suite during the wedding festivities. It had been curious to watch the emotions play out on Violet's face as she stood barefoot in front of her single trunk.

Dismay. Frustration. And finally shame.

"What is it?" he asked, trying to understand why she now wore such a pinched look.

"I just—it's that I never realized all of me could be packed up so easily. It's just one trunk. I bet the room I had looks like I wasn't there. This room won't bear any notice of me when we leave."

He came to stand beside her. "We can buy you more trunks."

She gave him a tight smile. "It's not just about the trunks, but thank you."

He hadn't understood the sadness in her eyes. It had to do with more than possessions...that much was certain, but that didn't guide Julian in what course to take in remedying it.

He glanced at her now. They were off to see Stark at his workshop, the matter of railroad planning at hand now that Violet was an asset to their venture. She had been excited about the plan, thrilled he had even considered her for the position of cartographer, and Julian's heart swelled at the thought of working alongside her.

She fussed with her cuff. It was a simple dress of blue, more at home on a workday than for leisure, but it suited her and he had never been so proud to have anyone in his company. He tucked his hands behind his back and walked alongside Violet as they stepped out from the boarding house and into the afternoon light.

He hesitated after a few steps and cleared his throat. When she looked at him he offered her his arm and smiled.

"It would honor me greatly," he told her, making sure

to offer the perfect picture of chivalry. Violet deserved nothing less.

She blushed and Julian wished he was as gifted as she when it came to drawing. He possessed no skill when it came to capturing color or moments on paper, but this color, this one, he wished he could commit to memory. Somewhere between a strawberry and the blush of a sunset. His wife had a lovely dark complexion made more lovely by the blush painting her skin.

"Thank you," she murmured, taking his arm. The feel of her palm on his arm, despite the layers, warmed him considerably more than the late summer sun could hope to.

He glanced about them and frowned when he saw no signs of an approaching fall. It was now late August. The leaves in the city would be changing, and his parents would be on their way back to New York soon. Their stay had already been prolonged due to his mother's inability to be apart from Seylah for more than a few hours, but soon they would leave to settle into their place among society for the end of the summer season.

There would be fall outings to the countryside, balls, and new shows from Paris and London to take in. His mother would thrive in the environment, and he knew she would ask after his plans to return now that he was wed.

His parents would do their best, or his mother would, to bribe Julie away from the frontier. Futile, but Julian commended his mother's efforts, which would no doubt be balanced by his father's live-and-let-live attitude. The man supported them always, even if it sent them to the far reaches of the country.

"You must live for you. I will not be here forever. Make a life you are happy with," his father had always advised.

Julian had never questioned his father's advice. The older Baptiste man had served as a wellspring of wisdom and guidance for his son. Julian had soaked up each moment of tutelage, and now he was hard-pressed to find himself outmatched by life's twists and turns. Julian suspected he would pass on the gift of independence to his own children...should he have them.

He looked at Violet once more and saw her frowning as she started down the street.

"What is it?" he asked her, touching her hand.

"It's just, I hadn't thought about life after our wedding. It was all so...rushed," she said, emphasis resting squarely on rushed.

"That is a mild description but yes, it was. And, ah, we could do that now—what do you wish for us to do?"

She blinked owlishly at him. "What do you mean?"

"Would you like to stay in Gold Sky?"

"But I—" She fiddled with her cuff nervously again, picking at the fabric. "I thought we were going to return to New York?"

"Why would you think that? I do have a vested interest in the town now."

"Yes, the rail depot and your sister."

"Yes, that, and now you. This is your home, after all."

"But that isn't of great importance."

He stopped dead in the street and raised an eyebrow. "Your wants are of great importance to me, Violet."

"But, I just mean to say that you are important in New York, and to give that up for a frontier town is just ludicrous."

"It's...unconventional but not out of the question. After all, my family knows its way around unconventional arrangements."

"True, true. Then what do you aim to do in the meantime?"

"I aim to continue with my plans on the railroad. I suspect my parents will be leaving before too long, and then you and I can decide what our future holds, hmm?" He brushed the backs of her knuckles with his fingers one more. "Do you have an opinion on that?"

"I like it very much," she replied shyly and her eyes darted up to meet his. "Even if it does you no good to know what I think."

Julian breathed out a little chuckle and shook his head. "Ah, that is where you are wrong, my dear, but worry not. I will teach you the ways of happy matrimony."

She laughed. "Oh you will, will you? And tell me, what is the first rule of such an engagement?"

He drew himself up and made a show of clearing his throat. They were attracting glances from nearby townsfolk, but Julian cared little what they thought of his childish antics if it kept the smile on Violet's face.

"First," he said holding up a finger, "is to keep your bride happy at any and all costs. If the occasion demands naval warfare, there may be concessions to negotiate, but on the whole you must endeavor to keep a wife blessedly happy."

Violet hummed in approval. "I will do my part to avoid naval conquests, I suppose."

"It would make for far less eventful evenings, I daresay."

"Do continue. What is the second?"

Julian held up two fingers and drew in a deep breath. "Secondly, one must always solicit the opinions and preferences of a wife when it comes to matters of occupation, geographical location, extravagant spending, the question of children, and the general size and description of homes?" The last of it came out as a question and Violet laughed.

"Oh is that all?"

"Thirdly, there is also the business of 'to have and to hold,' and I do believe communication, fidelity and honoring have something to do with all of it. But of course, that is if you refrain from naval warfare. That is a sticking point for me, darling." He winked at her and Violet once more blushed, a hand lifting to her throat.

"You, sir, are a charmer. I see now how you left ballrooms littered with broken-hearted girls."

Julian gasped in jest and released her arm. He held his arms out at his side and fixed her with another playful look. "Are you alluding that your husband was once a degenerate?"

Violet clasped her hands in front of her, the ring on her finger, a modest work of white gold filigree and yellow diamond, flashing in the sunlight.

Julian found that he liked the look of his ring on her finger.

"I have said no such thing, and quite honestly I find your baseless accusations comical," she told him, a laugh shaking her voice, though she strove to maintain a severe expression. They both knew she had no hope of maintaining her frown, and already the corners of her lips turned up in mirth. Julian saw his opening for victory and stepped closer to her, closing the space between them in rapid succession. Violet's eyes widened at his sudden movement. Her feet stutter-stepped and in her surprise she wobbled, a happenstance Julian knew to use in favor of pressing his advance and he caught her around the waist with an arm holding her flush against him.

"Do you now?" he asked, catching her left hand in his and raising it to his lips. The glittering yellow diamond on her finger flashed between them as Violet's mouth opened and closed, though no words came out. Instead she nodded her head vigorously and managed a squeak that sounded to Julian vaguely like *yes.*

"I suppose I can allow the affront to my honor to stand, on the grounds that it brings you joy," he said, unable to keep his eyes from dropping to her mouth. Her pouty lips begged him to kiss her, but even Julian knew there were bounds of propriety that not even newlywed bliss could excuse. Properly and passionately kissing one's wife while holding her thusly would cross at least one of them.

"Does it?" he asked, and she started as if he had caught her in the midst of a scandalous undertaking, and not for the first time Julian wondered what went on in Violet's mind. He tilted his head to the side and looked at her anew. Perhaps he *had* caught her in a scandalous moment, even if it only occurred in her mind. Her pupils were dilated, he saw when he looked closer, and a shiver moved through her body despite the summer air all around them.

Ah, yes, his dear wife was most certainly caught red-handed in her fantasies.

He would have to remember to ask her what exactly she had imagined him doing at this juncture.

She flushed a deeper scarlet when she noticed how he looked at her. "What?" she asked, reaching up a hand to tuck her hair behind her ear. She was still pressed to him, and the gesture forced her breasts against his chest in a way that made him bite back a groan.

"I, ah, I've quite forgotten, which I presume entails it had nothing to do with naval warfare," he admitted, and cleared his throat before regretfully releasing her.

"No," she said, her voice low, "I do not believe that was what I had on my mind."

Because Julian was a gentleman he did not press the matter, but he did hum in what could only be categorized as 'thoughtfully informed,' and he informed her as much when she inquired what the sound meant.

"Informed on exactly what?" she asked, her hands going to her hips in a show of bluster he found endearing, since it lacked the necessary bite to hold weight.

"On matters of, well, you know," he said, tapping a finger against his temple as they once more set off in the direction of Stark's workshop. As he faced away from Violet he did not see her reaction, but he did hear it—a very audible splutter and cough.

"What do you mean?" Violet asked, but the waver did not lie and Julian glanced over his shoulder at his wife, who stood red-faced, wringing her hands in front of her.

"Darling, now is not the time to reveal such things, but later." He cleared his throat and let his eyes slowly roam over her form—a form he had intimate knowledge of, one he had caressed and stroked to beautiful completion more than once throughout their first night together. A body he was eager to have laid bare before him once more that night. "But later, I will disclose my full knowledge to you, if it would please you."

Her eyes grew round as saucers. "It would," she blurted out before she winced. "I mean to say that it would be—that would be agreeable. A fine idea."

He winked at her once more. "I thought as much."

"I've changed my estimation of you, Julian," Violet said, coming forward to stand close.

"Oh?"

"Yes," she told him, "you were no degenerate. You, sir, were a Lothario."

He chuckled. "Is that your estimation?" He licked his lips and Violet's eyes followed the movement, her own tongue moving in a mirror movement of his, and he had to take in a steadying breath.

She nodded at him and moved closer until their arms pressed against one anothers. "But that suits me fine," she said, looking up at him.

He met her eyes. The pair were oblivious to all around them, and for all they knew the town of Gold Sky had fallen down around them. They would be none the wiser, not with the other standing so close. "And why is that?"

"Because I quite think I like having a seducer for a husband. It does make everything that much more enjoyable. Don't you think?"

And this time it was she that winked at him before she moved away and set off with far more sway in her hips than was decent or Christian.

Julian suspected Violet did not care much for either, and that suited him perfectly, as such topics were the last thing on his mind as he hurried to catch up to his wife.

CHAPTER 14

"Do you think you will be able to have it done in time?" Stark placed a hand on the table and gazed at Violet who sat at his desk. Her head was bent forward, considering the map entailing the swath of territory that needed the attention of a talented cartographer if Julian and Stark had any hope of succeeding in bringing the railway to Gold Sky.

She paused, her hands moving over the map's surface before she nodded and lifted her head. "I can do it. It will take me a few days to scout the area properly. I have some notes of my father's to work from, but I can do it."

"A few days to scout?" Julian asked.

"Yes, I'll go by horseback and travel light. A few nights camping, and I should be done covering the ground from Butte City and beyond Gold Sky."

Julian balked. "Horseback? What do you mean, travel light? Do you intend to stay out there?"

"If by out there you mean make camp as she details the

area—by what other means did you expect her to do it?" Stark asked, giving Julian a confused look.

"I hadn't—I suppose I had not worked out the logistics of what we were asking her to do. We do not need her making camp on the wilds of the frontier."

"It's hardly wild, Julian," Violet sighed, but she smiled at him.

"If it is not wild, then what is it? There are no beds or roofs to keep you comfortable. There are no doors to keep you safe from whatever man or beast one finds away from civilization."

Stark nodded in agreement. "He does have a point there."

Julian nodded, pleased. "Exactly, which is why I do not think we should have Violet go out to do this work."

Stark nodded again. "Absolutely not. You are entirely right."

Violet's mouth fell open in shock. "You cannot mean to keep me in town simply because you think it is too rough for a lady. Do not think I don't know what you're about, the pair of you. If I was a man, you would let me go as I please."

"Now that is simply not the case," Stark said, and Julian broke off the nod he had been in the process of vigorously executing. Hadn't Stark just been agreeing with him?

"What do you mean?" Julian and Violet asked, rounding on Stark.

The man rubbed his hands together, giving Julian a grin that Julian had fast become worried at seeing. It meant the carpenter had a plan.

A plan Julian wasn't entirely sure he would agree with or...to. He braced himself to wait and see which would be the case.

"Violet should not be expected to traipse across the wilds of the frontier alone. She should have an escort, and as her husband, that escort should be none other than you." He flicked a finger at Julian.

Ah, yes, it was not agreeing *to*.

"You are newlyweds. What a splendid way to enjoy your honeymoon, unmolested and in the unreachable wilds, making camp together, sleeping beneath the stars, dining over campfire. It's positively laden with romantic charm."

Julian cleared his throat. "I had quite imagined spending my honeymoon in more civilized quarters," he said, but the look Violet sent his way made the protest die on his lips. Her dark brown eyes pleaded with him and her hands were clasped together.

"Oh, please," she said, and it was then that Julian came to terms with the fact that Violet had him securely wrapped around her finger.

Gone was any argument that a honeymoon should be comfortable, that it should involve breakfast in bed served to them and not cooked over an open fire, that it would not demand them to be on guard against attacks from animals or thieves.

None of that mattered, because Julian could see how much it meant to Violet.

"This is such an opportunity for me," Violet went on, fingers tightening against each other. "I wish to prove that I am my father's daughter. That I am capable of more than cooking and cleaning. That I have skill."

"I know you do," Julian told her. "You are incredibly talented, Violet."

"But now I can show everyone," she replied, standing from the desk. "I can show them all if I do this. Your railroad will come to town and my map will be the one to make that happen. I will do what my father set out to do."

He squeezed his hands at his sides. She was right, he knew it. Stark knew it by the way the other man went silent and stepped back from the couple. The legacy of her father, the man who had never made it to Gold Sky but had taught his daughter and given her his skill…

Julian sighed and nodded. He could understand the urge to please a father, to show that what they had given you had been for a reason. This railroad depot, the expansion of a line to Gold Sky... it was in part a way of Julian showing his father that he too was able to seize new business opportunities successfully.

That he had the ability to make the Baptiste name successful in his own right.

Why shouldn't Violet also want that for herself? More so, given that her father was no longer alive to see. It was then, when one was alone, that victories meant the most, and he could see it meant a great deal to her if the shine of her eyes was anything to go by.

"What would we need to make this...frontier honeymoon successful in terms of covering enough ground to complete the project?" he asked, and Violet clapped her hands in excitement.

"You won't regret this," she exclaimed, hustling around

the table and hurrying toward him. "I will take care of everything—you just be ready to leave by three!"

He blinked. "This afternoon?"

She nodded and paused, one hand on the doorframe. "Yes, tonight would be best if I am to have the whole affair done in five days' time. We won't ride far, just a bit down the road to a high ridge that I know will give us the perfect vantage point for me to create an outline of the area. You'll see. It will be perfect."

"Are you sure you don't need help?" He started toward her, but she surprised him when she pushed away from the door and crossed the room to him. Her arms went around his waist and she hugged him tightly to her.

"No, I will take care of everything. I swear it. Even your packing. Stay here and work on the finer details with Stark, and before long we will be off!" She leaned up and kissed his cheek. "You'll see."

"I have no doubt that you can handle it," he said, lifting a hand to cup her cheek. "But I can help to make it easier."

"Thank you." Her eyes softened and she turned her face to kiss his palm before she stepped away. "But I consider it my right as outlined in your rules to happy matrimony. You've kept to your end by making me happy. Letting me plan the excursion will continue to do so."

He held up his hands in acquiescence. "You are right. My apologies."

"Now that is much more like it. You almost had me wagering on naval warfare for a moment."

Julian laughed while Stark looked on unfazed. "I have no idea what either of you are going on about," he said, moving to clean his glasses with a sigh, "but it seems as if the infection of wedded bliss has already addled your brains."

"Quite. Now if you'll excuse me, I have plans to make and a man to see about a horse!" She flashed Julian one last smile before she bounded from the room, and he was left staring at her in what he supposed was a version of lovesickness. That feeling that was confirmed when Stark snorted at him.

Julian snapped to attention and wiped the look from his face. "Let's go over these plans once more before I go?"

"You are married to her, you know," the man said, coming to stand beside him. "If anyone should be free to stare besottedly at a woman, it is her husband."

Julian colored but only hummed at Stark's observation, and the two commenced reviewing the plans for a third time, but not before Stark teased him once more on the newness of marriage's pleasures. Julian shrugged it off. This venture would go off seamlessly if Julian had anything to say about it.

Before long there was a rap on the door and Julian righted himself from the approval for funds he had just been signing and blinked around the room. The sun had shifted, indicating that it was later in the afternoon, and he shook his limbs out, marveling at the stiffness that had settled in. He'd been intent on completing as many tasks as he was able to before he left Gold Sky with Violet.

Stark nodded at the door. "I believe that is your fair lady."

"It would appear to be that time," Julian remarked, stretching his arms overhead. "She said she would take care of it all, but I can't help but...worry."

"Don't worry, Violet is capable. You'll enjoy the time if you allow her the space to stretch her legs."

He swallowed hard and forced himself to nod. "True. I suppose I'll see you in a week's time."

Stark was already bent over a missive he'd been writing to an investor, and waved an arm over his head. "Try not to fall prey to anything bigger than you, or with venom at its disposal."

Julian rolled his eyes while he yanked on his coat and headed for the door. "If that isn't a heartfelt send-off then I haven't the faintest idea what is."

His friend chuckled and lifted his head. "Be safe. Enjoy your wife."

Julian inclined his head. "I intend to. Goodbye, Stark."

He turned and stepped out into the afternoon light, and smiled when he saw Violet standing between two mares, one chestnut and the other dappled grey, their leads in her hands as she waited for him. He saw that the two animals had been packed neatly, precisely, and perfectly outfitted for a trek into the Montana expanse.

"I have your horse, sir," she said, offering the chestnut mare's reins with an exaggerated formality that made him chuckle as he stepped off the boardwalk and toward her. "She is a worthy steed who will see you through any obstacle."

"And what a noble animal she is." He nodded and patted the horse on his nose. "What shall I call her?"

"Marbles. Marbles the mare."

Julian could hear the smile in her voice. The effect was infectious and he grinned as he turned around. "Marbles the mare will be a good companion for our adventure."

She tipped her head at him a wide smile on her face. "Only the best for you. It is your honeymoon, after all," she said, earning another laugh from him.

"Too true. And what is a honeymoon for if not a bit of indulgence." He went to mount his horse but Violet moved forward, catching his hand.

"I, ah, I know that I pressed the issue before in Stark's workshop, but we can stay in town. I was so excited that I hadn't given much thought to what nights would be like."

"This is more than fine," Julian told her, and lifted the hand resting on his arm to his mouth. He dropped a kiss against her knuckles and perhaps took a bit more time than was proper to release her hand. "I aim to uphold the rules of happy matrimony without fail, and besides, a few nights under the stars with you only means we will have to be creative."

"Oh, is that so?"

"Without question. But I have full faith that we can manage it together, darling." He dropped his voice an octave, leaning forward to whisper the last word, that endearment he could see quickly becoming a favorite of hers.

Violet's eyes fluttered closed and she swallowed hard before letting loose a shuddering breath. "You rake," she whispered back.

"Your rake," he corrected, kissing her cheek gently before he pulled back and cleared his throat. "Now then, Marbles and I have much to discuss and a ride will be the perfect way to do it." He nodded at her horse. "Shall we?"

"Let's," she replied, moving to her own horse. "I wouldn't dream of keeping the pair of you from making your greetings." It was only when Violet went to pull herself astride her horse that Julian realized he had forgotten the most basic of all gentlemanly behavior.

Helping a lady mount her horse.

He sprang forward, his mind flying to what Julie's archaic etiquette teacher would have to say on the matter of him leaving a woman to her own when there was a horse to mount. He could practically hear the shrieking now.

"Violet, allow me to—" he began, extending a hand, but he stopped short of his bride and her mare when Violet swung herself up into the saddle effortlessly. She grinned at him once she was seated and shoved her skirts out of the way with a flick of her hand.

"I've been riding since I was a girl, but I appreciate your concern, husband." She settled into her saddle more firmly and then asked "What?" when Julian did not immediately answer her.

"That was...quite handy of you," he replied.

"Handy?"

"By which I mean attractive. I never thought that seeing a woman mount her horse unassisted would have an effect on me, but…" He ran a hand along his jaw and then looked at the horizon. "Now that I give it a moment, I think seeing you do anything handily has that effect on me."

Violet bit her lip and then nudged her horse forward. "Then I must advise you, you may feel faint when you see me prepare a cookfire later this evening."

He made a show of slumping forward and clutching at

his chest. "I shall never survive this trip without swooning myself into an incoherent state."

Violet giggled and the pair leaned toward one another, she in her saddle and he where he stood beside her horse. The sweet playfulness between them simmered to a far headier thing that reminded him of how one's skin felt after too many hours swimming beneath the bright summer sun. She made him feel as if he were burning up from within, and all with the simplest of things: a smile, a giggle, her genuine excitement.

He adored that about her and would go on enduring the threat of swooning over his wife for as long as she would allow it.

"Take it to the frontier," Stark hollered from inside his workshop, and the pair sprang apart.

Violet jerked upright in her seat while Julian blew out an exasperated sigh and raised a hand in acknowledgment to Stark. He turned to see the carpenter leaning against his door, eating an apple with a smirk on his face.

"There is work to be done, I'll have you know," he told them with a laugh.

"Yes, yes," Julian muttered, turning to his horse and swinging up into his seat. "Come, Marbles. It's high time we leave behind the work-obsessed tyrants of Gold Sky," he said with a sniff and urged his horse forward on the road leading out of Gold Sky. Violet joined him, a smile playing on her lips at Stark's incredulous "What horse is named Marbles?"

"Isn't it beautiful?" Violet asked, her dark eyes moving over the valley beneath them.

He stretched his arms overhead and smiled, joining her at the cliff edge. "It is," he said, and reached out a hand to take hers. "But not as beautiful as you."

"Charmer." She grinned at him and leaned close to kiss his cheek. The light brush of her lips made him sigh with pleasure. She pulled a spyglass from the leather bag she wore at her hip and set her sights on the prairie below.

"From here we will be able to make a plan for the next four days. We should be able to cover the ground necessary for making a more than adequate map to suit our needs for the railroad."

Julian hummed in agreement and stepped back from her. He let himself enjoy a moment of admiration and smiled at the intent and animated way she went about surveying the land below. The Montana territory proved to be an example of wild beauty both sharp and soft all at once. Inviting but unyielding in raw power, it reminded one to mind themselves while traveling through the mile after mile of wilderness.

They had ridden at a decent pace for the better part of the last few hours. The city limits of Gold Sky had vanished long ago and now the pair stood on the heights of a ridge that offered them an advantageous view of the land below. The stretch of Montana territory that extended in front of them was lined by mountains on one side, and the glittering band of silver that signified the presence of a river shone in the distance, while the darker green trees extended to the horizon line and vanished out of sight.

A honeymoon enjoyed with such a view could be considered second to no other place on earth.

No place could ever be second, with Violet at his side.

"I'm thrilled we made such wonderful time." Violet shut her spyglass and grinned at him. "We can make camp here tonight and then head in the direction of the river you saw in the distance. The territory between here and there is what we need to take stock of for the railroad depot."

"Why is that?" Julian asked, unsaddling Marbles.

"There are no proper settlements between here and that river. Beyond it is the way to the Idaho territory. The township of Coeur d'Alene is of decent size, and the silver mine's success there means it would be a smart move to consider for the railroad. We already know what lies between here and the end of the Butte City line, but no one has taken an interest this far west."

He nodded, picking up the eagerness in her voice. She was right. A move toward Coeur d'Alene was prudent. A lucrative move. "It would be a point of interest for investors," he added, and she practically bounced on her toes in excitement.

"It would. Not one of them would think us unprepared or a poor investment choice."

"Us?" he asked, his interest piqued by her use of the word. Us. He quite liked the sound of it when it came to the matter of Violet and himself.

"I, ah, well..." Her voice trailed off and some of the excitement left her under his questioning gaze. "I only meant that our efforts here...well, that they would be profitable. I hadn't meant to include myself in your business venture with Stark. I'm sorry if I overstepped."

He set the saddle down and frowned. "You weren't overstepping. You are a part of this. You do understand that, I hope."

"As the cartographer, of course."

"No, not as the cartographer. As my wife."

She gave him a thin smile. "I think I much prefer my role of inclusion to be that of cartographer…"

He dipped his chin and his frown deepened. "I'll endeavor to not take offense."

Her eyes widened. "I did not mean...well, I am very happy to take part in this as your wife. But my role as a cartographer is a chance to prove myself on my own."

"What do you have to prove?" he asked, his voice soft. "Is this still about your father's legacy?"

She twisted her fingers in the coat she wore and looked away. "How do you mean?"

He took a step toward her. "I mean, are you proving yourself for the sake of your father's legacy, or is this about—"

"About how people view me?" She gave him another thin smile. "You aren't wrong in your estimation on that. No one ever dreams of growing up to be a servant. Not when there are stories of princesses and princes filling a little girl's daydreams."

"Who cares what anyone thinks of you." He came to a stop in front of her, and watched her close her eyes at his words.

"It's not always easy to remember that, when your

everyday is filled with constant reminders of folks who they are better than you. Worth more than you are."

"Those people are small. Mean in their worldview. You are not beholden to them now, and you never were."

Her mouth fell open in a slight O. "How do you keep managing to make me feel like this?"

"Feel like what?"

"Like the most important person in your world."

"It's easily done," he told her. "Perhaps because you are just that."

Violet let out a shaky laugh. "There you go again," she whispered, lifting her hands and placing them on his shoulders. She gave him a squeeze. "How are you real?"

He leaned into her touch. "Well, when two people love each other very much, they make a decision to have children, you see. And once upon a time, my mother and father decided to do just that. And voila." He gestured to himself with a finger while she giggled at his explanation. "You were blessed with my sister and me. Of course, I am the superior twin, but never breathe a word of it to her. She's quite sensitive on the matter."

"Of course not," she swore, eyes dancing with merriment.

"Now that the matter is settled I'd like to see you prove yourself handy once more. Shall I gather wood for the fire while you make preparations for the night?"

"That would be perfect. The weather is clear for the night. I thought we might sleep under the stars. That is, if you'd like to?"

He gave her warm smile. "I'd like nothing more than to do just that. I'll be back in a bit." He set off towards the copse of trees a short walk away, but not before he heard her call after him.

"Prepare to see me being quite handy!"

He laughed. The light feeling in his chest was refreshing. He took in a deep breath and sighed when the air smelled of nothing but the rich Montana soil: sage underbrush and the delicate floral scent of summer's wildflowers.

It was nothing like summer in the city, or even a summer abroad in Europe. Each locale had their own attractions: old-world charm and avant garde events in Spain, a vibrant cosmopolitan scene ripe with networking opportunities in New York—and now there were the wild places of Montana.

If asked to choose, Julian would always choose the wild places.

He gathered an armful of sticks and kindling perfect for a cookfire, his mind more at peace than it had been for quite some time. Even with a new business venture and the uncertainty that came with mapping the territory to their specifications, he felt none of the pressure he did when doing business in the city.

Violet had a large part in the peace he felt, but he was also aware that it was this place. The town of Gold Sky was rough around the edges, but it was still a gentle and accepting place where it felt safe to breathe. It was a place he could imagine escaping to every so often with Violet, or even permanently if she wished to stay.

If he had learned anything from his parents' happiness, it was to always choose one another. The world would not always be kind, but it would be bearable when one could wholly and completely lean on their spouse. No matter what the world had thrown at his parents, they remained steadfastly devoted to each other.

Julian hoped to find that with Violet.

He emerged from the treeline to see Violet busy at work making camp. Already their bedrolls had been placed and the site selected for their fire, and she was busy preparing dinner.

Handy, indeed.

He smiled when she waved enthusiastically at him. He returned the gesture as he approached and felt his heart warm a little more toward his wife.

The woman was gentle, caring, and warm. Julian could not have asked for a better match.

"Is this enough?" He held up the wood and kindling for her to look over. "I defer to your expertise, as I have done nothing more than a handful of camping excursions and day trips."

She gave the bundle in his arms an assessing look. "I'd say you're a natural forager. It's perfect."

"Good to know I have some wilderness survival skills."

"Never fear. I promise to look after you."

He set the wood down and set about working on the fire. "Then I am in good hands, but count your blessings, darling. I am more than proficient at starting a fire."

The evening passed peacefully. The pair worked together and enjoyed a delicious dinner, wonderful conversation, and a happy round of stargazing that lulled Julian to sleep with a smile on his lips. When they awoke at dawn to break camp, Julian and Violet fell into a companionable rhythm that saw them on the move at an enviable speed.

The Montana scenery stole Julian's attention more than once, as there was no shortage of places to draw his eye during each day's ride. The land was some of the most beautiful he had ever witnessed.

Too often his mind wandered into a daydream captivated by the mountains and vibrant flowers stretching as far as the eye could see. Violet, on the other hand, looked at the land with a more disciplined eye. Her interest was focused on capturing the elevation and detail of the miles they logged each day. She worked the theodolite surveying apparatus with a deft hand that resulted in Julian gazing longingly at her with a laughing comment of "handy" offered between the two of them.

Diligently, Violet recorded elevation changes and the distances between them in the ledger she carried in a leather bag at her waist. While Julian would lose himself in the scenery as the pair conversed after dinner, Violet would open her sketchbook and began drawing. The pencil would move almost lazily while she laughed with him or pointed out a particularly interesting constellation in the night sky.

It was peaceful. Simple. Perfect for a honeymoon.

The nights spent beside her as she drew in her sketchbook with sure deft strokes of her pencil were blissful. She would go back and use them to compile the finished product. These were her "rough looks," as she called them. The final product would be painstakingly done in ink with the help of protractor, levels, and pen compass.

It would go a long way to convincing investors that

the Gold Sky depot was a viable and profitable investment. Change would come to the town, the region would transform from endless wild, people would come, the population of Gold Sky would double as new faces arrived eager to start anew... And through it all Violet would be beside him. He was happy she was here to see it begin. It would be the start of something new for not only Julian, but for both of them.

Them. That one word had the power to warm him through at the possibility of a future where Violet was beside him for each new venture. It was as exciting as it was thrilling, but would require much from them both. Long hours, sacrifice in where they directed their energies—the end result would be a life they were proud of.

A life with each other.

It made these slow days where their world consisted of only the other all the more precious.

By the fourth and final day, Julian was loath to think of leaving behind the bubble they had existed in for the duration of their trip. The roaring of the river as they approached served to remind him of the business that awaited them when they returned to Gold Sky the next day. He smiled at the thought of the small frontier town classifying as busy, but after so many days in the quiet solitude of the plains and mountains, Gold Sky would seem like a burgeoning metropolis.

It was just before sunset when they arrived at their chosen campsite. Julian estimated they had another two hours of good light, though an approaching storm signaled by the darkening sky of clouds in the distance made him wonder how much time they truly had left to settle in and ready themselves for the final night together.

He frowned at the thought, in time with a rumble of thunder. It wasn't their last night together, just their last without the interference of life and others. Those were two entirely different things, but it didn't mean that his mood lightened at the realization.

"What has you in a mood?" Violet asked from where she combed her horse. Wood for the fire had already been gathered, and he was fixing in place the final stake to finish securing their tent in preparation of the approaching storm.

They had been lucky enough to sleep under the stars every night, an activity that had offered another opportunity to talk and laugh with each other as they stared up at the night sky. Tonight there would be no stargazing or pointing out favorite constellations—no sharing of myths to go along with particularly interesting stars. Just the ceiling of their tent and the promise of a soggy decampment.

He glanced over at Violet and raised an eyebrow at the pinched expression on her face. "What?" he asked, not quite sure what he had done to deserve such a look.

"Your mood," she said again, hands going to her hips.

"Is fine," he replied, raising his mallet and driving the stake down the final few inches. He made a show of checking the stake's stability, of testing the rope's strength, and retied it once more when she said nothing.

When he looked at her again he saw that she hadn't moved and was now frowning at him.

"Why are you lying?"

He rose, twirling the mallet in his hands. "I'm not."

She huffed. "Though we are newly wed, do not think I can't spot a lie from you at a hundred paces."

"Ah, that close, is it?" he asked, but his tone was off from the normal lighthearted way he had always managed before. This didn't sound like a joke. There was little joy in it, and it fell flat between them like a heavy stone.

She swallowed and crossed her arms. "Given enough time, I suspect you'll scarcely be able to tell a white lie at ten times that distance, but seeing as we are well within my current range of detection…" She gestured between them with the hand that held the curry comb. "What is it?"

"Nothing," Julian maintained. His voice stayed even and he cleared his throat, glancing over his shoulder at the approaching storm. "We should hurry with dinner or we won't have any before the storm arrives."

Her lips pressed into a thin line. "Fine. But this isn't over."

He said nothing, but he had an inkling of what she meant at *this*. *This* primarily being his displeasure at the thought of returning to Gold Sky, of going back to their responsibilities and decisions. All of it should be exciting —*was* exciting. There was no shortage of good to their return from the exploration save for one.

It was just that Julian was greedy.

He sighed and chastised himself. He should not feel irrationally angry about sharing his time with Violet. Should not feel the loss of their time together as keenly as he would an injury. But he supposed it all came with the logic of greed, which was that there was very little of the latter involved in the entire affair.

The tense silence that had descended on them at Violet's first question over his mood lingered, which only served to darken him further. He wanted her liveliness, the easy way they laughed and spoke. Not this stilted mood which stole their words and forced their bodies into rigid shapes that stumbled clumsily around the camp in an effort to avoid touching the other.

He licked his lips, letting his eyes move over Violet as they cleaned up dinner. He wanted nothing more than to touch her now, to pull her dress and riding coat from her body, to feel the soft and supple body beneath it—yet here he was, longingly gazing at her and feeling as if he had no words to speak. Every one he uttered only further pushed him away from her until it was like they were hardly present at all.

He wondered if Violet felt the same way—she must, given the tense way she held herself throughout the evening as they made ready for the approaching thunderstorm.

It was only when they were sitting in the tent with thunder rumbling overhead that Violet showed how much the strained atmosphere had affected her.

"I'm going out," she blurted, rising to her feet and making for the tent entrance.

He leapt to his feet in surprise. "Where are you going? The storm is nearly here." Thunder pealed again, louder this time, to demonstrate the truth of his words, but she shook her head.

"I need air," she replied, yanking open the flap with a jerk of her hand. "A little rain will be fine."

She stepped out into the twilight and let the tent flap swing shut behind her.

For a moment he did not move. It was one thing to admit greed when it came to one's spouse, but it was another thing entirely to encroach on the other's space when space was needed. Yet, Julian was willing to wager that concessions on when or when not to follow a spouse were easily enough made when a thunderstorm was at hand.

The soft pitter-patter of raindrops hitting the tent canvas spurred him to action, and he followed her out into the evening.

"Violet!" he called, turning to look for her when he didn't see her form immediately. Where had the woman gone? Why had she chosen now to run off, just as evening arrived and a rainstorm descended? Didn't she know how dangerous it was to take off like this? And just what did she mean by doing so when emotions were already high?

He strode forward, mind spinning endlessly through the reasons why she should have stayed put before the thought of what might happen to her before he found her entered the ever quickening spiral of thoughts.

"Violet!" he yelled, voice now at full volume, but it failed to carry as the storm's strong wind whipped it away. He ran his hands through his hair and fought to keep his composure. There was a treeline and the river just beyond it, and perhaps she had gone that way to clear her head. It was the only place she could have gone that would not have revealed itself to him.

He ran toward it, all the while futilely calling out her name. He burst through the treeline and at first felt his stomach hollow and drop when he didn't immediately see her, but after another frantic second of searching a movement down by the river's edge caught his eye.

There she was. Hunched forward and sitting far too close to the moving water for his liking. She was on her haunches, arms wrapped around her knees as she stared at the water, seemingly oblivious to the storm nearly overhead.

"Violet!" he called again, and this time she lifted her head in his direction, though only for a moment before she looked away and back to the river.

Did she mean to ignore him? What did she intend to do? Endure the storm in the open, and by a river no less?

He strode toward her, steps quick in his eagerness to get them both back within the confines of the tent. It would be calmer there. He could explain to her why his dark mood had suddenly overtaken him.

"What are you doing?" he asked, when she didn't move.

"Thinking," she said, and he had to strain to hear her over the wailing wind. The rain was now falling faster, fat drops that came at increasing intervals. Before long it would be a downpour fit to soak them through.

"We have to go inside. You can think there." He held out a hand to her, but she made no move to take it.

"No."

He blinked at her. "Pardon?"

She looked up at him then and gave a slight shake of

her head. "I'll not go anywhere with you. Not with you in this state."

"And I'll not leave you here!" he yelled back, but this time the wind did not steal his voice and she jerked back at the volume at which he spoke. "You will come inside with me. Now!"

"No man tells me what to do."

His eyes narrowed. "I am not just a man. I am your husband."

Her mouth dropped open at his response. "Excuse me?"

"You said no man may tell you what to do, but I am your husband and you will—"

She shot up to her feet and he didn't miss the fire that flashed bright in her eyes. "What? Obey you?"

"Heed me," he corrected, and flung an arm out toward the sky. "Will you be reasonable? There's a storm overhead and you wish to stay by a river! Of all the foolhardy things to do!"

"I much prefer it to spending another moment around your brooding."

He glared at her. "I was not brooding."

She laughed bitterly. "We are well within my hundred-foot range, Julian. Do you wish to keep lying?"

He hated how easily she read him. The woman barely made sense with her current survival instincts, but for all that she was still able to see right through him. It was infuriating, but he said nothing of it. "Get away from the river," he bit out, jabbing a finger toward their camp, "and we will continue this discussion inside."

When she made no move toward their camp, he took a step toward her. "Violet, come away from there."

She shook her head. "No."

"It's not safe to stay where you are. I do not care if you are angry with me for...for brooding. Which I was not," he said, emphasizing his final word. She rolled her eyes at him.

"I'll not take one step until you admit that you were, and—and you must tell me what is bothering you."

"Nothing is bothering me!" he insisted, voice rising.

"Liar," she shouted back. Wind whipped past, kicking up her hair, making them both squint at the other through the rain that had become a true and proper downpour. Lightning cracked overhead, and he ran a frustrated hand over his face.

"It doesn't matter! What matters is your safety." He reached forward, catching her wrist, and made to pull her up with him, but Violet dug her heels in.

"I'll not go until you tell me!"

"You're being absurd!"

She pulled her arm back and he relented for fear of hurting her. He let out an exasperated growl and looked at her. Her dark hair had come loose from the plait she'd worn it in, and it clung to her face and neck. The riding dress she had put on was barely recognizable, soaked through as it was.

Parts of it clung to her legs and breasts in a manner he should not be noticing. The banks of a river with a roaring storm overhead was not the time and place to become fixated on how enticing she looked. Even as he gave himself a mental shake, he was unable to look away from her chest, which rose and fell quickly in time with her ragged breathing.

Had yelling at him really caused her to lose her breath this easily? Was she ill already from the rain? The latter forced his eyes up to her face in search of more clues, but it only took one look for him to realize the cause of her breathlessness.

She was blushing. That familiar color flooding her cheeks left little room for error. His wife was not ill, nor at risk of it. He suspected she was quite warm from the way her blood rose to her skin.

The woman was aroused.

Her brown eyes, those lovely eyes he adored, had darkened, and her pupils were blown wide in desire. Even in the dim light afforded them by the storm, he could see the want on her face.

"I'll not go," she rasped as a shudder stole her breath. She gave her wrist another yank, but this time he came with it. He moved forward until he crowded her space, their bodies pressed close, warming the other in the onslaught of summer rain.

"Then I will come to you," he said, moving closer still to her until they were toe-to-toe. He still held her, fingers collaring her wrist, and he flexed his fingers, drawing her closer to him.

'What are you doing?" she asked, eyes dropping to where he touched her. She leaned into his touch despite the lingering anger in her eyes.

"Staying with my belligerent wife," he told her, and her eyes widened.

"Me?" she all but roared and gave her arm a sudden

jerk that yanked him forward and into her unexpectedly. "You would call me belligerent after your incessant brooding?" She pulled her arm again with a strength Julian hadn't anticipated. She stepped back, her feet meeting the river's edge, and he had no choice but to follow the motion forward when she again moved back.

"Sonofa—" he groaned, desperately trying to find his footing on the riverbank, which until that moment he had paid little mind to. Now he became painfully aware of the scattering of riverstones and uneven ground below them. The toe of his boot caught on the edge of a stone and he stumbled blindly forward, the added momentum of his body carrying them both. Her skirts tangled around her legs and she reached forward, fingers latching onto Julian's coat as she fell back into the river.

"Oh," she cried out as she hit the shallow water with a splash. He fell forward, his hands outstretched as he did his best to catch his weight. Even so he struck his hand on a rock outcropping. He winced in pain but was immensely relieved as she had only just missed hitting the obstruction herself in their sudden tumble into the river.

"Are you all right?" they both gasped, hands reaching for one another where they half-lay, half-sat, limbs tangled together. Violet gasped again when Julian winced at the brush of her fingers on his wrist.

"Are you hurt?" She surged forward until she was able to inspect his wrist, the tantalizing swell of her breast teasingly close to his mouth. "Answer me!" she demanded with what could be classified as an unladylike growl, but in Julian's estimation it suited her. The urge to kiss her, to taste her warm skin buzzed in his mind so intensely that he did exactly that. He hooked an arm around her waist and pulled her close enough to drop a kiss to her skin. He moaned and huffed out a breath against her as he kissed her again.

"Julian, your wrist!" She moved to the side, trying to examine him.

"My wrist is not my most pressing concern at the moment," he managed, using his uninjured hand to stroke her cheek. She now straddled him, a leg on either side of his hips as he sat in the coursing water. It didn't matter that water was pelting them—pouring down, in fact—or that the river was freezing and his wrist was most likely sprained.

Cold water, pain, and torrential rain be damned.

What mattered was the warm press of Violet's thighs, the supple feel of her against him, the heat of her core as it pressed snugly to his hardening cock.

"Julian..." she said again, but this time her voice was softer. Her hands wandered from his wrist to his shoulders, and she arched her back at the brush of his lips against her neck. "Why won't you tell me what's wrong?"

"I'm greedy for you," he admitted, fingers twisting in the material of her coat.

Her palms went back on his shoulders and she leaned back to look at him, blinking hard against the sheet of water that continued to fall. "Greedy? What on earth do you mean? You have me."

He laughed bitterly and looked up at her. "That's precisely what greed is, darling. Having something but always wanting more. I want more."

"M-more?"

He nodded, breath coming faster now. "God, yes. More. More of you. I want nothing but you, Violet. I love you. I was brooding earlier because I loathe the thought of leaving this. Of leaving a world that consists of only us."

Her mouth parted and he felt her hands slide up to cradle his face, thumbs resting against his cheeks, fingertips resting against his scalp. She leaned forward and pressed her forehead against his. "I love you too," she told him.

His eyes closed and he laughed, the sound of it lost in the rumble of thunder. The cold rush of the river current and the flash of lightning around them ceased to exist at those few simple words.

I love you too.

A fire was lit within him, and he flexed his good arm around her before he gathered her close to him. "Hold tight," he told her, working to be heard above the rush of the river.

"What are you—oh!" She gasped in shock when he pushed up and stood, dragging her with him. For a moment he wobbled but remained on his feet, and uttered a silent prayer at the small favor. It wouldn't do for him to injure his other wrist in a show of strength to his bride. River water dripped from her waterlogged skirts, but still he marched forward, bringing them both out of the water and to the safety of the river bank.

A clap of thunder sounded, a bright jagged finger of lightning following close behind, but he saw none of it, was aware of none of it, because she was in his arms.

He kissed her again, his mouth slanting to fit hers as he carried her to the riverbank and beyond it. She lifted her head to look around in a bewildered moment, but scarcely had time to voice her concern before he claimed her mouth again in another passionate kiss. He sighted the tent in the distance and made for it, his arm clamped almost painfully tight around her waist. He pushed his way into the tent and only then did he set her on her feet.

In the dark of the tent with the muffled rain sounding overhead, the pair began to undress. His wrist was bumped at awkward intervals, a muffled hiss escaping his mouth each time. But he was a man possessed in his need for the woman touching him. He shushed her concerned inquiries but did acquiesce to the lighting of a lamp, if only to better see her as she laid herself bare to him.

"I fear I am not much help," he said, holding up his injured wrist, and winced when he made to flex his fingers.

"Oh, I quite forgot," she admitted with a shake of her head. "Sit." She gestured to the bedrolls at the center of the tent. Dutifully he dropped down to the bedding and watched in awe as she made quick work of her traveling coat and dress. Soon she stood in front of him in nothing save her drawers and corset, which had grown soggy and hard to remove.

"Come here, I am only injured, not incapaciated." He reached for her and she husked out a laugh but lowered herself to her knees and allowed him access to her stays. She reached for his hand and placed them on the top knot.

"Hold this," she said, giving the corset string a tug. "I can undo the knot." Wordlessly the pair worked at the knot and little by little it gave way until she was finally able to slip it free.

He breathed a sigh of relief. "Thank god. I was quite ready to cut it from you," he admitted.

"You wouldn't dare."

"I would. There isn't a jury that would convict me."

She smiled, the shadows from the lamp playing over her skin, and he knew not where to look. The curve of her cheek, the length of her neck and the way her collarbones caught the faint light, the swell of her breasts or the way her remaining garments were like a second skin...it was enough to make him hot beneath the collar. He reached up, pulling at his coat, and then sighed at himself. He had been so preoccupied with her state of undress that he had entirely forgotten to see to his own attire.

"Blast," he muttered, ripping his jacket off with a muffled curse when the cuff caught his injured wrist.

She bit her lip and reached out to touch his arm. "If it's too painful…" Her voice trailed off and he shook his head vehemently and yanked his belt free.

"I could be told that I must lose my hand and it would still not be too painful to be with you," he told her, his words rushing over one another as he hurried to undress.

"Then let me help you, stubborn man." She nudged his hands away and he huffed out a laugh when he felt her fingers deftly work the buttons of his shirt.

'I am not a stubborn man, I am your stubborn husband," he remarked, holding his arms out to help her undress him. She lifted her eyes to meet his, and the shadows cast by the lamplight made his pulse leap. He watched her lick her lips, her dark eyes moving across the bare skin of his chest.

"So you are," she said, laying a palm flat against his sternum. Her fingers were warm against his skin and he shivered when she stroked his skin lazily. Silence fell between them and exploring hands continued their path. He kissed her jaw, her cheek, smoothed his hands along her sides, the material of her drawers and chemise allowing his fingers to tease and cup her breasts. Only once did he hiss out a gasp of pain when he lost himself in an earnest caress, but a stern look from her served as all the reprimand necessary for him to mind his injury lest his wife put an end to their activities.

He would rather lose his arm than stop touching her.

Of course he would injure himself the first time they touched each other freely and without the hindrance of clothing. The injury wouldn't deter him, but he would have to be creative in their lovemaking, a problem he solved by allowing her to take the lead.

He guided her hands to his shoulders. "Show me what you want," he told her. Her hair was loose, falling in curling waves around her bare shoulders, and he leaned forward, breathing in the scent of her, burying his face in the dark tresses. "Show me, darling."

She leaned back and gave him a smile, just the curve of her lips visible in the flickering light of the nearby lantern. "Lie back," she murmured, pushing on his shoulders until he was flat on his back. He felt a rush of desire wash over him, like the slow raw heat of a fresh sunburn that left one's skin buzzing and sensitive to touch. Every inch of his was electrified, and her hands were the conduit that set him alight.

"I love you," he murmured to her, reaching up to brush his fingertips over her collarbones. A sigh of pleasure escaped her full lips in acknowledgment. She swung a leg over him, their naked skin heated and pressed closed, her hips rocking forward, pushing the head of his cock closer to her. He groaned when he felt the wetness of her desire sliding over him. She felt so good, warm, pliant, the weight of her grounding him and making him want to thrust up into her, but he held himself back.

He had given control to her. He would not take it back now.

"Keep going, darling," he encouraged her when he felt her falter. But a quick dip of her chin and he saw that her smile was back. She reached for him, her fingers wrapping around the thick length of him.

"Julian," she whispered, guiding him to her entrance, thighs flexing on either side of him as she moved back to take him. "I want you."

He hummed in pleasure at her words. "Take what you need. Take it all."

She sighed again and lowered herself, easing the first inch of him inside of her. "Julian," she gasped, sinking another inch lower, her hands on his chest, fingers flexing as she moved tentatively. Another rock of her hips and he lifted his own to meet her movement. The feel of her around him, on him, under his hands, was overwhelming.

Beautiful and rising.

Their movements became less ginger and unsure, a hunger and need taking possession of the lovers as they found pleasure in the other's touch. Outside, the thunderstorm continued to rage on but his world consisted only of the space within the confines of the tent. Extended only as far as the light of the lantern shone. Was only made real by what he could touch.

And all he could touch, both in hands, body, mouth, heart, was Violet.

There was only Violet.

He found it hard to think of what it felt like to be without her, to not have the pleasure of lovemaking in this new world of intimacy. It was uncharted territory for him, but he willingly took to it, knowing she was the one he would learn it with.

Faster and faster they moved, the thought of where one ended and the other began lost. Her thighs squeezed his as she moved closer to her orgasm. He thrust his hips up, matching the speed of her movements. She was nearly there, he could feel it from the way her body tightened, how her fingernails scraped his skin and her cries drowned out even the falling rain.

"Julian!"

She shouted her release, eyes squeezing shut as she climaxed and fell forward against his chest. He wrapped an arm around her, catching her and gathering her against him as he continued to move, though it took precious little more to finish him. The squeeze of her around his cock, her breasts on his skin. Oh, the smell of her was intoxicating, and he groaned as he found his pleasure. His arm tightened around her body as he orgasmed, and she moaned with him, her hands coming up to stroke his skin as he came back to himself.

"You were lovely," he gasped, not bothering to catch his breath.

"You are so good to me," she told him, propping herself up on a hand to look down at him. The lantern light painted her brown skin golden, and he knew that for as long as he lived he would never see a more beautiful sight than his wife smiling down at him.

CHAPTER 15

The soggy decampment and muddy ride back to town Julian had been dreading was not at all the ordeal he had anticipated. In fact, he was in good spirits, with a smile ever present on his face as they journeyed and finally arrived in Gold Sky. It was not for lack of mud or rain, for those were to be found aplenty. It was the simple fact that he had never felt closer to Violet. Their previous night had opened new possibilities of what the future would be like.

His wife wanted him. Had given herself to him completely, and he to her. There was, in Julian's estimation, nothing more fulfilling than being completely known to one's spouse.

He glanced over at Violet and chuckled when he caught her staring at him. She blushed, but smiled and looked away from him.

"What?" she asked, eyes now firmly on the boarding house as they approached.

"Nothing," he replied, striving for innocent. He knew he had been found out when Violet laughed.

"You are a terrible liar."

He shrugged and swung down from his horse. "Only with you." He came around to her horse and extended his hand up to help her down.

"I think I quite like that," she said, reaching down to him, but stopped when she saw he held out his injured hand to her. "Your other hand," she told him, pointing.

"It's really not that bad," Julian sighed, but extended his uninjured hand to her.

"You fell into a river and landed on it," she huffed, letting him help her down. "We need to get you to a doctor, or let Alice take a look at it at the very least."

Julian pulled a face at her suggestion. There was much to be done now that they were back in Gold Sky, and he hated to think of losing any time to a doctor who might suggest he refrain from using it entirely.

Violet's eyes narrowed, and he suspected the woman had read his mind. The eyes were the windows to the soul —damn his eyes for telling on him. He cleared his throat and looked away.

"I am quite well, I promise," he lied.

She scowled at his answer. "You lie."

"What is he lying about this early in the nuptials?" Alice asked, appearing beside them and making Julian yelp.

"Where on god's green earth did you come from?" he gasped.

"From the boarding house that I run," Alice replied,

jerking a thumb at the building. "The one you are standing in front of, or does love have you that addled?"

"Perhaps it does have us addled, but we come by it honestly," Violet told her, and then pointed at Julian. "He was injured, and now he refuses to see a doctor."

Julian's eyes widened and he turned to her. "You are making baseless accusations. I was merely saying I did not believe I required medical attention."

"Because you were plotting—"

"I am a gentleman. We do not plot."

"—on how best to avoid a doctor so that—"

"I would never."

"—you would not have to sacrifice work!"

"Groundless. All of it."

Violet wagged a finger at him. "You forget that I can detect any and all of your untruths up to a hundred feet. You are well within my range of detection, sir."

"Then allow me to remedy that immediately." He made to take a large step back but Violet caught his coat lapel.

"You cad! You need a doctor."

Julian sighed, eyes going heavenward. "Perhaps," he finally said.

Alice laughed, the sound breaking the silence, and she reached out a hand to them. "Oh, the pair of you are carrying on as if you've been married for years, not a week. What happened out there?" she asked, nodding in the direction they had come from.

"Well, a lot," Violet said when Julian made no move to speak. He nodded in agreement with her.

"A lot," he echoed.

Alice smirked knowingly at them. "Where are you hurt? You look well to me, or is this…" She lowered her voice and leaned closer to them. "...one of those intimate injuries?"

"Who is hurt?" Rosemary asked, bounding into the group and causing Julian to jump once more. "I heard lowered voices and came immediately," she said, holding up her pencil and a pad of paper.

"Where are the women in this town—are you all dropping from the sky?" he asked, clutching his chest. He would not survive another surprise appearance and he looked around warily lest he be caught unaware once more. "Are you taking notes on this for the paper?"

Rosemary nodded at him, her pencil scratching away at the pad of paper in her hand. "The news never rests."

Violet groaned and rubbed her temples. "Well, put it down for a nap, Rosemary. This is not to be published."

"She's prickly on account of Julian being injured, but I cannot see where," Alice told Rosemary, who hummed knowingly.

"An intimate injury?" she guessed, tapping her pencil against her chin.

Alice tutted. "Perhaps. I suspect as much."

"Alice!" Violet cried, cheeks going scarlet.

"It is not an intimate injury," Julian hissed, stepping closer to the women and thrusting out his injured wrist. "I fell and sprained my wrist, and perhaps something else with my hand as well."

"How did you manage to fall?" Rosemary asked with far too much interest than was necessary for polite conversation. Julian wagered the woman was committing the conversation to memory for use in that evening's publication.

"There was a river. It was a small accident," he explained, omitting the rainstorm or the argument that had occured in said river.

"I was too close," Violet said, adding to the story and placing a hand on his arm, "and Julian, ah, pulled me back and went in himself."

"What were you doing near a river?" Alice narrowed her eyes at Violet. "You know far better than to take a risk like that."

Julian snorted but said nothing when Violet jabbed him in the ribs. "I got lost in thought," Violet replied, but Alice remained unconvinced.

"Hmph." Alice shook her head and then held out a hand to Julian. "Let me see it. I'll save you a trip to the doctor."

When Julian made no move forward, Violet urged him toward Alice. "It's either this or the doctor, and I will support the doctor in his recommendation, even if it includes bed rest."

Julian balked but moved forward then, holding his wrist out to Alice. "It isn't all that bad. Just tender."

"What's tender?" his sister asked, looking over Alice's shoulder as she examined his wrist. "How did you injure yourself?"

"God above!" Julian barked, jerking in surprise at his sister's sudden appearance. "Is *Maman* with you?" he asked, looking around the side of Alice where his sister stood. "Perhaps she is lying in wait in your bustle with little Seylah."

Julie wrinkled her nose. "What on earth? What happened to you in the wilderness? I thought it was a simple expedition."

"He injured his wrist. Rosemary and I first supposed it to be an intimate injury, but it is benign. Though I suppose it could have have sti—" Alice began, but Julian's groan of exasperation cut her off. These women would be the death of him if any more of them showed up unannounced.

"It *was* a simple expedition," he said tersely, pulling away when his sister made a grab for his wrist. "I assure you I am fine."

"He's lying." Violet crossed her arms and frowned in his general direction. "He could scarcely put any weight on it last night or this morning."

"Well, come along then, I'll fix you up," Alice told him, turning toward the boarding house door. "It won't do for you to lose a limb from rough handling by your bride."

Violet flushed. Rosemary perked up, her eyes dancing from Violet and back to Julian again. "This evening's edition will be a crowd pleaser," she muttered, pencil flying over paper.

"And that is our cue." Violet urged Julian forward and he readily went. Anything to put space between himself and the pack of Gold Sky women hellbent on discussing the how and why of his injury.

"Cue for what?" Rosemary called after them, pencil held aloft in question.

Violet rolled her eyes and pushed the front door to the boarding house open. "Goodbye, Rosemary," she called over her shoulder.

"Our readers will want clarification!"

Alice cast an apologetic look at Rosemary, but Violet was undeterred in her march forward. "Goodbye, Rosemary," she said again, punctuating her words with the slam of the door as she shut it in the reporter's face. Julian turned to see Rosemary's face scrunched in consternation through the door glass as she tapped on the pane with her pencil.

"Ignore her, she will give up eventually," Alice advised, walking ahead toward the kitchen. "Now let me get a look at that wrist. Did you splint it?"

"Ah, no," Julian sighed, removing his coat with a groan.

"And why not?" Alice asked, crossing her arms. "That should have been your first action."

"Because my wrist is fine, and this is—ah!" he yelped when Alice poked his wrist with more force than necessary.

"If that were so, then you would not have reacted."

Julian cleared his throat. "You took me by surprise."

Alice narrowed her eyes at him. "Is that so?" she asked.

When Julian made a show of looking away and clearing his throat with an indiscriminate mumble she shot Violet a look. "I suspect it's only sprained, which is fortunate. His hand will be sore from bruising but it doesn't feel terribly swollen. I'll put it in a splint and fashion a sling for him. It'll heal in a few weeks."

Julian's mouth dropped open. "A few weeks! A sling? There's far too much work for me to do without the use of both of my hands."

"Thank you, Alice." Violet breathed a sigh of relief. "I

have been so worried since he fell on me in the river. I knew it was—"

Alice raised an eyebrow. "Since he what?" She looked at Julian. "Since you what on her in a river?"

Julian face darkened with a blush while Violet spluttered her way through an explanation that left Alice with more questions than when she began. The woman needed help, and since Julian had taken a vow to love, honor, and cherish her, it was up to him to provide relief. It was his injury under scrutiny, after all.

Sucking in a breath, he turned to Alice and thrust his arm out to her. "I see now that you are right. Please, help me tend to it."

"I thought you said a few weeks was far too long to go without both hands."

"I was mistaken?" he tried. Violet gave him a relieved look and relaxed against the table she stood beside.

Alice hummed but went about gathering the tools necessary to help splint and bandage his wrist. "Docile as a lamb now," she mused while she worked.

Julian said nothing but he did not miss the smile Violet hid behind her hand. She was quite lucky Julian had felt the need to fulfill his husbandly duties despite Alice's curious looks.

She was interested to know how the injury came about, to be sure, but Julian would not be the one to offer more details of the circumstances of his injury, nor the events that had followed. He swallowed down the memories of Violet pressed close, the feel of her skin under his palms, the way she moaned beneath him, the curve of her lips in the dim light… it had all been intoxicating. Addictive, like one night too many spent at the tables. The woman lingered on his lips like a fine cognac, had him flustered from the simple memory of what it was like to touch her.

He dropped his eyes to his wrist; the injury, while interfering with his plans, would serve as a reminder of his night with Violet.

There would not be a moment he did not recall the taste of her on his mouth or the echo of her moans against his lips.

"Salacious activity!" Julie's voice echoed from the hall, and the sound of the door slamming shut accompanied her hurried footsteps toward the kitchen. All eyes were on Julie as she entered the kitchen, waving a newspaper in hand. "Is it true that you hurt your wrist due to salacious acts?"

"What? Where did you get that?" Violet cried.

"Rosemary rushed out an early edition," Julie told her, giving the paper a little wave. "The ink is still wet, so do be careful," she advised when Violet grabbed for the paper.

"They are not considered salacious if said acts were done with my wife and were consensual," Julian pointed out, making the entire room go silent. The women all turned toward him with conflicting looks. Alice looked chagrined, Julie mortified, and Violet...Violet was a mix of blushing and speechless.

Julie grimaced and dropped the paper on the table. "I wish I had not heard that."

"Be careful asking questions to which you are not ready to know the answer," he advised her, and nodded his thanks to Alice for her tending. He held out his uninjured hand to Violet. "Would you accompany me to Stark's shop?"

"I'll just need to grab my measurements ledger," she murmured, following him out of the kitchen. They walked in silence, fingers intertwined, when Violet hesitated before the front door. "What if others are reading Rosemary's paper?"

"Well, it *is* the truth…" he sighed.

"Julian!" She elbowed him in the side and he laughed, shying away from her. He caught her hand again and stilled her when she made to pull away.

"Even if the whole town reads it I don't care. I will remind them exactly the way I did my sister, and I assure you not a single one of them would be able to say a word against us. I am happy to have you as my wife, and if that means the circumstances of my injury are made public then I am quite fine with it."

She worried her bottom lip. "You are?"

"I am."

She relaxed at his words and let loose a deep sigh Julian hadn't been aware she had been holding in her lungs. "Then so am I," she told him, and took the hand he held out to her. "So am I."

He opened the door, and hand-in-hand the pair walked out into the afternoon light. It mattered not if the street was papered with the early edition of Gold Sky's periodical, or if every person they encountered on their way across town had already been privy to the paper's contents, as they saw no one else but the other.

CHAPTER 16

The next few days in Gold Sky saw much progress for the happy couple. A change of residence, from the boarding house to the Wickes-Barnes homestead, was in order. There were, after all, no shortage of rooms—five rooms at last count, even with parents and new baby Seylah in residence.

The completion of the map was accomplished in wonderful order. Local investors had been impressed by the skill of it and by the cunning of the new railroad scheme. They were eager to join Stark and Julian in their bid to make Gold Sky the frontier's premiere destination in both a commercial and residential sense. There would be no shortage of jobs, nor hands with which to do them. Though lucrative as it was, Julian took care to emphasize the importance of preserving Gold Sky's unique and accepting nature.

The town would not lose what made it a safe haven for those who did not quite fit society's expectations. No matter the financial gain or the impending power grabs

Julian saw in the town's future with such rapid growth, it would remain, first and foremost, a place where all people were safe and welcome.

The revelation pleased both Julie and Violet, though if Julian were honest he cared more for Violet's opinion than his sister's. Julie had both Forrest and Will to put a smile on her face, which left the care of Violet's smile to Julian. He intended to excel at the matter, and set to it with a fervor that left his mother and sister sighing in approval and his father and brothers-in-law working to keep up.

"You're driving us ragged," Will muttered, setting yet another bouquet of flowers on the mantle for Julie. The taciturn man held a stern expression for a moment before he grinned at Julian. "Been a lot more creative around here thinking up ways to match your energy. Keep it up."

Julian blinked at his brother-in-law and then swallowed. "I'm not going to ask what you mean by creative, but thank you."

"Means you might be expecting another little one to spoil."

He blanched. "And with that, I will take my leave."

Will's laughter followed him into the kitchen where his family had gathered for breakfast. He smiled at seeing Violet at ease, her arms full with Seylah, sitting rather than bustling around serving everyone.

"You will miss this food on the train," Manon advised her daughter-in-law. "They scarcely stop the train long enough to stretch your legs, let alone find a decent bite to eat."

"Always so dramatic," Julie chimed in. "I quite liked the fare on the way here from New York."

"I am not being dramatic. She must eat if she means to make it to New York in one piece." His mother huffed with a put-out look, but it lasted only a moment before she brightened and sat up straight. She grabbed Julie's hand. "You won't reconsider your decision on staying here? We would have such a lovely time in fall in the city, and little Seylah would be this season's darling."

"Mother, if I went with you, then who would teach the children?" Julie asked.

"A substitute. Do they not have those here? Someone to manage the class in an interim capacity?"

"The town does not have the budget for a second teacher."

"Then we will pay it. How much do you want?" Manon asked, earning a sigh from Julie.

"We do not need another teacher because I am not going to New York. I want to spend the fall here with Forrest and Will. I'll not leave them, and what would you have us do? Have the town absent of law as well?"

Manon pursed her lips. "The town would be fine… everyone here is quite reasonable despite what the tabloids say of the frontier."

Violet and Julie laughed at that. "The town would not be standing when we returned if you removed Forrest and Will from it," Julie informed her mother.

Violet nodded along and bounced Seylah on her knee. "Even losing Julie would be disastrous. The children would be left to their own devices, and I suspect they would overrun the town before the week was out."

Manon groaned and crossed her arms. "All my fun is spoiled. I only wanted my children together for the fall."

"We will visit at Christmas," Julie told Manon. "Besides, you will have fun aplenty with showing off Violet to society. She will need all of your focus if she is to make the right impression and endure the season successfully."

Violet paled. "Endure?" she asked, her voice meek. "I, ah, did not suppose society was endured?"

"And survived," Julie said, holding up a finger. "You must keep your wits about you when you are in such company."

Violet shrank into her chair, eyes wide, and sank her teeth into her lip nervously. Julian bit back a swear and strode purposefully forward.

"Now who is being dramatic?" he asked.

Julian had planned on showing Violet only the finest side of New York. He would smooth the way with the Four Hundred, and she would enjoy herself in the very best way. But Julie's words had the opposite effect Julian had hoped for his new bride on their return home.

"You liken New York to surviving a battlefield," he told his sister, plucking a piece of toast off of a platter and serving himself a cup of coffee.

"It is," Julie shot back.

"Not everyone has your experience or point-of-view when it comes to New York. Violet has never been to a city so large, and you, my dear sister, have made her nervous. She is not a debutante as you were."

Julie's eyebrows shot up. "Oh, I hadn't thought—" She

cleared her throat. "I'm sorry, Violet. I didn't mean to spoil it with my sour talk."

Violet shook her head and looked down at Seylah. "I would have been nervous in any case. I've never been anyplace like it before."

"There is good food," Julie supplied, giving her a smile. "And, well, the bookshops are divine. I have a list, if you wouldn't mind making a few stops for me?"

"It's no trouble at all," Violet said, cutting off Julian when he made to protest.

"Oh, how perfect!" Julie clapped her hands and jumped up from her seat. "Just give me a moment to get my list. I'm so excited." She rushed from the room and Julian sighed, leaning against the counter at his back.

"New York is quite enjoyable," he told Violet, giving her a reassuring smile. "You'll see."

"There is something for everyone if you keep an open mind. And you are with family," Manon told her, touching her arm. "We will have a wonderful time."

Violet smiled at Manon. "Yes, I think we will."

THE FAMILY MOVED their belongings into the wagon they would take to Butte City. And, for a little while at least, Manon achieved her wish of having her children with her on the road. Julie, Violet, and his mother, clutching Seylah tearfully, rode in the wagon. His sister gleefully drove the horses along as her husbands shook their head at her antics.

Julian, his father, Forrest, and Will rode alongside them on horseback. It was a fine ride, the weather pleasant and the sun shining brightly overhead. Their departure from Gold Sky was short, a tearful parting that involved Julie and her husbands promising to visit at Christmas. Manon wept openly at leaving, his father looked little better, and Julian felt an unfamiliar pang of loss strike him as their train set off.

He had never missed anywhere, not truly. But now, with the familiar curve of the mountains fading into the distance, he was melancholic.

Violet's sniffling broke him from his reverie, and he turned to see her dabbing at her eyes with a handkerchief. She had spent much of the previous day with Alice. He frowned, knowing how much it wore on Violet to leave the other woman behind.

He stepped close and wrapped an arm around her waist, drawing her to him. "I'm sorry," he told her, leaning close. "I'm sorry."

"What are you sorry for? This is...this is what I wanted." She smiled, but it was tight-lipped, and she blinked back tears. "I wanted this."

He caressed her cheek, his hand settling at the nape of her neck. "That does not mean you aren't sad, Violet. I'm sorry for that part."

He felt her body tense slightly under his hand before she blew out a sigh and relaxed against him, the tension leaving her. They stood close, his arm around her waist, hand still cradling her head, until she wrapped both arms around him and hugged him.

"Thank you."

"We can send for her to visit at Christmas. She could

come with Julie."

Violet's head lifted, hope shining bright on her face. "Truly?"

He nodded, his heart lifting at the happiness he could see reflected in her eyes. She was lovely like this. "Yes, well and truly. It would make for a very merry Christmas."

She bounced on her toes, raising herself up to press a kiss to his lips. "You treat me very well," she told him.

"I should hope so," he said, leaning back to look at her, "since you are my wife."

She hummed but said nothing, dropping her head to his chest again and hugging him. They stood in silence, the gently swaying train lulling them into a peaceful trance as the Montana scenery began to shift and change outside of the window.

He swallowed hard, watching as the terrain became less wild, flatter, less green, more...civilized. It pained him to leave such wild beauty behind—but it was only momentary. The freedom he had found in Gold Sky would not fade or end, not when he had tied himself to the town in such a fundamental way. If only in the capacity of commerce, he would return to the frontier.

He dropped his eyes to Violet, to her mass of shining black tresses gleaming in the sunlight. He raised his hand, fingertips sifting through her hair as he relished the feel of it in his fingers.

She was as much as part of the frontier as the crown of mountains behind them. The unforgiving landscape that possessed a raw beauty he had never known beat in the heart of the woman he had given himself to.

Julian loved Violet with fierceness that surprised even

him. He was excited to show her New York City, to walk the halls of his childhood home with her at his side.

But it was just that. His past. Violet was his future.

There would be no staying in New York City among the Four Hundred. Not so long as he was Violet's and she was his.

Julian's future had inexplicably followed in his sister's footsteps, and it seemed Gold Sky had claimed the heart of the other Baptiste heir.

~

WHAT HAD ONCE BEEN a test of fortitude and patience was now a welcome stint of solitude for Julian. The journey by train from Butte City to New York was a time of quiet. A time when he was free to enjoy his wife and family with no distractions. There was little opportunity for business when constantly in motion, and Julian resolved to enjoy the reprieve to the fullest extent.

His mornings were filled with slow breakfasts at Violet's side, long conversations with her, and books he had put off reading for the sake of work. Afternoons consisted of tea with his mother and father while Violet sketched the newest scenery flying past. Then there were the enjoyable dinners, and cognac with his father in the evenings over a card game or two.

And the intimate nights with Violet once they had retired to their compartment.

The quarters were cramped, but the newlyweds made it work.

There was love in each slow and lingering touch

shared between them. Julian had always heard that love was silent, that it was a language communicated by hands and lips, formed with bodies and exchanged freely.

He had never understood it.

Not until Violet.

There, love was understated. It was patient and kind. Quiet, but deep in its ferocity. Julian had never felt anything like it, and when they stepped off the train in New York City, he was loath to leave the confines of the locomotive.

His mother bustled past with the kind of intensity that only came from pent-up energy. "Freedom!" She extended her hands with a happy laugh, turning her face up to the sky. "Jean! Breathe it in! We are home."

His father stepped beside her and laughed along with her. "The only thing I smell is the smoke of it all, but I am happy if you are this joyful."

His mother smiled and looped her arm through his father's. "Does that mean we can go for lunch at my favorite bistro?'

Jean chuckled, adjusting the shawl on Manon's shoulders. "We can buy the bistro, for all I care. Just keep smiling at me, hmm?"

His mother giggled when his father leaned close for a kiss, and Julian shook his head, turning away from the scene of his parents acting like besotted youths. He turned toward Violet to see her gazing at his parents with a soft smile playing on her lips.

"They're incorrigible," he told her conspiratorially as they watched his parents giggle and kiss. His parents had always been a couple to get lost in each other. It mattered not if it were at home or under the public's watchful eyes. Everyone knew Jean and Manon were tenderly and utterly in love as much as they had been on the day they met twenty-two years before.

"I quite like it," she told him with a grin.

"They act like newlyweds."

"I suppose a city so full of energy keeps one youthful. I cannot possibly imagine growing old in such a place!" Violet shook her head, eyes wide with wonder. "New York is just..." Her voice trailed off and Julian guided her through the crowd until they were free from the crush of bodies.

"Just what?"

"So alive. I can't imagine ever being able to see it all, even if I never left it. How did you ever leave?"

"The city can wear on you," he replied, stepping closer to shield her from being shoved aside by a group of boisterous businessmen.

He watched the group as more than one man turned back to look at Violet. She was lovely, he knew. Julian reckoned he had fallen for her then, back on the front steps of Alice Hill's boardinghouse. That didn't mean he would stand idly by while men ogled her.

A heavy coiled feeling in his chest reared up and Julian stepped in front of her, blocking her from view. It was then that the men focused on him, on his face, and they blanched. Julian was recognizable, well-known, and given the area, held enough influence that even one worth their mettle avoided giving him offense.

Though Julian carried himself without the brash overbearing nature he observed in many of his heavy-handed peers, he was not a man to be trifled with. Not with the calculating and methodical way he went about his business. Not with his seemingly infinite resources, both in connections and currency. Julian was able to make his decisions with the knowledge that he could allow for patience and timing. He would, could, and had crushed more than one adversary since he had come of age, each one dealt with more severely than the last, which had garnered him a reputation as merciless by necessity.

Family was a necessity, and Violet was now his family.

He raised an eyebrow at the men, causing their eyes to drop, and they turned away.

He glanced down at Violet and felt the rigidness of his posture soften. She had blessedly missed the subtle exchange, though it had occurred in front of her, which suited Julian's tastes perfectly. He would prefer for his wife to not see such things, even if he knew he could not protect her from it forever.

That did not mean he would not try. Love motivated such efforts.

He smiled at her, brushing back a curl of her hair while she continued to look around in excitement.

Love at first sight. How like a Baptiste, given his mother and father's love story.

Violet threaded her arm through Julian's, leaning into his side as they walked. The touch garnered looks and attention from countless passers-by who recognized the Baptiste clan on sight. None of their attention was so forward or lingering as the earlier men, so Julian gave them a slight nod of acknowledgment but kept his attention squarely on Violet.

The public would know soon enough that he had married. He would be surprised if they hadn't already been alerted by Rosemary's industrious reporting, though news traveled slowly from the frontier. New York society would know soon enough that he was now wed. There was no need to feed the onlookers' curiously, with Violet happily chattering on his arm. She hadn't so much as noticed the attention, her eyes darting to and fro, sweeping across the skyline and buildings as they walked. They followed his parents through the crowd to the bistro his mother favored. It was a French eatery that paid homage to Creole roots. Julian knew she enjoyed it for the reminder of a home she had left, a place that still existed geographically but had forever vanished with the war.

His mother didn't often speak of the war but when she did it was with intention and purpose. There was oft a time when she had told him a story of her childhood or the days that followed her escape from Preacher's Point.

In those rare times she would smile though Julian could see the smile was tinged with sorrow.

"Remembering is hard but necessary. The people I loved are gone, scattered to the wind, lost or dead, even before the war. But there are times that I can feel them. Home isn't a place, it's something you carry with you."

That lesson he learned well. Home indeed was a place that you carried rather than walls and a roof.

Gold filigree on the window proclaiming Caroline's Bistro welcomed them as they entered the establishment. He smiled, watching his mother greet the bistro owner, Caroline Ravenel, a bright-eyed woman with a warm smile. She was younger than his mother but not by much, and could remember the world his mother had fled though she'd been a child.

Julian didn't miss the way their eyes often wandered, sometimes drifting to the side as they recalled events. How they touched hands without even seeming to notice, as if to assure themselves that the other would not vanish. There was a bittersweet air particular to their interactions, and Manon made it a habit to visit the bistro as often as she was able, because even if remembering was difficult, it was necessary.

Memories were always worth it. Even at the price of hurt. Julian glanced over at Violet to see that, unlike the wide-eyed awe she has displayed at the New York skyline, she was intent. She paused and sniffed the air, a focused expression on her face.

"It smells wonderful in here," she murmured. "Do you think the chef would tell me what spices they use?"

He nodded at his mother, who still happily chatted away with Caroline. "I would expect so, given that *maman* is on more than friendly terms with the owner, Caroline."

Violet followed his gesture and then nodded, smoothing her hands over her skirts. "I shall make my introductions, then." She lifted her head and marched off, leaving Julian behind along with his father. Jean came up beside him and laughed.

"I see you are settling into married life splendidly," he said, gesturing to a server for a table.

"Is it normal to be left behind so?" Julian asked, taking a seat across from his father, who merely shrugged.

"When they are excited? Yes. But they'll never go too far, just as you won't be inclined to."

"Meaning?"

Jean pointed in the direction of the women. "That your lovely Violet is already looking over her shoulder for you."

Julian looked over his father's shoulder and was met by the sight of Violet glancing over at him. She blushed when their eyes met, and after a quick smile she looked back to the women she stood with. He suspected his wife would have entry to Caroline's pantry before long.

"It's nice to see you happy."

His eyes snapped back to his father at the simple statement. The server bustled over to fill their glasses with water. Julian leaned back in his chair and waited for the server to depart before he responded. "How do you mean? I'm always happy."

Jean cracked a thin smile. "Not in the city you're not. Not like this."

"And what is *this*?"

"You're free," Jean replied. "As free and light as you were in Gold Sky. It's remarkable."

Julian cleared his throat and sipped from his glass. "I would not…" He hesitated, the denial he had been about to offer his father dying on his lips. "Perhaps it does not seem so oppressive anymore."

"On account of Violet." It was a statement, not a question. Julian nodded in agreement.

"Yes."

"You truly love her."

Again Julian nodded. "I do."

"And she loves you?"

"She does," Julian answered, but this time it was he who spoke matter-of-factly.

Jean's eyes drifted closed and he sighed deeply. Like this, his father looked younger, more carefree, like the man he supposed his mother had met during the war. A moment of quiet passed between them at their table before Jean opened his eyes and leaned forward, palms flat to the table.

"Then I am happy for you. That is all that I have ever wanted for you. To know love, true and honest, is a rare gift. It warms my heart to know that you too will enjoy it, as I have with your mother."

Julian inclined his head, his eyes moving past his father to the trio of women. He saw Violet laughing, her head tossed back, and just as he predicted Caroline hustled her forward toward the kitchen, Manon gleefully following behind.

"I have always wanted that," Julian replied, his voice soft. "I was overjoyed when we arrived in Gold Sky and it was apparent Julie had found that for herself. That love you speak of."

"I was happy to know it as well. Often it's easy to paint a different picture when it's only words. Actions and deeds are far more important. The men Julie chose love her unfailingly. I hoped for that type of commitment in your own life." His father leveled him with a meaningful look. Julian knew his father was trying to estimate his happiness, if he was as happy as Julie was.

Julian cleared his throat. "I am happy. I have found a partner to live and enjoy my life with just as you have. Just as Julie has."

Jean drummed his fingers on the table, eyes moving over his son's face, before the man relaxed and gave Julian an easy smile. "Then all of my hopes and dreams for my family have come true. Marriage is...marriage is hard work. It will not always be easy, nor will it always feel good, but it will be worth it. Never lose sight of that, no matter who or what comes up. There will never be another half to you like her."

The *her* was Violet. His wife. His partner. The woman he loved.

Her.

Julian's heart swelled in his chest. His father's words rang in his mind. There would be obstacles and rough moments in his life with Violet, but it would be a life of immeasurable value.

It would be a life worth fighting for, as so often the best things in life required.

CHAPTER 17

Julian stared at the crackling fire. It was the end of their second day in the city and he was, in a word, exhausted. There had been no shortage of business to attend to, accounts to balance, payroll to double check, missives to answer.

Much had happened in the two months since they had first taken their leave of the city for Montana—though not unmanageable, as the stewards left to manage their affairs were skilled and trusted, men and women the Baptiste family had relied on for years.

Already the news of his marriage had begun to circulate, though the finer points concerning it were unknown to the polite society of New York.

He shifted in his seat, eyes straying from the crackling fire to Violet. She sat at her dressing table, a brush in hand as she combed and plaited her dark thick hair.

It felt natural to him that she should be seated there at her dressing table with him in their bedroom. He could not fathom the evening without her presence. In seemingly the blink of an eye, Violet had become an indispensable facet of his life. He refused to consider the days before he had met her. All of them were cast in shadow without her warmth and care.

That precious tenderness that had blossomed between them in the quiet halls of the boarding house continued to thrive within the confines of the city's seemingly endless expanse of concrete and steel.

Violet's hands moved, her waist-length braid sliding over her shoulder and down her back as she stretched her hands over head. She was sweet, like the delicate scent of flowers on a summer night, like the wild expanse of frontier they had left behind. The late August heat had turned to fall now. The brisk cool of autumn evenings and mornings would soon settle into the days until winter came upon them.

He wondered if they would spend the spring in the city or if they would make for Gold Sky once it was warm enough for a prolonged stay.

The holidays with her in the city would be enjoyable in a way he hadn't known since he was a boy. It would be impossible not to enjoy such a festive occasion with Violet. There would be so much to show her, so much to share and enjoy, that Julian found himself looking forward to the holidays for the first time in years.

He wondered what she would think of the way his mother spared no expense in decorating their family home to within an inch of its foundations. How would she enjoy walking with him in the falling snow? How would she respond when he kissed her amid the horns and bells celebrating the New Year?

He hoped she loved the city and enjoyed her time with him here, though it was far removed from her home on the frontier.

He frowned as the single thought returned to him: how long did they have until the particulars of their nuptials arrived from the frontier?

There would be a scandal, to be sure. That could not be avoided, but perhaps with careful planning he would be able to control the flow of information. The shaping of perception was all in the ability to proclaim the news oneself. Julian would have to find a way to tell the public that he had indeed followed his sister's legacy and become a mail-order groom of sorts, even if it was not quite the same method as Julie.

It would be a delicate affair, telling the general public the why of his sudden marriage. The sooner he found an opportunity to address the matter, the better. It would be the most prudent course of action if they hoped to achieve a semblance of normalcy by the time Julie arrived in the city for the holidays.

"What's wrong?" He looked up and saw Violet now regarding him with concern. "Are you all right?"

Julian rubbed his temples and gave her a tight smile. "I'm fine."

She crossed her arms and huffed. "Need I remind you that you are well within my range of detection?"

He laughed and shied away from the shrewd look she gave him. How had his wife learned to read him in a matter of weeks? The best businessmen in the city still had trouble pinning him down in matters of business. He had played poker with the best hands in Europe and escaped unscathed. He was able to coolly read a room of debutantes and their mothers without giving away so much as an inclination of preference, but now?

It was all for naught. Violet was able to read him as easily as if he had written down his thoughts for her in perfect penmanship.

"I am well aware of your powers, darling," he told her, shifting in his seat so that his chin was braced against his fist. He leaned against the arm of the chair and watched her as she rose from the dressing table and came to stand before him.

The dressing gown she wore was silk and slid over her body like a skin of paint. There was no one dip or curve that Julian wasn't privy to, which made for a distracting sight when his wife pinned him with narrowed eyes.

He reached out a hand and ran a finger along the side of her robe. The gold silk sliding beneath his touch would normally be a delicious sensation to savor, but now it was a cause for frustration as it blocked his hand from Violet's bare skin.

He frowned and began to undo the tie of the robe. The sight of her lovely brown skin, flushed from her recent bath, pulled a sigh from him, and he flattened his palm against her side with a satisfied nod.

"Julian!"

He startled at the sudden shout of his name. "I, ah —yes?"

Her hands on her hips, she leveled him with a glare. He licked his lips at the sight of it. He had observed that look before. Such a look did not ultimately point to danger, but could also signal a more passionate encounter.

"You did not hear one word I said, did you?"

He cleared his throat and looked at where his hand still rested on her. "I wouldn't necessarily say that," he told her, resuming his lazy stroking of her skin.

"You haven't," she said with a shake of her head. He leaned forward and pressed his lips to her skin where he touched her and she gasped, the kiss stealing her breath. "You've been—been…"

"Been what?" he asked, lips dragging across her soft skin.

"Distracted."

"Or do you mean distracting?" he asked, nuzzling closer still. She arched her back with a moan, fingernails scraping his shoulder.

"Both."

He smiled and kissed her again. He pushed apart the robe until it hung open at her sides, baring her body completely to him. "You are so beautiful."

"What were you worried about? I saw your face," she whispered, rubbing his shoulders. She looked down at him, her braid moving into his line of vision as he continued to kiss her.

"It was nothing," he told her, and this time he forced his voice to stay steady. She opened her mouth to say more but he pulled her forward, drawing her into his lap so that she sat straddling him. "It was nothing, darling," he said again, kissing her collarbone and working her robe down her shoulders until it pooled by her thighs. The brush of the cool material provided a sharp contrast to the heat of their skin as they embraced in the chair. She turned her head and slanted their mouths together, rocking her hips against his, and he gasped at the sensation while a moan sounded in her throat.

He moved away from her lips, his mouth dropping to the swell of her breasts. "You're lovely," he whispered, laving her skin with his tongue and closing his lips around her nipple.

Her eyes drifted closed at the sensation, her hips rocking again until the hard warm length of him pressed against her, leaving them both groaning with pleasure.

"Julian...mmm." She slid her hand from his shoulder and hugged him closer to her, arching her back in offering. He hooked an arm around her waist, hitching her further up his body, the friction between them perfectly agonizing.

He kissed her again, fingers replacing his lips to play with the aching bud of her breast. She wiggled against him again, her arm sliding behind his head as she pressed closer still to him.

"Julian, please." Her breath was a ragged mix of moan and plea. "Please."

"What is it you want, darling?"

He knew what she wanted. What they both wanted. And from the heat in her eyes she wanted it just as much as he did. Ached for it, in fact, as he did for her.

But he wanted to hear her say it. Needed to have those words fall from her lush lips, like a dying man in the desert needed water.

"I want you," she said, moving her hips with his again. The thin material of his trousers thwarted his need to feel the entirety of her as she rocked against him. "I want you inside me." She kissed him, biting his lips as she pulled back. "Now."

He groaned, the hand he had at her hip tightening. "Now? Here?"

"Yes," she gasped, raising herself up slightly, thighs squeezing him as she did so. "Yes, please." She dropped a hand to the waist of his pants and tugged at them until he moved to help her.

The pair worked together with clumsy fingers and pulled at the tie at the top of his pants until it loosened enough to free his hard cock. Ragged breathing filled the room as they continued to move together, shoving his pants down and bringing the tip of him to her entrance. There was a frantic energy to their movements and neither spoke until she sank down on his length.

"Oh, Julian," she crooned, thighs flexing and lowering her another inch and further still until she was flush against him.

His head fell back and they went still, the fit of their bodies perfect in their juxtaposition, hard muscle and soft curves joining to make one. It calmed the storm that had overtaken them, fed the need to come together in such a sudden manner. All earlier worry of what society would think of their marriage's unique circumstances left his mind as they began to move together.

"I love you," he whispered, opening his eyes to look up at her. She leaned forward, pressing her lips to his forehead while he thrust up into her.

"I love you," she gasped, hands coming to cradle his face. "I love you."

Their lovemaking was one of ardor and want, the frantic energy that had driven them together disappearing to patient tenderness. They touched, caressed, and kissed every inch of the other as they moved closer to the edge of pleasure. When they reached the precipice of their passion it was together, their mingled moans and cries filling the room.

He swore he had never heard anything so sweet.

They slept soundly and, at least for that night, he was able to put his worries aside. All the rest could wait till morning.

~

JULIAN PAGED through the portfolio he had just been handed and frowned at the reports inside. They concerned the most recent investor's comments about the Gold Sky depot. The maps had been beautifully done, the plans and already existing connections and infrastructure promised the venture would be a successful one, but the investor wanted...well, *more.*

With such a detailed map of the area and clear outlines for production, investors clamored for another stop on the depot, another extension of the rail to California.

There is a world of wealth at our fingertips if we seize it.

Julian rolled his eyes at the note from the investor. Everyone fancied themselves a philosopher on a deal with little risk.

He was well aware of the sound investment this depot would be, and knew the security his name imparted to the venture. Investors were assured a return on their investments, but now hungered for more.

He dropped the papers on his desk and rolled his neck. The familiar tense feeling of overwork had already crept back into his muscles after only a week back in the city. Things hadn't slowed down for any of them, but he was aware of the increased interest and pressure that now existed where the Gold Sky depot was concerned. Word of it had gotten out in the business circles he moved in, and the response was almost too much for him to keep up with.

Stark would be pleased by the turn of events. Julian would have to write to the man as soon as he was able, but for now he would have to get ready for the gala tonight: the event that had been put together, albeit hastily, to officially announce his marriage to Violet.

It was her coming-out, so to speak, and everything had to be perfect. His mother hadn't stopped working on it for days, and the obsessive air had leaked over to the household. If the event weren't tonight he didn't know how any of them would manage another day of it, his father especially. The man had borne the brunt of the frenzy of planning with a stalwart fortitude that Julian knew could only come from military training.

As for Julian, he has done his best to stay clear of his mother and her army of party planners.

The house had been absolutely transformed into an autumn wonderland. Just that morning he had stumbled into what could only be described as a forest. Birch and elm trees had been brought in for the occasion, making for a far more arduous trek to the breakfast table than one might expect in their home. Garlands of fall leaves and all manner of gourds has also appeared on the steps and any other available surface. The spice of cinnamon and clove hung in the air, though the source remained a mystery. Violet had stared wide-eyed at it all.

"Is every party like this?" she had asked, trying to parse out where the dining room entry was with the sudden forest barring the way. Unlit lanterns hung from the tree limbs, and Julian shook his head, giving one a poke that set it swinging merrily.

"No, not every party. Just this one."

"But why?"

He looked away from the lantern and brushed a tendril of hair away from her face. "Because this party is your introduction to society, my darling."

"Oh." She nodded and then bit her lip. "I hadn't considered it." Her voice wavered and Julian stepped closer.

"It will be alright," he assured her. "They are all vying for an introduction to you. Not the other way around. You owe them nothing. You are a Baptiste now."

She relaxed into him, her lips turning up slightly. "I will do well to remember that."

Julian wrapped an arm around her, fully intending to take advantage of the privacy the trees afforded them, but the flicker of activity that announced his mother's presence interrupted his efforts.

"My dears," Manon exclaimed from outside the corpse of trees. "Do come out of there and give yourselves over to me."

"For what reason?" Julian called out.

Manon sighed, exasperated. "I have a lady to dress. Your lady, to be exact. Now hand her over so that we may be off for a fitting."

When Violet's eyes rounded he gave her a pitying smile. "It's best to do as she says with little resistance. She will not relent until she has her way."

Violet laughed. "Oh, it's not bad. You're being dramatic."

"You have yet to experience my mother in the throes of event planning. Keep your wits about you, darling."

"I'll manage just fine." She leaned up and kissed his cheek before setting off to his mother.

"Godspeed," he called after her, earning him a huff from Manon.

"I heard that," she called out to him, hands on her hips as Violet joined her.

"You were meant to," he informed her.

"I am put upon so dreadfully by my ungrateful progeny. You will be the crown jewel in my crown as a mother," Manon told Violet, linking their arms together. "Now come and let me pamper you so we might stun the city."

His wife turned, casting a searching look at him, and Julian only dared to lift his hand in goodbye from his safety in the trees. The crowd of workers trailing behind Manon had enveloped them, blocking them from sight.

Julian hadn't heard from them since.

He rose and stretched, moving to the side table where a decanter of whiskey stood at the ready. He poured himself a drink and turned to survey the rough sketch of territory that had been completed that afternoon. He had realized all too soon that they would require more than one set of hands and eyes to accommodate the growth demanded by investors. Violet was soon to be engaged in other areas of their depot planning, and besides, there was all of the Four Hundred for her to deal with.

Julian had grown up navigating the often changing and endlessly fickle social scene, but for a person like Violet, who had been well removed from such an environment, the learning curve was sure to be steep. He did not envy her one bit, and it was his duty to make the transition as seamless as possible. That entailed delegating the more mundane and inconsequential aspects of the business to another, namely an assistant of sorts for Violet and her work. He did not want to monopolize her talent, not when they were in such a well-connected and busy place. She would do well once she gained her bearings socially, he knew, and it wouldn't do to have her redrafting territory maps when the world was at her fingertips.

His wife would do great things, of that he was sure. He tapped a finger on the sketch.

It had been done by a recommended artist, Lorn Dupree, a man slightly older than the pair of them, a bit eager and over-the-top for Julian's taste but meticulous in a way that would be more than sufficient for their work. He had seemed agreeable enough when Julian told him of their aim with the new territory map. Violet had noted the necessary information on their surveying expedition and Julian had found her workbook for Dupree to work from. He had never anticipated that the man would produce a rough finished piece with the new additions so quickly.

He rubbed a hand along his jaw and sipped his drink. He had hoped to discuss it with Violet and let her guide the process of the sketch, but Dupree had been ambitious and more driven than Julian counted on. It hadn't seemed like an ordeal to allow the man free rein for the afternoon. There could be no harm in a bit of extra work. Right?

He swallowed his drink, the burn of it sliding down his throat and into his stomach like a heavy stone. Something felt...off. He couldn't put his finger on it, but supposed it had to do with the gala that evening and his mother's incessant planning, which had put them all on edge for the better part of the week.

It had to be that. Or nerves rubbing off from Violet's fretting.

He downed the rest of his drink and put the glass away. Tonight would go off perfectly. He would not allow anyone to make his wife feel inferior. The matter of their marriage would be addressed and all would be well.

Society would welcome Violet with open arms, and they could finally get back to the business of being them. He would welcome the peace once more, and perhaps they could begin planning an impromptu trip back to the frontier before the holidays.

He knew she would enjoy it, and seeing Alice would put a smile on her face. It would be good for them after the whirlwind of New York. He nodded to himself and left the study, careful to look cautiously down the hall lest he was ambushed by his mother and her party planning army. Thankfully, he encountered no one and made it to his room in peace. He dressed for the evening and was surprised when he saw no evidence that Violet had been there.

His mother must still have her captive, which could be both a wonderful and terrible fate. Knowing his mother's overzealous nature, he hoped it was the latter. A knock at the door startled him, and he turned from the mirror where he had been giving himself a once over. There was only one opportunity for Violet's introduction to society, and he wished for it to be perfect. All details must be flawlessly attended to, even if that detail was his waistcoat.

He crossed the room to the door and opened it, and the sight that greeted him pushed away all thoughts of waistcoats and pocket squares. None of that mattered, not when his wife stood as she was in front of him.

Violet was more beautiful now than on her wedding day.

She wore a dress of royal purple with burnished gold trim, the deep hue highlighting the tan of her skin while the gold accentuated her brown eyes and the ochre he knew to be there. Her dark hair was curled and piled on top of her head with gold blossoms pinned throughout. Julian knew not one thing concerning women's hairstyles, but he knew that Violet's hair was the finest he had ever seen and would ever see. The low scoop of the dress drew his eyes to the tantalizing expanse of flesh that made his blood run hotter than normal.

At her cough he drew his eyes up to her face. He smiled at her, giving his best rendition of a gentleman doing anything but entertaining impure thoughts.

"Hello, darling," he all but purred, making her cheeks

color though she did not avert her eyes. Instead she lifted her chin and met his gaze with a steady look of her own.

She smirked at him and dropped low into an exaggerated curtsey. "Hello, dear. Do you like the dress?"

"Adore it," Julian told her, bending low into a formal bow with one hand extended to her. "You are a vision of loveliness."

She placed her hand in his, allowing him to press a kiss against her knuckles. "And you are the picture of a gentleman."

He raised his eyes to hers, lips skimming her knuckles as he spoke. "Then appearances deceive. Do not fall prey to it, darling." His fingers traced the sensitive skin of her wrist and she shivered, licking her lips and swallowing thickly.

"And tell me, sir. Why would there be an occasion for deceit?"

"Propriety," he told her with a weary sigh as he stood from his bow, "Christian mores, and a chaste lifestyle. It is in vogue, you know."

"I've often found myself to have little use for what is considered an acceptable lifestyle."

He chuckled and stepped closer to her, offering her his arm. "Then perhaps I shall extend an invitation to you to shirk both in the near future."

She took his arm and smiled sweetly, though she turned to press her body against him, breasts soft and full against his arm. He almost groaned at the touch but kept his veneer of civility in place. It would not do to let her know just how effective her teasing him was. Not with the night just beginning.

There would be time enough to explore the reach of the other before the night was over.

"Oh, I do like the sound of that," she whispered, kissing his cheek in the picture of chasteness.

He hummed but said nothing as they approached the dining room, or rather the dining hall. There was a certain size and grandeur that often eluded him until new eyes or circumstances pushed him to see his home in a different light.

Tonight's gala event was just such an occasion. Manon had turned the halls of the house from the tastefully appointed, if mundane, place he had grown up in, to the personification of autumn. A copse of trees barred the way to the dining hall, which he suspected held no trace of the space where his family enjoyed their meals in relative peace. The chatter of voices and laughter mingled with the merry sound of violins playing a waltz and the clinking of champagne glasses.

He would find an event in full swing, not a place to breakfast or end his day when Violet and he made their way out of the trees. For all he knew there was an entire forest floor his mother had created awaiting them. He expected nothing less than extravagance from his mother on such an important event.

Raising his head, he moved to enter the trees, but Violet slowed and faltered beside him. She was nervous, he could tell by the tremor in her hand as she held onto his arm. Turning, he gave her a reassuring smile.

"It will be alright. There is nothing to fear."

"What if I—what if I say the wrong things?"

"Impossible. This is *your* party."

"What if I make a fool of myself and drop my glass or forget the steps to a dance?"

"Then I will throw my glass on the ground as well. We will make a new dance and force the others to follow."

She shook her head, looking down at the floor, brow furrowed. "But I—"

"There is nothing you can do or say tonight that will change the fact that everyone gathered here has come to meet you. We will introduce you to them. They are eager to gain your favor. You owe no one anything you do not wish to give."

She fell silent, but when her look of consternation persisted he touched her cheek. "You are safe, Violet. I have you. I promise."

"Forever?"

He nodded, fingers moving gently against her cheek. Her eyes fluttered shut at the soft touch. "Forever."

She smiled, chest rising with a deep inhale before she opened her eyes. "Thank you. I'm ready."

He nodded at her, giving her another warm smile. "Then let us make our entry to *your* party," he said again, stressing the word so much that she laughed.

"Let us."

Into the trees they went together, the lanterns hanging from the boughs casting a gentle glow upon them as they walked. So encompassing was the forest that for a moment he forgot about the gala, forgot about the evening ahead or the hours of socializing at hand. All he could think of was how beautiful his wife looked in the shifting shadows of the trees and lantern light.

The rest, in its entirety, were simply details.

~

It was mayhem the moment they entered the dining room, now resplendent in a riot of oranges, crimson and varying shades of gold that called to mind what might happen if King Midas had been set loose in the Garden of Eden. There was no other way to define the experience than pure, unadulterated mayhem.

Of course, it was the kind of mayhem that only the gently bred and well-to-do citizens of New York City were inclined to participate in, but Julian was able to recognize it for what it was. Violet's introduction as his wife, as "Mrs. Julian Baptiste," had caused quite a stir among the gathered guests. She had been thrown into the veritable deep end of things.

Unsurprisingly, Violet was an astute swimmer.

"I had no idea we would be treated to such a connection," said Lady Pim of Lady Pim's Fine Etiquette and Finishing School for Young Ladies. Julian had nodded along and gave the headmistress an apologetic head nod.

"This is her introduction to society then, yes?" Lady Pim asked, raising an eyebrow and giving Violet a thorough once-over that made Julian bristle.

"It is," he gritted out, taking his wife's hand. "We are so very glad you were able to make it. We have not kept your fine company since Julie's graduation from your institution."

Lady Pim sniffed, turning her attention away from Violet, and gave him a raised eyebrow. "Yes, yes," she said with a distracted wave of her hand, "do not think I haven't made note of your absence at my yearly gathering. But worry not, I have taken into account the unique nature of your sister's...*lifestyle.*"

That was the delicate way of discussing Julie's decision to take two husbands. It still wasn't talked about openly in society, mostly because Julian was convinced no one truly believed it. But there were those, such as Lady Pim, who did believe it to be true. These people skirted the subject with a sly wink or sidelong glance held for a beat too long when Julie came up in conversation.

Julian did not miss it, though he often pretended he did. Oftentimes it was easy to compartmentalize.

But now...now it was perhaps a touch too difficult to manage.

He clenched his jaw, a scathing reply on the tip of his tongue, but Violet remained all smiles and soothing tones. "Well, Julie is a remarkable girl. She, no doubt, owes much of it to your careful instruction."

Lady Pim paused, her look thawing when she turned her eyes to Violet. "Yes, this is true…" She cleared her throat and then asked, "Has she talked of me much, or her time with me?"

Violet bobbed her head and handed Lady Pim a glass of champagne from a passing tray. "She has. I can tell you she thoroughly enjoyed her time as your student."

The other woman snapped her fingers and gave Julian a smug smile. "I told your mother she was having a grand time." Lady Pim wagged her finger and took a healthy sip of her drink. "I did, mark my words. I *told* Manon, though she doubted your sister's affection for our lessons."

Julian nodded and took a glass for himself, if only to hide the grin on his face at Violet's smooth maneuvering of the older woman. "Always the astute judge," he said, tipping his glass in acknowledgment as Lady Pim continued on.

But this time she slipped an arm through Violet's and steered her in the direction of a family she just had to meet. Lady Pim was, of course, all too happy to provide a personal introduction.

Violet turned and gave him a quick smile before vanishing into the crowd on Lady Pim's arm. It had been hard to relax since, with him keeping a careful eye out for his wife—though when he did see her she seemed relaxed and in her element. He trusted her to signal him should she need rescuing.

The woman was, of course, new to the ways of high-pressured socializing. And hadn't he assured her that all would be well as he would be at her side? *Him*. Not Lady Pim, a stranger she had only just met.

He frowned, moving through the crowd and making for her head of dark curls. She was in conversation with Dupree. It was fortunate they had found one another in such a crowd as this, but Julian would be remiss if he did not join them, if even for a superficial presence in what he assumed would be talk rife with terms unfamiliar to him.

The two would get on well, *were* getting on well if Dupree's animated face was anything to go by. He stood facing Julian, a wide smile on his face as he threw his arms wide and gestured wildly at what Julian assumed was the area he had just sketched.

Julian's step faltered. Ah, yes, the map. He had quite forgot to broach the subject when he'd encountered Violet before the gala.

"Julian!"

He turned to see his mother bustling up with a bright smile on her face. She enveloped him in a tight hug and then leaned back to gesture at the almost magical room around them. "Isn't it wonderful?"

"It's beautiful," he told her, and nodded at the entryway behind them. "How did you transport the trees here?"

"No autumn playground would be complete without a bit of foliage."

"It isn't just a bit. It's a forest, *maman*."

She shrugged at him. "Violet deserves a forest."

He sucked at his bottom lip and then finally sighed in concession. "That she does. You outdid yourself with all of this. Thank you."

"No need to thank me. I was blessed with the pleasure of dressing her up this afternoon. I cannot tell you how refreshing it is to spend time with someone who listens—"

Julian held up a finger. "I think you mean obeys you."

"And considers my wisdom and—"

"Lets you dress them up."

"Truly appreciates my taste."

"Allows you to do as you please," he corrected.

A smile played over Manon's features before she lost the fight at keeping a stern face and laughed, looking away with a little shake of her head and a sigh.

"Is there anything so wrong with that?"

"No, *maman*, nothing," Julian conceded, leaning close and kissing her cheek. "Nothing at all." He looked over at Violet, still standing with Dupree, and said, "I was on my way to check in with Violet. Would you care to join me?"

She held up her hands and waved him off. "No, go on. I've noticed you giving her space to stretch her wings. Quite admirable, given your penchant for lurking."

He frowned and gave her a narrow-eyed look. "I do not. Gentlemen *do not lurk*," he said, taking great care to stress his words.

Manon only rolled her eyes. "You are a veritable mother hen."

"I merely aim to keep the peace and—"

"I know this is a trying time, but I assure you she is doing wonderfully."

"At times it can be overwhelming, so if I linger it's for her—"

Manon crossed her arms. "You have been tracking her all night."

"And I have taken great care to let her know that I am readily available should she need me," he insisted.

"Of course, dear one."

His lips turned down in a frown as he huffed his displeasure. "You are not as entertaining or insightful as you like to believe."

Manon hummed and then reached out, nudging him toward Violet. "Go on. I'll not keep you from your lady love a moment longer."

"Are you sure I am not stalking as a hunter does?" he asked, but he did turn as she instructed and set off toward Violet, his mother's laughter ringing in his ears.

"I do not hover," he muttered, stalking forward. He ran a hand along his jaw and then frowned. "Do I?" Perhaps there was truth to his mother's assertion that he had a tendency to...*linger.*

He would have to ask Violet's opinion on the matter. If she wanted him near then he wouldn't care too terribly what his mother observed. Not if it pleased his wife. If she preferred he lurk — er, linger—then he would continue to do so with impunity.

Julian cleared his throat as he approached Violet and Dupree. "Hello, how are the both of you?" he asked with his best smile in place.

He was not lurking. Absolutely not.

Violet was the first to turn toward him but she was not the first to speak. She bit her lip as Dupree moved forward, holding out a hand toward Julian. "Good evening, my good man," he exclaimed, giving Julian's hand a touch too much strength. "Quite an affair you've put together. I cannot say that I have been to a more tasteful one."

"Thank you," Julian said, giving the man as firm a handshake as he was able to amid the vigorous shaking Dupree engaged in, and managed to pull his hand back with barely a grimace. "I hope you've enjoyed yourself tonight?"

"I have." Dupree nodded at Violet where she still stood silent and staring. "Your new bride has been incredibly helpful on that end, and I thank you for the kindness, Mrs. Baptiste."

Violet's lips pursed. The slight twitch of her mouth drew Julian's interest and he raised an eyebrow at her, but she said nothing, looking away with a murmured, "Certainly, Mr. Dupree. I hope you find the Gold Sky project to your liking."

Dupree winked at her, his hands going to the lapels of

his coat. "Oh, I shall, I shall. Of that I have no worries, my girl."

"Ah." Julian cleared his throat. "You will be able to talk business tomorrow if your schedule still remains free." He gave Violet a meaningful look, but she studiously avoided his gaze and only shook her head with a jerk.

"I haven't the faintest idea why my input would be needed. It seems you both have it all firmly in hand," she said, finally turning to look at him with eyes that shone far too bright.

Something was wrong. But what?

"Violet..." he began, but she had already moved away from him, the violet and gold of her dress gleaming like jewels beneath the soft candlelight his mother had filled the space with.

"If you'll excuse me, gentlemen," she said, voice wooden and flat. She turned from them with barely a nod of goodbye and strode away.

The interaction hadn't gone unnoticed by those gathered nearby, but Julian paid them little mind when they turned their curious gazes on him as he watched Violet make a swift exit.

"Women are strange creatures," Dupree observed, sipping from his champagne glass. Julian's eyes moved over to the man beside him and he frowned.

"What exactly do you mean?"

Dupree lifted one broad shoulder in a shrug. "She was fine until you came upon us. And then...." He blew out a whistle, rocking back on his heels with a shake of his head.

"And then *what?*" Julian pressed, turning to face the

other man. His voice held an edge of flint Dupree couldn't have supposed Julian had within him. He straightened up and blinked, looking suddenly alert in the face of Julian's ire.

"I just—ah, I mean that she left so suddenly," the other man tried.

"Yes and that begs the question of why." Julian took a step closer to Dupree, his mind turning over the curious wording she had used to him before taking her leave.

I haven't the faintest idea why my input would be needed.

"I hired you to be her *assistant.* That means you do not answer to me. *She* signs the checks despite my hiring of you. My money is her money. From the looks of it, you were getting along perfectly well before I arrived."

It seems you both have it all firmly in hand.

Julian continued, "But I know all too well looks can be deceiving. If you have upset my wife in any capacity, I will find out."

Dupree's mouth dropped open slightly and he blinked owlishly at Julian.

"I do care for my wife being upset," Julian informed him. "I will speak to her. You will be compensated for your work on the territory sketch. Beyond that, it is at Violet's discretion."

"But I—"

Julian tipped his head and lifted his champagne glass. "Enjoy the gala, Dupree."

"I did nothing wrong," Dupree protested, but Julian wasted no time in hearing him out. He cared little if guests were treated to a slice of gossip.

This was his home, tonight was his wife's party, and

she was not in attendance. Something had happened before his arrival. He knew it. And Julian intended to find out the reason for her sudden departure before he concerned himself with saving face.

That included smoothing over the loud dramatics currently taking place behind him. Specifically, the dramatics of one would-be cartographer. He was vaguely aware of the ruckus being kicked up in the dining hall by Dupree, and he kept moving as he navigated the crowd and then the copse of trees at the entry.

He knew she had gone. He hoped it was to their rooms. When he arrived at the bedroom door he slowed and stopped, brow furrowed as he took in a deep calming breath and knocked.

No answer came, but he forced himself to wait patiently and knocked once more. Still no answer came, and he gave himself permission to enter the room. There was a stillness he hadn't anticipated but which firmly spoke of Violet's absence.

He paced the room, hands in pockets, and worried his bottom lip. Where would she have gone?

She was safe here. No harm would come to her within these walls...and she would not go outside, not without him, or without telling someone...would she?

His mind began to race—what if she had gone for a walk in the neighborhood? What if she became lost? What the devil had Dupree told her?

That damnable man.

A light knock at the door broke through his thoughts and Julian nearly sprinted to it. He ripped it open, expecting to see Violet, but frowned when he saw only his mother in the hall.

"Oh," he said with a frown, sagging against the door.

She raised an eyebrow at him. "Oh. What a greeting that is."

He sighed and looked down the hallway. "She isn't with you, I suppose?"

Manon shook her head and gave him a kind look. "No, she isn't. But she is waiting for me."

"Where?"

"My suite."

He stood up straight and made to pass her. "I must speak to her at once."

Manon caught his arm and gave him a warning look. "You will wait," she told him. "She isn't quite herself at the moment."

"It was that man, wasn't it?"

"It was hard to discern, but I do know this. She will be better tomorrow."

"But I must—"

She touched his face gently and gave him a soft smile. "You must do nothing but give her a night of space. It will help, dear. Trust me on this."

He sighed, leaning back against the door. "Fine. But I do not care for it."

"Your consternation has been duly noted. Please get some sleep tonight, it will make everything ...better."

"Thank you," Julian told her, and she caught his hand, giving it a squeeze, before she stepped back from him. After another meaningful look she started down the hallway, leaving him staring after her.

“Sleep...sleep,” he mused, drumming his fingers against the wood of the doorway. He squeezed his eyes shut and shook his head. “Impossible,” he whispered, pushing away from the doorframe and making for his study in the opposite direction Manon had departed in.

There was no way he could sleep. Not while his wife was upset. Not while he was powerless till morning to rectify it.

His study was a place of action, the center of his being and purpose. It was there he would find the answer to his need to be useful, to feel as if he were not impotently standing by as events continued on around him.

Work was just the way to fix the feeling, and he knew precisely what he would do with the hours until morning. There was much to be done, and it would all require the presence of both a solicitor and a notary.

CHAPTER 18

It was just before dawn when Julian took a break from the stack of papers on his desk. The bleary-eyed notary had departed only moments before sunrise. Where the man had been prior to being summoned had been of little interest to Julian, but Julian supposed he had been slumbering, if the man's state of dress was anything to guess by.

It would at least make for a speedy return to bed upon his return home.

The pair had been at work for the past two hours, Julian's solicitor checking over the documents that had been drawn up in triplicate before handing them to the notary for officiating. The scratch of pen on paper and the subsequent stamp of the notary formed into a singular sound perfect for lulling Julian into a wakeful dozing state.

It had only been with the last stamp and snap of a briefcase that he had truly jerked awake and blinked sleepily around the brightening study. The pink and yellow hues of the rising sun painted the carpet of the room in a beautifully soft light that made him think of Violet.

He groaned at himself. Everything reminded him of Violet, so there was little surprise in him thinking of her when faced with the day's sunrise. Rubbing the sleep from his eyes, he rose from his desk with a stretch of his arms and made for the fresh pot of coffee that had just been delivered along with his breakfast.

There was a rasher of bacon and fresh bread, but the coffee was the only item worth holding his attention. Coffee, and plenty of it, would be essential if he had any hope of surviving the day ahead.

There would be no time to sleep after his night of work. Not when he had to speak with Violet, or at least try to. He had done his part as his mother advised and waited until morning, even if he had not stopped in his work.

Violet.

He poured a cup of coffee and stared into the depths while his mind churned, moving restlessly over the memory of Violet storming away the night before.

I haven't the faintest idea why my input would be needed. It seems you both have it all firmly in hand.

What had the damnable man said to her? He had taken Dupree for overzealous and eager, if a bit heavy-handed in their interactions. But he had not pegged the man for overstepping or for being capable of angering Violet.

Julian had badly erred, if last night's scene was anything to go upon.

He was determined to make it right.

He sipped his coffee, eyes moving back over to the window to watch the sun make its ascent above the horizon. Even if his mother advised him to wait, that did not mean he could not seek her counsel. Surely after a night with his wife she would have insight into the matter.

A soft knock at the door made him stand ramrod straight, and he whirled so quickly toward the door his coffee sloshed over the cup's edge, but he paid little mind to the sting of the hot liquid.

It was her, he knew it, could feel it in his bones from that slight sound at the door.

He rushed forward, spilling more of his coffee in his haste. He really should have put the cup down, but it was as if his body moved of its own accord. Before he could think, he threw the door open.

"Yes?" he breathed as the door banged open.

He had been right. There she stood.

Violet.

Her hair was down from the previous night's finery, the dark thick strands pulled into a single plait. She had foregone the richly appointed clothing his mother had dressed her in, wearing instead one of her simple muslin dresses, this one a soft yellow with cream linen along the throat and cuffs. The glint of the plain gold chain she had worn the first night Julian had met her flashed, and it was as if he were back in that moment once more.

All these nights and countless miles of travel, and Violet stole his breath just the same.

The only difference was that now he stared at her with open want and longing. Then, he had wanted her. Oh, the dark-eyed cook had made him want. But it wouldn't have been proper to give evidence of it. Now she was his wife, and he looked his fill of her. Lack of sleep perhaps made him stare longer than usual, but he paid it no mind. He sighed in relief at the sight of her.

"Violet."

She swallowed hard and looked away from his face, her eyes sliding just over his shoulder and focusing on the space there. "May I come in?"

"Yes, of course. Please." He moved away from the doorway and motioned for her to enter.

She gave him a nod before coming forward and into the center of the room. "You've spilled your coffee," she observed, nodding at the dark splotch on the hardwood and carpet.

"Ah, yes, it seems I have," he said, looking down dazedly at the cup he still clutched. "I did not...rest very much. My reactions are a bit spotty."

She nodded and looked away again, this time to the window he had just been staring out. "I'm sorry for that. I realize I had a part in that."

"It had nothing to do with you." Her eyes jerked to him, and he swallowed hard. "I mean to say, you have nothing to apologize for."

It was he who desperately wanted to make amends. Not her. What was she going on about?

"So you say."

"I do."

He moved toward his desk and deposited the half-empty cup of coffee with a thud. He would make do with no sleep and no caffeine. There was no helping it. Not when he could feel that something wasn't quite right still.

"I spent time working last night," he said, rifling through the papers on his desk and pulling out a portfolio. "I made great progress on the Gold Sky depot, but that is not what I want to discuss at the moment. I have these for you to sign."

He produced a stack of papers and watched as Violet recoiled from them, as if she had been presented with a snake ready to strike. "What are those?" she asked, eyes narrowed and focused on the papers.

He held them out to her. "Read them."

"What is it?" she asked again, her voice rising. "I'll not sign it until you tell me first."

He sighed, stepping around the desk, holding the papers aloft. "Violet, sign the papers."

She shook her head and took a step back from him. "I refuse."

"You—but why?" he asked in confusion. "A signature is nothing to worry yourself about—things will be so much better for us."

"For us or for you?"

He tilted his head to the side, trying to make sense of the words. "Us. This is good for the pair of us. Sign them."

He held the papers out but she shook her head again.

"Never," she bit out, surprising him with the venom in her voice.

"Violet…" he began, approaching her slowly, but he jerked to a stop when she darted forward and yanked the papers from his hand.

"Violet! What are you doing?" he asked, eyes going wide as he watched her storm toward the fireplace. It wasn't the roaring fire it had been through the night, mostly embers now, but there was still heat and flame aplenty for what he saw she intended to do.

She was going to burn the papers.

"I spent all night on those," he protested as she held them past the fireplace grate. "Stop!"

"Stop? How am I to stop when you mean to divorce me? I'll not sign these papers, even if you have to spend the next hundred nights making new ones. I shall burn every last one of those as well!"

"Vio—what?" he gasped, pulling back from her. The words had landed with all the force of a slap. "Divorce you?"

"Yes, and if you think for one moment I'll go peacefully then you are mistaken. I made a promise and so did you. I'll remind you of your vows, Julian!"

"Why would I divorce you?"

"Marrying me for the sake of the depot venture was unexpected. But now that you have Dupree you think to dispose of me? I think not!"

He threw out his arms. "What?" he roared, startling her to the point that she dropped the papers in her hand with a gasp. "I would never do such a thing. I love you!"

"Then what did Dupree…." Violet's voice trailed off and she licked her lips. "He said he was replacing me. That he had already done so."

"He what?"

"Last night, he said that he was replacing me. That he had already completed the territory sketch and that I had been employed out of necessity," she said, her voice small. "Then I heard guests talking about us. Saying that it would never last. That they were convinced you would have it all annulled."

His eyes fluttered shut and he opened them when he was sure he wouldn't tear the room apart with his bare hands.

"Who dared say that?" His voice was low, akin to a growl, and she blinked in surprise at the dangerous sound coming from her husband.

"I don't know," she admitted. "I didn't—it was hard to remember names."

"I will ruin them when you tell me who they are."

"Please don't," she whispered. There was no mistaking the metal in his words. He had seemingly become a different man before her very eyes, and she swallowed hard, saying again, "Please don't."

"I would never divorce you. Why would I have—do you not know what you mean to me?" He took a step closer to her, forcing the hard lines of his body to relax. He took in a deep breath and worked to drop his shoulders as he approached her. "I adore you. I love you, Violet."

"You've been distant. Keeping secrets. I know something has been on your mind. It has been since we arrived."

"Ah, yes, your penchant for knowing when I tell untruths."

She tapped her temple and smiled ruefully at him. "It is unfailingly accurate. What have you been hiding from me?"

"Nothing," he blurted out, and then sighed at the frown

she gave him. "I was worried about your introduction. About getting in front of the story from Gold Sky. Rosemary's zealous spirit in the way of journalism was bound to reach New York any day, and I did not want to put you in a precarious situation in society." He sighed and ran his hands over his face with a groan. "I did not want you to worry about being an outsider or feeling as if you did not belong. That is why I kept it from you. I wanted to take care of it for you."

"That is what you have been keeping from me?"

He nodded, hands still on his face. "Yes. I wanted you to feel at ease here in our new home."

"You didn't want me to feel like I didn't belong?"

He dropped his hands. "Of course not. You do belong —you belong with me. With my family. You *are* my family."

Her face softened and she sighed, coming to his side. "Forgive me. I reacted when I should have gotten the truth of the matter from you."

He caught her hands in his. "How could you have, when I was already keeping my worries from you. It was an impossible situation."

"We should have both done better."

"We *will* do better."

She turned her face up in offering and he leaned forward, his pulse quickening as their lips met in a kiss that reminded them both of their first. The one shared in front of a crowd in a chapel on the frontier.

That simple kiss had spoke of passion and want. But it had also demanded from each of them, pulling and yanking on them until they were helpless but to give all that it asked for.

Lips and hearts met, speaking the language of endless tomorrows and time spent learning to live, to love, to grow, and to do so at the other's side.

"I'm sorry," they both breathed when they parted. The couple chuckled at the shared sentiment, and they came together again, lips brushing once more before Violet asked, "What were those papers?"

His eyes snapped open. "Oh god, the papers!" he yelped, springing away from her and rushing toward the slow-burning embers the portfolio of papers had landed on. He fell to his knees, reaching for the smoking folio.

"Julian! Be careful. What are you doing?" she exclaimed, running toward him with hands outstretched, as if she meant to pull him back. But he was undeterred, and reached into the fireplace, grabbing the papers and working to smother the flames. "You'll burn yourself. Have you gone mad?!"

He yanked off his jacket and smothered the flames with it. "These are important!"

She dropped to her knees beside him, a look of panic on her face. "Whatever it is, it is not worth burning yourself over."

He looked up at her then and laughed the laugh only the sleep-deprived and determined denizens of the world were capable of producing. "These, darling, are worth an injury. These are for you," he said, unfurling his coat and presenting the papers to her.

"What are they?"

"Half of my wealth."

Her eyes widened and she fell to the side, her hands catching her weight. "What?" she gasped.

"I worked all night to have them drawn up. You own half of my property and any future property or wealth. It will all be entailed to you in the proper percentages. You have access to my bank accounts. All of it."

"But why?" She looked up at him from her position on the floor and shook her head. "Why would you do such a thing?"

"Because now we are equal in all ways," he said, and then held the papers out to her again. "Sign them."

"I can't," she insisted, but he shook his head and reached forward, hauling her up with him and tucking the papers under an arm.

"You can and you will." He maneuvered them toward the desk and dropped the papers in front of her before pressing a pen into her hand. "Once it is done, then you will never again believe such a foolhardy thing as me divorcing you. I give you your freedom, darling. I pray you choose me."

Her eyes left the papers and moved to his face. She stared at him for a long moment before she pointed the pen at him. "Thank you." There was a world of feeling, of emotion, in those two words, and he felt them at his core.

She loved him, he knew. As he did her.

They would not part.

Not now. Not ever.

He kissed her cheek and brushed his fingers along her jaw. "Of course, darling. Anything."

She undid the string securing the folio edges. The thick folio the papers were bound in had protected them fairly well. He breathed a sigh of relief, seeing they were only singed. Slowly and painstakingly he directed her through them, showing her where to sign until they were finished in their entirety.

Only then did the tension in his body leave completely, and he smiled warmly at her as she set her pen down.

"Now what do we do?" she asked when he slipped the folio into the drawer of his desk and locked it with a satisfied nod.

"Now?" he asked, stepping towards her and wrapping an arm around her waist. "There's only one thing I can think of doing."

"What is that?"

"Sleep. I would like to sleep."

She tilted her head, glancing up at him as they walked toward the door. "Am I to leave you to it?"

He grinned and shook his head. "You will do no such thing. I intend for you to be there as well."

"To sleep?" she asked, when she felt his hand move away from her waist, his fingers trailing lightly against her as they traveled up her side. She turned into him, her hands moving in a mimic of his, and he grinned at the feel of her lingering touch.

They were of the same mind and interest when it came to the matter of what to do next.

"So to speak. Do you agree to sleep?"

"I agree."

Unsurprisingly, they did not sleep.

EPILOGUE

Christmas in New York City was a gloriously beautiful occasion. The city was decked out in its finest decorations and a thick coat of white snow blanketed the whole of it, hiding any of the ills one might find in a city as large and as crowded as New York. Even the most cynical New Yorker was in good cheer.

For all of its faults even Julian had to admit that the city did have a certain beauty and charm during the festive season. A roaring fire and a fir tree decorated for the occasion set the scene. Stockings hung along the mantle and the smell of fresh baked cookies hung in the air. The tray of cookies Violet had just set on the side table was already half empty, and she eyed the platter with a satisfied smile from where she had tucked herself beside Julian.

It was a joyous season made even merrier by the presence of the Wickes-Barnes family.

They had arrived a week prior to Christmas, and had settled in at lightning speed. Manon was all too happy to make room for her daughter and sons-in-laws, though they were all of a lesser concern than Seylah's comfort. The tiny bundle had grown by leaps and bounds since Julian had last seen the infant. Seylah was now crawling and constantly on the move.

The fact that she was in possession of not one but two watchful fathers meant that the infant was held in check when she was not in her grandmother's care.

Even now, with the family gathered, it proved Manon's arms were the only pair little Seylah would stay still long enough to linger in. The child stared up at her grandmother as the woman bounced her in her lap with a smile.

"You're a little darling, yes you are," Manon sang, eliciting a laugh from Seylah.

"She's something, all right," Forrest hummed from his perch on the settee near Julie, who sat knitting a scarf. She nodded in agreement and looked up from her work with a shake of her head.

"She's a handful, is what she is."

Manon shook her head in disagreement, all the while still smiling at the baby. "No, she's just darling. Sweet as anything. Aren't you, love?"

"She is what you say she is," Jean said, coming into the room and working on the pipe he held in his hands.

"You always agree with her," Julie pouted.

"Of course I do," Jean replied without looking up from the pipe he was now in the process of lighting. "It's the secret of a happy home."

"He wasn't always so agreeable," Manon chimed in with a roll of her eyes.

Jean's eyes cut to her and he grinned, puffing away on the pipe. "I have always been agreeable, my sweet. You have the reputation for being cantankerous."

Manon scoffed. "Lies. All of it. I've always been sweet-natured."

"Shall we go down memory lane, love? I seem to remember a less than sweet start to us."

"I have no recollection of said events."

Julie perked up at the exchange and looked over at Julian. "It's starting!"

He laughed, raising his glass of mulled wine to her. "So it is. A Christmas tradition lives on!"

"What tradition?" Violet asked.

"They tell the story of how they met. But this bit is always my favorite," Julie answered, leaning forward and abandoning her knitting with a grin. "They are adorable when they bicker so."

"We are not bickering. Your father is simply forgetting history. *Again.*"

He raised an eyebrow at her. "You pulled a knife on me when we first met."

Violet's eyes widened and Forrest's mouth dropped open in shock. Will, on the other hand, doubled over laughing.

"Sounds about right for the women in this family," he muttered, earning a narrow-eyed look from Julie.

"*If* I pulled a knife on you, it was in defense," Manon insisted. "And besides, you were in possession of a sword and a firearm."

"Right you are on both accounts," he said with a wave of his pipe.

Violet threw out her hands and sat up, making Julian groan at the loss of his wife's warmth against him. "Please tell me you will give us the story in its entirety. I must know."

Forrest and Will nodded along. "You have our attention as well," Forrest said, urging them on. "Please tell it."

Manon and Jean shared a meaningful look across the room. She settled back into her seat and looked down at Seylah. "Shall we?"

He puffed out a breath of smoke and moved toward her. "I thought you would never ask, love."

She sucked in a breath and patted the space next to her. "Then come and sit. We have a story to tell."

THE END

EXCERPT: SEYLAH'S STORY

Seylah had never been a particularly elegant girl, had little interest in frippery or the latest fashions, and had never been one given to minding her manners. That did not mean that she was uncouth, but simply that her edges may have been rougher than most of the other girls of her age.

After all, Seylah had grown up in an unconventional household. With a former debutante for a mother and a pair of Gold Sky's lawmen for fathers Seylah's upbringing had been one that favored freedom, discipline and creativity.

Yet for all that, she was polite, pleasant and well-spoken. Seylah's mind was quick, nearly as fast as her tongue, though her fathers swore it would be a miracle if the two ever managed to pull even of each other. Her heart was bigger than she knew what to do with, the product of her warm family where affection and love were never in short supply.

Seylah had inherited her fathers' collective stubbornness, resourcefulness, and bravery. She was in possession of her mother's spirit, that particular strength of will; a character that had carried a debutante to the frontier.

Moreover, she had been given the gift of hope by all three of her parents and so Seylah saw the world as one endless experience of possibility. Adventure awaited her around every corner despite having grown up on the same collection of avenues in Gold Sky. But the influx of new money and people was rapidly changing the face of the town.

Gold Sky had developed from the burgeoning frontier town still finding its legs at her mother's arrival fifteen years earlier to a cosmopolitan oasis at the fringes of the frontier. The sheriff's department had evolved past her two fathers and now consisted of a force of ten men, there was even a fire brigade given the town now numbered upwards of thirty rctail cstablishmcnts and countlcss other homes.

And while Seylah loved adventure, lately she found it left a bitter taste in her mouth. She could have settled for less transformation and, quite frankly, for more of what yesterday had offered.

When that development had occurred she couldn't quite say.

Maybe it was that she had just had her fourteenth birthday and had noticed differences in herself that she'd rather not dwell on.. And maybe, just maybe, those physical and emotional changes were putting a strain on the one thing Seylah prized above all else: her relationship with her best friend August Leclaire.

The pair had been inseparable since childhood with

August only a month older than her. A fact that he never let her live down, despite her still being able to beat him in a foot race. Every day they had walked to school together and back again, spending as much time as they could after and in between with each other. Theirs had been a fast friendship, one that made Seylah feel at home, as if everything in the world were in it's designated place so long as August was on her left. But lately...lately, something had happened to their closeness.

What it was she was loathe to say aloud, but she knew precisely when it had occurred.

The night the main thoroughfare of town had suddenly become grander, more special, which was an easy task with the arrival of electric street lamps. That was the night something had shifted, or at least it had begun to for Seylah.

It was dizzying to watch the street light up like magic. There had even been a party that evening replete with a countdown to welcome the momentous occasion. Electric lights like this were common in the cities Seylah frequented with her family, such as New York and Paris. But not here, not on a frontier that was still a touch removed from civilized.

August had been with her then just as he always was for any event, big or small. They had stood together laughing with the townsfolk as the excitement mounted, until it was practically buzzing. Perhaps their fingers had brushed and Seylah had forgotten to breathe, her lungs suddenly void of air as the crowd around them gleefully counted down each new number until finally they were at one and Seylah was left blinking in confusion, because when the streetlights blazed to life so did another thing.

Her heart.

The light had formed a halo around August's dirty blonde hair making it gleam like the nearby river when the sun was high. His boyish features now seemed sharper, more of a man than the boy she had grown up teasing. His shoulders, she realized, had filled out since the summer before and when had he grown a head taller than her?

August wasn't a boy anymore. And if this past summer had told Seylah anything, it was that she was no longer a girl, was on the verge of blossoming into a woman. How had she not realized the same was true for August? Her eyes had moved over him taking in all the changes she hadn't noticed until they had, literally, been put beneath a spotlight.

It was enough to make her dizzy.

He had turned towards her and given a familiar smile, that same smile he had given her when they were 5 on their first day of school. But instead of smiling back she had been too wide-eyed, too focused on him that she hadn't realized he was calling her name.

"What?" she asked, stumbling back a step. She had been staring at him. Caught red-handed in fact when August had said her name. "What is it?"

"Why are you staring at me?"

"I'm not. I was stunned by the light."

He scoffed, reaching out and rubbing his knuckles against her head, mussing her hair. "Liar," August said.

"I am nothing of the kind. I'm a lady," she repeated

with a toss of her head and August laughed along with her, throwing an arm over her shoulder. She desperately tried not to notice the gesture as anything more than a friendly touch from her friend.

Her best friend.

She breathed in deeply and fixed a bright smile on her face when August blew out a huff of laughter and leaned against her.

"A lady are you?"

She nodded keeping her smile in place. "Truly."

"Then as the only lady I know, would you accompany me to the fall dance this weekend?"

Her heart warmed, lighting up brighter than the street lights around them.

"A dance?" she squeaked.

He hummed, tweaking her nose. "Yes, a dance. Do me the honor of attending the dance with me?"

"What?"

"The dance this month. May I escort you?"

Seylah nodded dumbly and managed a quick breathy "Yes."

"Then I shall call on you, my lady!" August's voice rang through the night, carrying above the din of voices and the stray sounds of the gathered band that heralded the lighting of the lamps.

He wanted to call on her.

She didn't care if he tweaked her nose or ruffled her hair like he had done when they were children, nor did she give any amount of attention to the old women giving them knowing looks from across the street. It was common knowledge around Gold Sky that you could not find Seylah without August in tow. Of course, that gave rise to more than a fair amount of gossip and well-intentioned wishes from the majority of the townsfolk. And until that moment, Seylah had brushed off the giggles and hopeful looks from the adults around her as meaningless.

She knew that he thought the same as she, the pair of them rolling their eyes and ignoring the pointed looks or playful comments whispered just loud enough for the friends to hear.

"The pair will marry when they grow up. I know it."

"Isn't it darling how they've always been together?"

"Young love is so exciting!"

Seylah would wrinkle her nose and shake her head while August blew out a weary sigh. The pair of them intent on carrying on as if the remarks hadn't been overheard. August was her friend and she was his. They had always been thus and would remain so until they perished, of that she was sure.

There would be no separating them.

Never.

Not even under the duress of incessant gossip from the townsfolk. She was happiest when she was with August. No other place she would rather be if given the choice.

Except that now...now it felt different to Seylah. As if her eyes had suddenly been opened, her heart made aware of something she had always known but hadn't possessed the words to express it. August. She looked up at him, the bright light of the street dazzling her nearly as much as the boy she had grown up alongside. Because suddenly he wasn't simply August.

Then I shall call on you, my lady!

He was the first boy to call on her. *Her.*

The first to set her heart pounding. The first to make her shiver with a feeling she couldn't quite place. Her cheeks heated with a blush that left her hot and shaky beneath the arm August had thrown over her shoulders.

Heart fluttering in her chest, Seylah felt dizzy with the still new exhilaration that accompanied August's touch. Not for the first time in Seylah's life, she happy to be at August's side for all to see.

That night had been startling. A realization in feelings that left Seylah bewildered about her relationship with August. Her fledgling confusion may have registered as nothing at all if August hadn't mimicked her behavior in perfect synchronicity.

In the two weeks that led up to the dance, their easy and steadfast friendship had become strained. The conversation was stilted. No longer did they touch with easy affection, nor was it possible for the two of them to ignore the comments that dogged their every step.

It felt as if the street lights had illuminated every dark and shadowy corner of Seylah's mind and there was nowhere for her to turn without being confronted by thoughts of August. She swallowed hard and closed her eyes, blowing out a sigh.

It was normal for friends to think of one another, especially best friends. Things were just...confusing right now, but it would go back to normal. She was simply nervous about the dance, nervous about dressing as she was now for the first time. She opened her eyes, taking in the image of her standing in a pale green gown that showed off her girlish figure to perfection. She smoothed her hands over the sumptuous material that was a far cry from the durable dresses she much preferred in her day-to-day life.

As was her hair, a swept up style replete with a pompadour. Such a look wasn't conducive to horseback or field surveying. She patted at her hair nervously and forced herself to not fidget.

A lady does not fidget.

Or at least that's what Mrs. Rosemary had advised her when she'd approached the woman for tips on how to conduct herself tonight. Her mother had also given her thoughts on fidgeting. but the former debutante had strongly advised her daughter to behave as she always did, that she was under no pressure to conform to expectations. That anyone that wanted her to do so was not worthy of Seylah's energies.

Seylah knew her mother only sought to help, but she much preferred Mrs. Rosemary's advice on how to approach her night with August.

Forcing her hands still at her sides, Seylah gave herself a determined nod and remained still. She would not fidget. She would not do it. She would not touch her hair. She would not shove August into a doorway if presented with the opportunity.

She. Would. *Not.*

She was a lady.

She was still giving herself a talking to when August arrived to call on her. Her heart fluttered like a bird against her breast at the thought of him coming to call on *her*. Her fathers answered the door while her mother fussed over the lace of her dress with a watery smile.

"You look so grown up," her mother whispered with misty eyes that had Seylah biting back an *"Oh mama."*

She was the oldest of her siblings, all girls to their mother's delight and fathers' horror and chagrin. The four Wickes-Barnes' girls, ages fourteen, twelve, ten and nine had inherited their mother's beauty. Tan skin and abundant curls were the markers of Seylah and her sisters, as was their eyes.

All four girls were in possession of differently hued eyes. Seylah had inherited her mother's dark brown, but the next Delilah had sky blue. Florence took after Will with her cool slate gaze, and then there was the youngest, Rose, whose eyes were the mirror of their grandfather's clover green. Seylah quite liked the reminder of their family when she looked at her sisters,. In each of their faces a reminder could be found of where they came from, how beautiful their family was, and for that she was happy---they all were.

Though Seylah suspected her fathers would have been a tad happier with the presence of an older brother, August had always filled the space where a son might find himself. This proved a gift for everyone involved, considering August's father had taken work out west when the boy was five, and had never been heard from again. It wasn't easy to be a boy without a father, but Forrest and Will filled the roles nicely, and so quietly, that none thought to show August or his mother pity at the loss of a man that had been flaky at best.

Forrest had taught August how to skin a deer and

chop wood, Will had taken care that August understood the importance of accounting as well as how to shoot a target dead on. The men had welcomed him as the son they had never had, and with four girls in the family, August's presence had been appreciated as a brother of sorts. Now that he was here for Seylah on the night of a dance, it was plain to see that both Forrest and Will were reconsidering their estimation of August.

"Are you bullying August?" Her mother's voice rang through the foyer and Seylah squeezed her eyes shut at the grumbling sound her fathers made at the question.

Of course, they were bullying August. Once a friend, now a foe given that he was here to escort their daughter to a dance. Gathering her skirts Seylah set her chin and cleared her throat.

"Leave him alone!" she called, rushing towards the foyer. She skidded to a stop when she saw her fathers looming over August with crossed arms and stern faces.

"You have her home by seven," Will said.

"You'll keep room for the holy ghost between the two of you while you dance, you hear?" Forrest ordered.

August nodded, his face and ears turning red. "Y-yes, sirs. I promise."

"Seven? That's when dinner is served! She won't have any time for fancy dancing!" Delilah cried from the staircase.

"She must fancy dance, papa!" Florence chimed in from beside her sister where she clutched the banister.

"Fancy dance!" Rose cried from the second floor and Seylah bit back a groan. This hadn't quite been the scene of romance and sophistication she had imagined when daydreaming about this moment. She had anticipated August looking gallant, herself like a maiden with effortless beauty, they would smile and go together, it would all be perfect but instead…

She blushed furiously at seeing her fathers crowding August further against the door. This was not romantic or what a lady imagined when being escorted to an event. At least, Mrs. Rosemary hadn't told her about this. She cleared her throat and took a tentative step forward. How she would restore order she wasn't rightly sure but she had to do something, and it must be done now. Thankfully, her mother appeared, effectively rescuing both August and Seylah from the scene of familial mayhem. Julie bustled forward towards her husbands with a frown.

"Stop that this instant," she ordered, hands on her hips.

Her husbands automatically dropped back, ducking their heads. "Aw, little bird, we were just givin' him a talking to about tonight and safety," Forrest supplied.

"I know precisely what the pair of you were doing. You were scaring August to death and embarrassing Seylah within an inch of her young life. You've scarred the poor girl."

Her fathers glanced back to see her standing red-faced, hands fisting in her green skirts. In unison, they cringed and stepped back from August, who looked as if he might faint at any moment.

"Shoo, the pair of you," Julie flapped her hands at them and then gestured for Seylah to come forward. "Come on, darling. Let's get you and August out the door before I have to put your fathers in line." She smiled at August, smoothing a hand over his suit jacket. “Don’t you look dapper, August!”

August offered a weak thanks as Seylah came forward to her mother’s side. “Now you two have a lovely time tonight. Come back by nine, not seven.” Her mother kissed their cheeks and bustled them towards the door with a warning look at the men who were still standing in the hallway, albeit with a recalcitrant look on their faces.

“Sorry about that sweetheart,” Forrest offered, giving her a quick peck on the cheek.

“Home by seven,” Will repeated, pointing at August as her father bent to hug Seylah.

“Yes, sirs.” August managed to get out. Seylah had had quite enough of her overbearing fathers and looped her arm through August’s.

“Come on. If we don’t go now we will never make it,” She said, stepping out of thc house and into the early evening. August stumbled after her and was silent as she continued to march up the path towards the lane that led to town. Quite a few homesteads had sprung up on the lane leading from the school to their home but it was still blessedly quiet, a respite after her family’s chaotic scene.

They walked in silence, August stiffly beside her as gravel crunched underfoot. Seylah glanced at him and winced when she saw that he was still pale and shaken looking.

“They won’t do anything to you, you know that.”

He blinked as if coming out of a trance and looked at her as if realizing for the first time that she was there with him. “I, ah, I know,” he sputtered.

She raised an eyebrow. “Do you?”

"They are the law men...sheriffs can't kill people right?" he asked after a moment and Seylah laughed.

"August…"

He cracked a smile then and relaxed slightly against her. "I know they aren't going to kill me."

She nodded, patting his arm. "Good then it--"

"Maim me? Possibly. Rough me up? More than likely, as they both informed me they would without your mother or you knowing."

Her mouth dropped open. "They did not."

"They did, but," he held up a finger when she went to protest, "I know it's because they love you. I understand."

She drew back, looking at him in confusion. "You do?"

He nodded. "Of course, I do. You're family. They'd do anything for family."

"But you're family too," she protested.

August smiled thinly. "Not like you, Seylah." There was a note of such moroseness in his voice that she nearly stopped walking.

"August," she put a hand on his arm and moved to stop him, "August what do you mean?"

"Don't worry about it, Seylah."

"But--"

"We will be late for the first dance. We can't have that. Not with how pretty you look tonight."

Her eyes widened at August's words. He had never said that to her, not ever. She hadn't even thought that he had noticed what she looked like with how little he commented on her appearance. And now, now she was pretty.

"You think I'm pretty?" she asked, a hand going up to her pat her hair.

He nodded and cleared his throat. "Prettiest in town."

Seylah felt simultaneously as if the air had been punched out of her lungs and that she was floating. It was on unsteady feet that she made it to the dance that was being held in their school, a favorite site for festivities. Tonight the building she saw every day was magical. Lit up and sparkling like a jewel box, ribbons and garlands hung from the trees nearby making it a picture of romantic perfection. This is where all of her wishful daydreaming would be made reality, she could feel it in her bones.

Tonight things would change between her and August. For the better, she knew it. The strained nature of their relationship would be understood, feelings would be communicated, there would be no lingering awkward nature to their friendship. Not tonight. There couldn't be. Not when he'd called her the prettiest girl in town.

She preened and simpered at August's side. The lingering looks they received were no longer covert but were out right. No one was surprised to find them together. After all, they were always together, were they not?

The only difference was that tonight it wasn't just the grown ups commenting and noticing. No, tonight the girls in their grade had taken equal interest. Seylah tried not notice as they danced their first dance, or again when August excused himself to get them refreshments. But it was plain to see that the girls had finally taken notice of

August, had also, like Seylah, realized that he was no longer a boy.

Their eyes followed his every move, but Seylah could not begrudge them as she found that her eyes followed a similar path. It was hard not to stare at August when he was the tallest and broadest of their year, when he was the only boy that could properly keep step in a waltz, or had the forethought to offer a drink after a spirited dance. August was attentive and kind, listening to her and laughing along with her jokes, rather than sticking to the walls in sullen silence as the other boys did.

Given this, Seylah understood why the other girls in attendance had noticed August and wasn't surprised to hear him the topic of conversation when she excused herself to freshen up. But what she didn't anticipate was August's voice joining in the din of girlish chatter. She was standing at the back side of the schoolhouse, about to round the corner to return to where she had left August waiting. It seemed he hadn't been alone long in her absence.

"She's just a friend," August was saying. The tone was unlike the soft, warm voice he had complimented her with, when he had said that she was the prettiest girl in town. This was nearly a scoff, so unlike her best friend in any nature that she stopped short as if she had been slapped.

Something was going on. Something big.

"Doesn't look like just a friend," a girl laughed. "Looks like you're her beau."

"M'not," August returned.

"Then why are you always together?" Another voice

asked, and Seylah leaned against the building feeling as if she was no longer walking on air, only punched in the stomach. There was no air to breathe and this time it wasn't from excitement.

There was a long beat of pause before August spoke again. "Because her pa's look after me, so I look after her."

"So you don't *like* her then?"

"No. I couldn't ever see her like that."

"You look after her for her fathers? They make you do that?"

"I do it to return the favor," August bit out, suddenly sounding uncomfortable. Seylah felt unshed tears pricking her eyes. "Nothings for free out here and I owe them a debt."

A murmuring of understanding arose from the girls gathered, and Seylah reached out a hand to steady herself as her knees buckled.

"Since you don't *like* her then and you're not her beau, will you dance with me?" The girl asked, but Seylah couldn't bring herself to hear August's response. Not with the sudden sick feeling that rose up and threatened to choke her.

The magic of the night, the imagined closeness and changing of their friendship to something more was lost to her. While she had been dreaming of a declaration of affection between herself and August, he had been merely performing a duty, a debt to her fathers for their care. A rushing sound filled her ears, choking off the jovial music that still played inside the school house, the sound of feet on wood turned into a single humming sound as did the chattering and laughter of the gathered merrymakers.

Seylah heard none of it. Not as she pushed away from the school house fighting back tears, not as she rushed towards her home, ignoring the instruction from Mrs. Rosemary that ladies did not run.

Seylah was no lady. Not with her best friend merely keeping her company in repayment to her family.

She was mortified, alone, and most certainly not the prettiest girl in town.

She would take care never to forget the lesson.

THANK YOU!

I hope you enjoyed Hearth and Home!

Julian and Violet's story is at an end but I couldn't bear to put aside Gold Sky or the Wickes-Barnes family, which brings us to little Seylah Wickes-Barnes who isn't so little anymore and embarking on her journey to happy-ever-after in the next chapter of life in Gold Sky!

Get ready for the next generation of love in Gold Sky with Seylah and August's story, a tale of best friends and first love, misunderstandings, and realizing the right one was there all along.

Thank you for making this series a labor of love. It means the world to share this with y'all.

Sign up for our newsletter e-mail list at https://bit.ly/2PCKCZl and *don't be shy about reaching out through social media! I pretty much live for that stuff.*

Reviews help eager readers find new authors to love and I welcome all reviews, both positive and constructive. Drop me a shout and I'll love y'all to the moon and back!

Turn the page and enjoy a sneaky peek at Seylah and August!

ABOUT REBEL CARTER

Rebel Carter *loves* love. So much in fact that she decided to write the love stories she desperately wanted to read. A book by Rebel means diverse characters, sexy banter, a real big helping of steamy scenes, and, of course, a whole lotta heart.

Rebel lives in Colorado, makes a mean espresso, and is hell-bent on filling your bookcase with as many romance stories as humanly possible!

facebook.com/rebelwrites
twitter.com/rebelwrites_
instagram.com/rebelwrites

ALSO BY REBEL CARTER

Heart and Hand: Interracial Mail Order Bride Romance

Love and Gravity: Multicultural STEM Romance

New Girl in Town: Older Woman Younger Man Romance

Auld Lang Syne: Highlands Holiday Novella

30217927R00194

Printed in Great
Britain
by Amazon